THE
EXPERIMENT

Also available in Hardcover and eBook

Hardcover ISBN: 978-0-9862834-5-1

eBook ISBN: 978-0-9862834-6-8

For Bella and Noah,
whose smiling faces make this all worth it.

1

It's comforting to let things out. To sit and talk and feel the weight of the world rise off your shoulders as you throw your words at someone else.

For Sarah Hart, this was certainly the case.

Her brown hair tickled her shoulders as she laid back on the stiff leather recliner. The recessed lights and bright white ceiling were glistening, free of any flaws. Sarah felt like it had to be some sort of trap. Like she was some caged animal put in an environment where she had no control – the bright lights were there to hypnotize her.

"I don't think this is a good idea," she said aloud, but barely audible.

"What makes you think that?" the soft voice from the gray-haired man with glasses said. "What brought about the change?"

There's never been a change, is what she wanted to say. *I never wanted this. It was forced upon me.* But she couldn't say that because she couldn't risk losing everything she'd gained. All she could manage to get out was, "I feel bad."

But as he'd done throughout this entire process, the man in the moccasins and corduroy pants said, "You need to remember the immense upsides to this." He said it like it was some sort of an optional enhancement.

"It just feels wrong. It was never supposed to go this far," she said.

Dr. Epplestein paused the way he always did – almost as if doing it for effect on a Hollywood set – and then said, "Is there a certain point where you thought we should adjust our vision?"

Vision? There was no vision. Sarah couldn't think of it as a vision. More like an experiment, with her husband as the guinea pig.

"I..." she opened her mouth to speak, but to say what? That this whole scenario, situation, process or whatever you want to call it was okay to begin with but not anymore? That she was fine with making her husband a test dummy before but now she's over it? What she should have said when she opened her mouth to speak was that she shouldn't have allowed this to happen in the first place. That she was wrong, and that her life of financial struggles had crawled into her head like a bug while she slept and took over her decision-making. But for some reason she couldn't admit to it. Couldn't admit the guilt. She felt the need to shove her finger at the man sitting on the chair beside her.

"It's normal to feel this way," Dr. Epplestein began. "You're afraid and that's normal. But when we first started, we discussed that this might turn out to be longer than either of us expected. Just hang in there a little while longer and things will all work out."

Just what her father told her.

Sarah hadn't sought out help for herself, it was her father who convinced her to do so. She and Brian were having marital problems – financial problems, really, in a marital problem disguise – and her father tried to help, but there was nothing he could do. There was only so long he could act as a shoulder to cry on before he decided she had to try something new.

Though he tried to convince her to leave her husband and to move back in until she and the kids could find a new place to live, she couldn't bring herself to do it. Couldn't bring herself to take the kids away from their father. He was always such an amazing father to their two children, and although the marriage was shit and the tiny apartment they'd stayed in for far too long was dated and in need of new tenants, Lacey and Mason loved their father. Cheered him on like he was a god, and in their eyes, he was.

With her unwillingness to leave Brian, Sarah's dad took the next-best step he could think of and paid for her to visit a psychologist. "I love that you can confide in me," her father had told her. "But I can't seem to help you feel better. Rather than just being someone to talk to, I want you to see someone who can really help you."

At first Sarah was happy about it. She was happy about the new opportunity and the chance at a happier life through whichever way a professional might be able to help her. But then Dr. Epplestein heard the story of Brian, and he became infatuated with Brian and seemed less willing to look deeper into Sarah's problems. But what could she do? Her dad felt happy about helping her and she couldn't leave.

"How much longer?" she asked Dr. Epplestein, eyes never leaving that bright white ceiling.

And that's when he sat up in his chair and leaned close to her. Sarah's stomach turned as she looked into the face of the man who was controlling this entire game. She wanted out, but it was too late.

2

Brian Hart had never been one to complain. Not when his mother and sister were killed in a car accident. Not when his dad killed himself the next morning because he couldn't live with the guilt of being the surviving driver. Not even year after year, as his life had become a road trip filled with nothing and the ideas of offing himself crept up. But on this specific day, he was in the mood to complain. He was in the mood to curse at the sky and wonder *Why me?* Because this particular day was the fourteen-year anniversary of the day he first began his writing career. And not a damn thing had changed.

A mug of coffee that sat beside his dimly-lit desk was once hot and comforting, sending waves of steam into the air. But it had since gone untouched and grown cold – the latter being an analogy of his writing career. He took a sip anyway, grimacing at the taste. But he needed the caffeine. The early morning routine he'd adopted was harsh, and had never grown on him.

He used to write midday, throughout the day, like a real

writer. He treated it as a full-time job, just as any real writer would. But that was back when it was just Brian and his laptop cooped up inside a one-bedroom condo. He bought it with Mom's life insurance money. He could have had a two-bedroom if he'd have gotten his dad's money, but Dad lost out on that stack of cash when he dragged the blade of a knife across his neck.

But the condo was enough. It was Brian's little place to write, and when it came time to pay bills, he never had any issues. Still, to get out of the house every day, and also to slow the pace of the dwindling bank account that couldn't stay fluffy forever, he took on a small job.

He never stopped writing during the day, but at night he worked as a bar back at Teeter's Tavern a few miles down the road. It helped him to keep his sanity, being able to talk to people after hiding away during the day. And it also helped him to meet some girls, though he found out the hard way that twenty-five-year-old bar backs who struggle to lift empty kegs aren't really what women fantasize about when they drift off into Magic Mike Daydream Land. And the excuse, *But I'm a writer, I don't have time to work out* went oh-for-twenty and was then retired.

The condo is also a distant memory, sold when he and Sarah married each other after only eight months together; when you know, you know, right? And the bar back position is only a former job with many cringe-worthy memories.

Up until the night before, Brian would have sworn to the stars that he wouldn't trade this life for the world. Funny how things can change on a whim.

He picked up that cold cup of coffee and forced the

caffeine into his body, knowing that without it no words would get written. When he put the mug back down onto the wooden desk, he adjusted the small lamp that hung sadly over his keyboard. The movement caused a creak in its neck, stirring the woman in his bed.

There had been many nights at the beginning where his early morning noises didn't bother his wife. Sarah thought of him as ambitious and dedicated. But recently, even his breathing seemed to piss her off. And on top of that, she was a pissy morning person to begin with. Each time there'd be a little noise, he found himself tensing up, waiting for some sort of a snicker or sigh or some other bullshit noise to prove to him that she was irritated. So the anger he felt when his writing sessions weren't going well would only be intensified at the thought of his restrictions. Sometimes he'd have the urge to curse, or slam his fist against the desk, or swipe everything off the desk itself and go on a maniacal rage of punching holes in the drywall. But he never could. He had to worry about the repercussions. So what could he do? He could take another sip of his cold coffee and grunt under his breath. And that's just what he did.

Most mornings blended together, all pretty much the same thing. For the thousandth time, he found himself looking down at the blinking cursor and wondering when it would just burn a spot into the damn screen already. Since he'd sat down in front of the thing, he'd thought of everything besides writing. Always seemed to happen that way. The most annoying part about that? The rest of the day would be filled with ideas.

He gave himself twenty more minutes of this torture, thinking maybe something would come along in his brain, but not giving himself enough time to become too enraged. Plus, he needed to start getting ready for work.

Turns out he wouldn't make it twenty minutes. It only took ten more minutes with zero production for him to call it quits and close his laptop. He walked his coffee mug out to the sink, tiptoeing past the kids' room. They'd need to wake up soon, but not just yet.

He took his shitty attitude with him into the kitchen, knowing full-well it would follow him around all day. He'd be behind his forklift at work, cursing at himself for not being able to sit and write all day.

Someday, he'd tell himself continually. But he'd been saying that for fourteen years now.

He put his mug into the sink and then walked across the living room to where the sliding glass doors gave him a view of the gray early morning hanging over the apartment parking lot. He ran his hands through his wavy black hair as he looked out into the early morning. Life hadn't yet begun, but it'd be bustling with nine-to-fivers soon enough.

Down the hall, he heard Sarah's alarm clock buzzing. *Must be 6:00.* She was probably happy to roll over and not see him. The days with her were so hit-or-miss that he never knew what he should expect. So for the past few weeks he decided just to expect for the worst, and if she was to somehow wake up happy, well that would just be a plus.

He made his way back down the hall with no idea how he should've expected his wife to greet him.

On some mornings, his wife of eight years is empathetic. She'll wrap her arms around his neck as Brian sits in his wooden chair and whisper to him that everything will be okay. And it'll cheer him up for the time being. But most mornings she just grunts and walks away from him, probably disgusted at the pathetic excuse for a husband and provider he'd become. And *most mornings* had recently turned into *every morning.*

Withering away behind a forklift was never in Brian's plans. He never aspired to let his writing fall face-first into a hot pile of shit. But that's just what happened. And Sarah had enough. Brian walked down the hall toward the buzzing alarm clock, replaying the previous nights' argument in his head.

"When will you give this up?" she asked. "Your kids need a better life. You need to prioritize."

The thoughts of her conniving and matronizing tone brought back the urge to slam her head into a wall, just like he wanted to last night. But the heat that filled his whole body last night as she sat on the couch on her phone, not even looking at him as she criticized and bashed every move he'd ever made and any risk he'd ever taken isn't there now. Maybe because it's only 6:00 AM and he doesn't have the energy to bicker, or maybe because he knows that how she concluded her argument last night was what really mattered.

It's to be expected after eight years of false promises, debt collectors, and rent payments that she'd be unhappy. Brian promised her the world when they first met. And she believed him. Believed *in* him. But then as time went on she became more skeptical. She agreed, though, to let him continue pursuing his dream if he'd do one thing: make sure they get a house with a yard before the kids started school. But now Lacey is seven and Mason is four and they're still forced to share a tiny swing set with the rest of the kids in the complex. It isn't how Sarah was raised and she'd be damned if her kids were raised that way, dodging rent payments and prying eviction threats off the door.

And as she crawled into bed last night without an ounce of desire for intimacy, the words came out that Brian knew would one day come:

"We're just two different people," she said. "I want a divorce."

And somehow, some way, as always seemed to happen when Brian thought he'd hit rock bottom, his life managed to become even shittier.

3

The guy sounded like a rat. Or maybe he just looked like one. Regardless, he was an annoying little fuck that could never stop talking. He thought he was high and mighty when really he was just a young punk with short-man syndrome, feeding off the ability to boss around a bunch of high school kids...

and Brian.

Eric Millford was his name, and declaring himself five-foot-four was being generous. But, like all short men, he had arms the size of tree trunks and a shiny bald head. He was the manager of Eats-N-Treats Pet Store but dressed like he was trading on Wall Street. There were many times where Brian would've liked to step out from his forklift's cage, walk up to Eric, grab his tie and twirl it around his neck until his white face turned red, then purple, then blue.

Maybe it was envy, because Brian was nine years older than Eric and had to take orders from him all day. Or maybe it was the fact that both Eric and Brian were the only people working at Eats-N-Treats who had college degrees, but Brian just chose to take a risk that didn't pan out and hated to have to listen to a guy who settled for being a manager at a fucking pet store.

Whatever the case, Brian hadn't had one decent interaction with the guy since he started there.

"I need all these pallets cleared out, Brian," Eric said, leaning into the forklift and placing a hand on the steering wheel. To stop it maybe? Make sure Brian didn't take off in the big, bad forklift while he was talking? Brian felt a smirk come across his face thinking of how often he and his two other co-workers in the warehouse made fun of Eric for proclaiming everything in the store as *his*. "*My* store," and "How are *my* shelves looking?" and "You can't skateboard on *my* ramp" to the kids out back. What a douche. It's not *your* store, you simply get paid a shitty salary to work here. Just like the rest of us.

"What's funny?" Eric asked.

"Nothing," Brian said, without removing the smirk. "Go on."

"I *said*," he paused for effect, "that I need these pallets out of the way before today's delivery comes in. You have about an hour until the truck gets here."

"Okay."

Eric nodded and then removed his hand from the forklift's wheel before stepping back. His action said, "You may carry on now," but his posture said, "Get back to work, runt." Or maybe, "Get back to work on *my* store, using *my* forklift, you runt."

Tommy and Stephen appeared out of who-knows-where several minutes later, looking just as they always did: dry-eyed and high as a kite. If you saw the two walking side-by-side, you'd never really expect them to be hanging out together. Tommy, white as a ghost with long, shaggy, brown hair, walking side by side with Stephen, black as night with one of those high-top haircuts kids are trying to bring back and pants sagging off of his ass. Maybe it was work that forced them to be together, or just the pot that did it. Regardless, neither seemed to mind each other's presence.

"Hey," Brian called over to them.

"Sup," Tommy said with a head jerk that sent his hair in a hiccup.

"Today's shipment's coming in an hour. We need to clear this shit out," he said. He didn't mean to do it, but he sometimes felt like he would dumb down his speech to their level.

"*His* shipment?" Stephen said. It somehow never got old talking shit on the guy.

But they did as they were told, Brian and the stoners, and they got everything put away nice and tidy just in time for another shipment to come.

Now they could start all over. Yippee.

The job was horrible, and barely paid the bills, but when Brian started there seven years earlier, he loved every second of it. It started as an early morning gig – come in at 4 AM and be home by noon with the rest of the day to write – but then became this day shift thing that Brian swore up and down he'd never succumb to. It was nice, though, not having to bring your work home with you. Unload some shit from a truck and go home, that's all. And that's what he and Tommy and Stephen did: they unloaded shit and then they clocked out.

This particular day went just as any other, with Brian driving the forklift around the warehouse while Tommy and Stephen moped about at snail's speed. Pallets of pet food here, toys there, colorful boxes and smiling faces on the cardboard containers. Same shit, different day.

The work day took his mind off of everything, as it always had. He'd try to brainstorm but always got caught up talking to people or being told what to do by the bald, waddling rock. Work allowed him to forget all about the fight with Sarah the night before. That was until he got to his car and thought about how he couldn't wait to get home to an excited Lacey and Mason, always happy to see their father, oblivious to the loser he'd become. And then it hit him that the days of walking in the door to his gleaming kids were limited. And pretty soon he'd be walking into a quiet, empty apartment.

4

There they were, as always – Lacey on his one hip and Mason on the other – as Brian walked through the door of their second-floor apartment. They would scream and stomp on the floor when they heard his footsteps coming up the wooden staircase, and for the millionth time, Sarah had to tell them to be quiet out of respect for the neighbors below.

But the kids were just happy to see their dad. Happy to be home from school and ready to have dinner and watch TV with their family. Happy. Happy and oblivious. Oblivious to what was going on between their parents. And oblivious to what was about to become of their lives.

Sarah looked on as they stomped around like a stampede when the door opened. How the hell had the neighbors downstairs never come up to complain? Was there even anyone living down there? Sarah seemed to be the only one who'd ever cared anyway.

Brian bent down and pried the kids off of him, smile on

his face the whole time. "Alright, kids," he said. "Let Daddy put his stuff down." And as they would every night, the kids would oblige to their father's command and their excitement would diminish. They would still excitedly ask questions as kids always do: *What are we going to do tonight, Dad?* and *Can we stay up late?*

Once the kids had run off, preoccupied by something else, he was able to take a few steps into the apartment.

"Hey," he said to her. Still less than twenty-four hours since her declaring she wanted a divorce, Brian was still clearly wearing the comment on his sleeve.

"Hi," she said. "How was work?" She wanted to respond to what she knew was on his mind, but she couldn't. She had just taken off on this race and it wasn't a sprint, it was a marathon. This run would drag her through the depths of hell.

Dinner time had come and gone and Sarah and Brian were able to act as normally as two people on their path could act. The pot was beginning to boil and Sarah knew it. But for this night at least, all was calm.

For the kids.

The same after-dinner routine took place that took place every night: Brian remained in the kitchen to clean the mess and Sarah took the kids off to get bathed and ready for bed. Some nights they'd switch, but Sarah loathed the idea of cleaning pieces of corn and rice off of the kitchen floor every single night. Besides, the kids were old enough now where they could bathe themselves. Sarah just had to sit on the floor and scroll through her phone while they did so.

Brian read Lacey a story and Sarah did the same with Mason, sitting on their respective kids' bed. And then the lights went off and the children were asleep and it was just the two people who once loved each other and made a vow to spend the remainder of their lives together. *Through richer or poorer.* Liars.

On a typical night, this would be the point where the two would share a small spot on the couch together, watching TV with the volume on low and an open bottle of wine in front of them. But on this night, it was straight to the bedtime routine. As Sarah put her brown hair up in a ponytail and leaned over the vanity to remove her contacts, Brian stepped into the shower – a multitasking technique new couples do to turn each other on, but married couples do with hopes of getting to sleep quicker.

Sarah wiped off her makeup in the mirror that slowly began to accumulate steam. The silence in the bathroom was uncomfortable, the tension seeming to build to the point that at any second Brian might come crashing through the shower curtains to attack her. But when the silence breaks, it's nothing like that.

"There's no changing your mind?" Brian asked from the other side of the curtain. His voice echoed around in the bathroom and the question repeated itself to Sarah several times before she could muster up an answer.

"We've grown apart," she said, glad he chose this platform to have the talk. Had it been face-to-face, this lie might have been more difficult to spit out.

"You mean I don't make enough money for you," he snapped back. That brewing pot had come to a boil.

"Think what you want. There's just nothing there anymore." The words came out so naturally. It was like another version of Sarah inside her was speaking. An actress playing the part. And playing it well.

The water shut off and his arm reached out from behind the curtain to grab a towel. "What about the kids?"

"Don't bring them into this."

"How can I not? It's going to ruin their lives."

"Ruin *this* life?" she asked with the most condescending tone.

"Fuck you."

She laughed. His assumptions were making it easier for her to play the game.

The shower curtain slid open with a squeal. Brian had the towel wrapped around his waist as he stepped carefully over the side of the tub. "You know what I mean. Kids that grow up with their parents divorced do a lot worse in school. In social situations... You know this."

"I don't know. My days aren't spent researching stuff to write down in some book."

"Well this *research* has been out for about twenty-some years. If you'd take yourself away from Facebook for five minutes, you'd be able to see."

She ignored the jab and walked out of the bathroom and down the short hallway to their bedroom.

Something about this was too easy. It was as if having the argument was relief in itself. Like she was able to get it all out. All the things she'd been telling Dr. Epplestein were now coming out. She was able to talk to Brian about their life. About the life she wasn't happy with. She loved Brian with all of her heart and not one single cell in her body wanted to play this game with him. But their life needed to be about more than love now.

If only he'd have had some initiative towards anything other than writing. Or maybe it was the writing itself that was the problem. What if he never started writing? What could he have done with his time if he wasn't spending it beating his head against his desk every morning trying to *make it* as a writer? He could have gotten a decent job right out of college. Could have been ten years into it by now. Could have had some minor leadership position working his way up the ladder. They could have had the house with the yard that Sarah craved so desperately.

Maybe writing was the problem and not Brian.

Sarah put on her tank top and Brian's boxers that she always wore to bed. And when she crawled under the blankets she wondered to herself that if Dr. Epplestein's plan somehow worked, this could all go away.

"There's no way you'll reconsider? For the kids' sake?" Brian walked into the bedroom to find Sarah had already crawled beneath the covers, lying on the far side of the bed, facing away from him. It was like the disgust she had in him now grew more and more with each passing second, and he could feel it growing on him.

"Look at us," she said without even having the decency to turn over, as if she was talking to the window. "You think this would be healthy for the kids?"

"We're only fighting because you're leaving me."

"No, I'm leaving you *because* we fight. All the time."

"About money."

"*Yes*, about money." She finally turned around. "Do you see where we are right now? Do you remember all the promises you made me? This isn't the life I wanted."

And to that, he had nothing to say. He knew the truth. He knew what he'd told her.

"I'm leaving you, Brian. I wish you nothing but the best of luck with your writing," she said with about as much compassion as an annoyed teacher. "I really do. But I can't do this anymore. There's only so long you can watch someone chase their dreams before it just turns into them chasing their tail. I'm going to take the kids and stay with Bethany until I can find another place to live."

Bethany. Her sister. Judgmental sister with the rich husband. Bethany who'd never worked a day in her life but still managed to look down on those who don't work corporate jobs and collect six-figure paychecks.

But once again, he had no response. He put on his gym shorts and crawled into bed next to her, but certainly not beside her. And as he stared up at the ceiling, she turned over again on her side, facing away from him. After a few moments, she spoke again.

"I appreciate you worrying about the kids," she said. And she said it with some damn emotion for once. Maybe she felt bad. Finally. "You're a good dad, Brian. But..." she paused. "Money can really influence things."

And there it was. The real answer. *You don't make enough money for me.*

He watched the ceiling fan go 'round and 'round and contemplated going out into the fridge for a beer. Or a couple beers. Sarah would usually cling to him once they got in bed, unable to go to sleep without him, but that was then and this was now. She didn't need him. Didn't even want him. So why lay there and pretend to be tired?

He envisioned throwing the covers to the side, going to the kitchen and cracking one open, sitting on the couch and watching TV in his underwear like he used to do when he was living alone. Envisioned staying up well past midnight watching a movie or some late-night Adult Swim. But then he looked over at the alarm clock on the nightstand beside him that read 10:27. In four and a half hours this thing would be going off. Was it worth it? Would it be so bad to skip a day of writing if it meant being able to stay up and drink? Just release all the worries of the world and watch some damn TV with a cold can in his hand?

It'd be nice. But he couldn't bring himself to do it. Especially not now. Because now he had something to prove. He needed to prove Sarah wrong. That he wasn't just some wannabe hack writer. That he was a damn good writer, but just hadn't found the right pair of eyes to read his work yet. So he rolled over and shut his eyes, thinking of the 3 AM alarm that'd be going off soon, and the work he'd get done once he was awake.

Sarah put her head on the pillow with her back to her husband. She'd done what she was told to do by Dr. Epplestein and it made her stomach turn. The seed had been planted and the experiment had begun, but Brian had no idea.

5

Brian didn't typically wear a suit and tie, but this was a special occasion. He sat at a round table covered in white cloth, wine glasses and fancy silverware. On one side of him was William Landay and on the other, Reed Farrell Coleman. Across the table was Stephen King and beside him, James Patterson. The five of them were invited to the night's Edgar Award ceremony, as they had all been nominated for Best Novel by the Mystery Writers of America.

Last year's winner, John Grisham, took the stage to announce *this year's* winner.

"It is an honor for me to be announcing this next winner, as I have become a true fan of his work. His prose...impeccable. His storytelling...brilliant. Ladies and gentlemen, the award for this year's Best Novel goes to Brian Hart."

Brian stood, feeling surprisingly cool and confident as he rounded the table and shook the hands of his literary idols. And then he took the stage, showing the same poise as he shook the hand of John Grisham and faced the microphone. And as he opened his mouth to speak, there was a technical glitch in the microphone – a buzzing sound going on and off, on and off. During the brief halt in the screeching sound, he leaned into the microphone. But as soon as he leaned in close enough to speak, the buzzing started again. He smiled at first, and the crowd got a chuckle, but then it grew more annoying with each passing second.

"Is someone going to fix this?" he said into the microphone, but no one could hear over the buzzing. He leaned in again and this time screamed in frustration, "Is someone going to fix this damn thing?"

And then he felt pressure on his shoulder like a vice grip and suddenly he was in his dark bedroom under the covers, looking at the ceiling, and the alarm beside him was buzzing.

"Wake up," Sarah said as she shook him. "You're going to wake up the kids."

The room was dark with a red tint funneling from the numbers on his digital clock. The red came in and out as the numbers flashed in unison with the buzzing. He looked at Sarah, at the dark ceiling and then back at his alarm clock before leaning over and ending the microphone's glitch. The buzzing stopped and the numbers on the digital clock now sat steady.

Brian flopped back down on his pillow and laid in silence. Within seconds, Sarah's heavy breathing was evidence of her unconscious state, leaving Brian alone to wish with everything in him that he could be back in that dream and never wake up.

He began his everyday routine, sliding swiftly out of bed and tiptoeing across the carpet and into the bathroom to brush his teeth and throw some water on his face. He lifted his head from the sink, dried off with the hand towel and looked at his reflection: *Not in the mood for this shit.* Some days he was excited to write and others he dreaded it. This was a dreading it type of day.

If only he could've gone back into that dream.

He shut off the bathroom light and went out to his small rectangular desk that could fit his laptop and notepad and maybe a pencil or two. The wooden chair squeaked as he sat in it and he scooted in before turning on the overhead lamp and opening the laptop. He took a deep breath, leaned forward, rested his forearms on the jagged corner of the desk, and wrote nothing. Out of the corner of his eye, he could see Sarah, and all he could think about was her.

Why did she have to do this? Why did she have to go and mess things up? Ruin the family? Why couldn't she just be supportive and let him carry out his dreams as a normal spouse would?

Or was this *his* fault? Was *he* the one to blame? Should *he* have called quits on this writing thing years ago and concentrated on supporting his family? He sat there thinking she should've been supportive like a good wife would, but maybe she was thinking the same about him. Maybe she'd been telling herself for years that a man should worry about his family first. I mean, they had two kids. Why weren't they put first? Why was writing always at the forefront of his mind? Why wouldn't he come through on the promises he made to Sarah when they married?

Brian looked over at the figure under the covers – the long brown hair now hung over the pillow – and he thought about that very moment. *How did it come to this?* It'd been eight years since they said I Do and Brian promised Sarah the world. "My writing will take off," he said to her. "I promise you. I'll work day and night until we're rich."

He meant every word. He just wasn't able to follow through. It's tougher to get published than he'd imagined. Either that, or his writing was terrible and he was simply oblivious to it. And now here they were, living in a rundown apartment with two kids. All because he had to prove he was different than the average Joe on his way to work in the city every morning, sitting in traffic and getting angry at the thought of being bitched at for showing up three minutes late.

The thought of nine-to-fiving still made him cringe. But as he looked at Sarah sound asleep in their bed for what may be the very last time, he realized he'd rather be average with an average family than to be a hopeful writer with no family at all.

All these years in one company could have landed him a pretty decent title by this point. Especially since he did have that "piece of paper" (his bachelor's degree). It's not like he was some janitor who'd come into a company and plateau. He'd be up for promotions, advancements...

Just a different path. One he didn't want or need at the pet store.

But the thirty-one-year-old mother of two lying in the bed beside him wanted to go down that path with him. She *wanted* the commute. Benefits. Suit and tie and briefcase when he left the house in the morning. *House.* That's all she really ever wanted. And now look where she ended up. With a thirty-five-year-old man making high school senior money to drive bags of pet food around on a forklift.

Brian stood from the chair and walked the few feet to the side of the bed where Sarah was lying. She had her entire face and body covered, as she always did once Brian would turn on his overhead desk lamp each morning.

He looked down at her and felt nothing but love. And compassion. He looked down at the mane of hair coming from beneath the covers, spread out on the pillow, and he reached down and removed the covers from her face. Her soft, pale skin was exposed. Her eyes were closed, but he whispered to her anyway.

"I'm sorry," he said. "For everything."

But what he did after is what he'd need to apologize for.

6

Thirty minutes into his three-hour writing block, and all Brian had done so far was make his coffee. He took the steaming mug and gingerly walked down the hall and back to his bedroom to his desk, then placed the mug on the one tiny spot where it would fit. One day he'd spill a cup on the floor and lose his security deposit, he knew it, but it hadn't happened yet. And he'd be much happier knocking it onto the floor and losing his security deposit than he would be knocking it the other way and losing his computer.

He sat again, trying his hardest to hide the creaking of the wooden chair as he backed himself into it. Once he was set, he looked over at the woman who wouldn't be his wife for much longer, thinking one more time of how beautiful she was.

Times were so good when they were younger, back when they first met. There were no kids involved and no stresses in life. At that time, it was intriguing for Sarah to tell people she was dating a writer. *Oh, that's different!* her friends would say to her with a twinkle of anticipation. *A writer? What kind of stuff does he write? Like in magazines, or books?* And she loved it. Loved the attention. The intrigue.

But as the years went on, the anticipation and excitement faded. No one asked about his writing anymore, and Brian could tell. She never had stories of people asking about him anymore. There was a look of discomfort on her face any time the two would even talk about his writing outside of the apartment. Like she was embarrassed. Maybe not embarrassed by his being a writer or the writing itself, but at the staleness of repetition when answering the questions. Each *How's Brian's writing going?* and *When will his book be published?* question started driving her crazy. And Brian understood completely. Because the same questions were asked to him, and giving the same *Oh, still working on it* answers all these years later was enough to make him want to climb under a rock.

And it all led them to this point. On the brink of divorce. No more fun nights out, taking shots of whiskey while listening to live music. No more sporadic trips to wherever Groupon told them they could visit for little money. No more nights spent on the couch wearing nothing and touching everything. The next thing they'd do together would be signing divorce papers.

He peeled his eyes from his wife and dragged his mind away from the memories of happiness, and what he saw when he came back to reality was the same blinking cursor on the white screen. That haunting image of no words written on a blank page and a cursor that pops its head out every second to let you know it's still there, waiting to move and leave behind a trail of letters. But even as he stared at the screen, knowing his story and what he wanted to write, his mind kept running back to those memories of a smiling Sarah.

He'd wished many times that he could afford to go see a shrink. To have someone to talk to. Someone besides Sarah, who was surely sick of Brian's cries for a good break. But although he couldn't afford the cost of a shrink, he did have his writing. And for that, he was grateful.

Writing had been therapy to him. It was nice to be able to pour things out onto paper. Take his insecurities and flaws and put them into characters. Then he could make the character have to be the one to expose it. Have a sick, twisted urge to go on a killing spree because your boss is a dickhead? Jot that shit down on paper. No need to go through with it in real life. Create a story and a character and let out all of your rage through that character. Same as therapy, was his assumption.

Finding his mind wandering again, almost an hour into his three-hour writing block now, he took a deep breath and let out a soft, quiet exhale, so as not to wake Sarah from whatever escape she was in at the moment. He leaned up and put his hands on the keyboard.

Don't overthink it. Just write.

After a few forced lines, he was able to get a flow, and his fingers started gliding softly along the keyboard. But this lasted only a few short paragraphs, until life crept up on him again. And he began to think about the rent that was due in six days and wondering how the hell he was going to pay it. He thought about the empty refrigerator and the electric bill that was three months behind, sure that any day now Sarah would throw a piece of paper his way and that paper would have a cut-off date listed. He thought about what life could have been like if he'd taken a different path, maybe never venturing into writing in the first place. But there was no going back now. It was too late. To start a career at thirty-five would mean retiring at eighty. It would mean always having a boss that's younger than you. It would mean having to answer *Why the career change?* questions and having to dodge the answer of *I never really had a career; just a hobby.* It would mean these last fourteen years of chasing his dream would be for nothing.

What if, he thought. What if he'd followed in society's line and got a nine-to-five after college. He may have hated his life, but at least he'd still have his marriage. And more importantly, he'd still have his kids.

What if.

Write that shit down, Brian, he told himself sitting at the desk. *Write down a story about a man who keeps his kids. That'll be the only whole family you'll be seeing.*

7

Sarah's arm popped out from beneath the covers at 6:00. She slapped the bedside alarm clock and then her arm disappeared into the abyss once again, like a game of whack-a-mole.

Brian was still in his wooden chair that slid underneath what was no larger than a school desk, and after the interruption, went back to reading over the few paragraphs he was able to write this morning. The short amount he wrote turned out pretty good in his mind, and he'd like to share it with someone. Whenever he felt like this before, he'd always shown Sarah. He'd have her sit down and read and he'd try to imagine which points of the story she'd be on and look for specific reactions.

Might be a little awkward to ask her on *this* morning, with divorce looming and all.

She crawled out of bed a few minutes later, stumbled to the bathroom, and looked like less of a zombie when she came back. When she walked into the room, he stood from his chair and said to her, "Read this."

"Really?"

"Yeah. Sit," he said with a smile. *I'm proud of it and I don't have anyone else to show,* is what he wanted to say.

It would've been nice to have more support. He'd often wondered what his mother's presence during these times could have done for his ego. Or his sister. Or even his father, though he was never the emotional kind. Times like these reminded him of the times when he was younger, and he *did* have a family. A loving one.

But with his mother and sister killed in the car accident and his father committing suicide shortly after, Sarah had been the only one he could show his work to. But she was also the only one he *wanted* to show it to. And once she finally did leave, he'd have no one. So while he still had her here, he'd utilize her.

"Okay," she said with a raised eyebrow.

As he always did when she read his work, Brian pretended to be doing anything but watch her, when, in reality, he'd focused in on her every expression. He was searching for a reaction, or some emotion.

"Another murder mystery?" she asked after a shorter pause than he'd hoped for.

She was done reading already? Where was the emotion? The excitement? Didn't she want to know what happened next? *Whose body was it? Why were they killed? How? Tell me!*

"Yeah," he said. "That's what I write."

She did that head tilt and eyebrow raise people do when they want to be an asshole and tell you that your idea sucks, but they don't want to be so blunt about it. He'd seen the look on her face before, but not to this extent. Was she being an asshole because she was leaving him?

How furious would she be if she left him after eight years of marriage, watching his writing struggles, just to see his next book take off and become a bestseller?

"I guess it's not bad," she said as she got up from the chair.

Why even let her read it? He knew what was coming.

"Just make it authentic this time," she added.

"Authentic?"

"Yeah. Like, more realistic. With the murders and stuff. The scenes where people are killed in your other books seem off. Remember? I told you that before. And some of my friends said it, too."

"Ok," he said. *No, you never told me that before. Why the hell didn't you tell me that before?* He remained calm, though. No need for push back. She gave constructive criticism. He can take it. But he sure as shit didn't remember her ever giving constructive criticism before. It was usually just head nods and groans.

"Don't be like that," she said. "I'm not saying it's bad. That's actually a really good idea," she said, pointing to the illuminating screen. "I'm just saying, research a little more than you normally do."

For eight years he'd been showing her his writing and the day after she asks for a divorce, she gives him the critique he'd been looking for. Couldn't be more ironic. But the feeling of doubt he had when asking her to read it had dissolved. A sense of relief took over, and he felt almost like he could hug her.

He didn't, of course, and she would eventually walk off to wake the kids for school.

It's a shame he couldn't have stayed that level-headed the final time those two would be together.

8

Sarah pulled open the wood-framed door. A snowed piece of glass filled a square hole in the middle of the door and on it were stickered black letters that read: Dr. James Epplestein, Ph.D.

This was a room she had been coming to more often than she'd liked. In fact, the first time she ever walked in here was against her will. Well, sort of. Her dad had asked her to do it and she couldn't turn the man down. She could see the hurt in her father's eyes – *why won't you talk to me?* But she couldn't. There was only so much she could say and only so many times she could hear *I told you so* from her parents. Even when they weren't saying it out loud, they were saying it in their heads, but she could still hear it.

"Good morning–" The receptionist prepared to give her a generic greeting, but then saw the person walking through.

Sarah smiled. "Hey, Alex," she said. "He have any free time this morning?"

The young brunette looked down into something that was hidden from Sarah's view by a chest-high countertop. "He doesn't have any available times…" she trailed off as she shook her head, still looking down and running her finger over what Sarah correctly assumed was Dr. Epplestein's daily schedule.

"Okay, I'll try again this afternoon, maybe?" she asked it as a question, but it was no question – she was coming back. She needed to speak with him.

"Is everything okay, Mrs. Hart?"

"It most certainly is not." She heard the words come out of her mouth like a stern old woman. "I really need to speak with him today. Something happened…"

"That's alright. Just have a seat," Alex said. "I'll be right back."

Sarah had a seat in an empty waiting room with chairs lining the freshly-painted walls that grew to meet an oddly-high ceiling. There were magazines and a fish tank and the curved receptionist desk with the marble countertop – everything you'd come to expect from a person with *Ph.D.* pasted on the door to their office.

Dr. Epplestein came out of his office followed by Alex, and they both shared a look of panic as if a kid had run off on their watch.

"Sarah, what's wrong?" He came up and knelt down in front of her, putting one corduroy pant leg down on the ground and leaning his forearm on the other. Sarah had always wondered if he dressed like a stereotypical shrink as a little play to ease his patients and get them to giggle and lighten up, or if this was one of those instances were stereotypes were in fact true.

"I did it," she said to him. "That planting the words in his head thing," she said, feeling nauseous about it.

"Yes. Misinformation," he said. Such a shrink. "How? What happened?"

"He wrote... started writing this chapter this morning, I guess, and he really liked it. So he asked me to read it." She took a breath because the guilt was starting to eat away at her lungs. "I did."

"And?" The doctor asked the question, but the receptionist looked more interested in the answer than he did.

"I told him to do more research."

"Research," he repeated. "Good. And the book? A murder mystery?"

She nodded and looked into the beaming eyes of Dr. Epplestein. The answer was obviously what he wanted to hear.

"A murder mystery," he turned and said, looking up to his receptionist standing behind him. Her enthusiasm matched his.

"Dr. Epplestein, do you really think this is going to work?"

He turned from Alex to Sarah and said, "Several colleagues and I have been studying this theory for... well, for many years. And I believe you walked into my door for a reason, Sarah. I believe this is going to work."

"And what about Brian? What happens to him if it does?"

Dr. Epplestein stood and put his hands on his hips. He looked at Alex once again when he said, "I'm not entirely sure." Then he set a reassuring hand on Sarah's slumped shoulder when he said, "But the only way we'll have to worry about that is if this theory proves right. And then," the smile came back to his face, "we'll be able to explain everything."

Sarah lowered her head, not knowing what the hell would happen if his plan worked. But she was torn because what he asked her next was what he asked her at the end of every session:

"You and the kids alright? Do you need more money?"

9

A forklift is pretty loud for such a little machine, especially when the sound waves are echoed off of the cinderblock walls and the concrete floor. It was always difficult to hear what was going on around the warehouse when it was running. It was why Stephen and Tommy used hand signals to direct Brian when he was driving a pallet across the floor, or getting dangerously close to the edge of the loading dock when the delivery truck came. It was also difficult to tell if others were in the room. If you wanted to break the rules around here, you had to have your head on a swivel.

Brian was well aware of this, and regularly defied the No Cell Phone Use rule implemented throughout the store. *One,* he thought: *Until you take over the payments on my phone, do not tell me when I can and cannot use it.* And *Two: People have other things going on in life besides stocking pet food and toys.*

Still, to avoid any write-ups, he'd always glance over each shoulder before pulling out his smartphone. He was behind the wheel of his forklift and had it in gear – you know, just in case he needed to pretend he was working –

when he pulled the phone from his pocket. The alert he'd gotten was a text message from Sarah: "I'd like to talk later if that's okay."

A smile came across his face and he didn't know whether or not to be happy about it. Did she have a change of heart? Did she want to stay with him now? It'd be great if she did, especially for the kids. But what then? Would he feel even more pressure to walk away from his passion and get a "real" job?

Was it the new story? The few paragraphs she read? Was it really that promising? Brian felt that way about everything he wrote. *This is The One!* But was it Sarah that finally felt this way?

Brian hated the idea of craving someone else's acceptance, but after his family died, there really wasn't much of it in his life. Besides getting Sarah to say yes to marrying him, he'd heard *No* more times than he could count. But to keep his family together, he subconsciously did crave her acceptance. Because he needed his kids. And that meant he needed Sarah.

He startled when he heard Eric's voice: "Let's go! Get back to work!" The bowling ball with feet yelled it from the double doors leading into the front of the store – those shiny metal swivel doors that seemed to mean acceptance into the Official Commercial Building Club with their presence. He quickly took his foot off the brake, sending the forklift rolling across the warehouse floor. In reality, getting written up for a safety hazard like that would have led to a much harsher penalty than simply being on his phone. But some things you don't consider until after the fact.

He gripped the steering wheel with one hand and raised his other in a *gotcha* gesture. But what he really wanted to do was raise his middle finger and explain to Eric that he may have been a manager at the age of twenty-six, but he was the manager of a fucking pet store.

Then again, Brian was a thirty-five-year-old forklift operator at the same store. *By choice*, he continuously told himself. *By choice*.

When he was a thirty-year-old making $11.25 per hour to operate a forklift for the early morning shift, Angela Ripper, District Manager of Eats-N-Treats, approached Brian with the offer to make him Regional Supervisor. The position entailed overlooking three stores within the region, ensuring all operations were running smoothly. "You have the Business degree," she said with a smile. "Why not put it to use?"

But he declined. And to this day, he can still see the look of astonishment on Angela's face. They'd offered him a salary of sixty-seven thousand per year to start, with full benefits and option in the company's stock that was set to go public within the year. And after hearing his rejection to the offer, Angela looked as if she may have missed something in her explanation.

She didn't. The offer was a great one. But there was one thing she mentioned that stuck with Brian, and that's that he would be on call twenty-four hours a day every other week. And that just wasn't going to work with his writing schedule.

Did he tell Sarah about the offer? Of course not. She'd have left him right then and there if she knew. But he wasn't ready to call it quits on his writing. So he continued to go to work every day, head hanging low, clock-watching and counting down the hours until he could get back to his kids and his writing...soon to be just his writing.

10

If Brian was certain of one thing, it was that there would come a day soon where his kids wouldn't be excited to see him. They'd be older and disgusted. They'd realize what a waste he was, and a loser. They'd be teenagers and upset with their mother that they have to go visit him from time to time. By then, Sarah will surely have remarried, and not for love this time, but for money. The kids would be spoiled, and show no enthusiasm when walking through the numbered door to their "biological Dad's" apartment.

He knew that one day this would all be true, so his plan was to take in every second of the moments he had: his kids both excited, yelling, screaming, and pulling at his legs as soon as the door opened and he walked in from work. Even Sarah sometimes shed a smile. For her, it might have been the knowledge that the days ahead would be some of the last they'd see of their father as he walked in the door with his lunchbox strap thrown over his shoulder.

With his kids draped at his side, all of his demons disappeared. There were no writing worries or financial stresses. No wondering what the conversation with Sarah later that night would hold or any other negative thoughts. For the time being, it was just Brian and his kids.

He knelt down to hug them, closing his eyes and wanting desperately to hit a pause button on life and keep that very moment forever.

His bubble burst when he felt the two of them squirming, giggling, unable to sit still and give a hug. *Kids, always so energetic.* They started climbing on his shoulders, wanting piggyback rides, wanting to wrestle, wanting to do anything but sit still and hug their dad. And as always, he gave them exactly what they wanted.

Brian removed the strap of the lunch pack from his shoulder and picked up Mason with a grunting laugh, getting him horizontally and running down the hallway making airplane sounds, the four-year-old's blonde hair flowing in with the breeze.

"Do it to me! Do it to me!" Lacey's turn. The seven-year-old was a bit heavier, but there's no way he'd deny her the excitement. Brian picked her up and did the same thing until Mason wanted back on the train.

After ten minutes of noise (those poor downstairs neighbors) and getting the kids all rowdy, Sarah played the bad guy – as she was usually forced to do when it came to rough-housing – and broke up the play session. "Okay, okay. Time to settle down. Kids, go wash up for dinner," she said, and with some moaning and groaning, they pouted off to the bathroom to wash up.

Still panting, Brian walked over and grabbed his lunchbox from the floor and brought it to the kitchen.

"Hey," he said to Sarah, startling her. She was standing in front of the stove, mixing up whatever was in the gigantic pot.

"Hey," she responded as if there was no ongoing dilemma.

Good sign.

"How was your day?" he asked as he cleared the remains of his lunchbox.

"Not bad. Work was slow so I was actually able to leave a little early and get the kids from school." She answered him nonchalantly as she went about her thing.

"Oh, nice."

"Yeah. They were excited."

And then there was an awkward silence, because the time was perfect to ask about the morning's text: *I'd like to talk later if that's okay.* Without the kids around, she could now elaborate.

"So that text," he started, but was immediately interrupted by the sound of footsteps coming down the hall.

Sarah looked at him with a smirk and said, "Later."

The four of them sat around the kitchen table and had dinner as a family. Twelve hours prior to this very moment, Brian would have thought of this certainly being their last night together.

But that text message...

He periodically looked over at Sarah whose demeanor would show anything other than a woman on the brink of a messy divorce. She was smiling, joking with the kids, happy. But then again, she wasn't the one about to have her kids taken from her. Brian was. And it was eating him up inside. He just wanted to know what that text was about so he could breathe again.

The longest wait of his life was finally over. The kids were in bed and now he looked at his wife, their future dependent on the next few words that would escape her mouth. There they were, sitting on the couch like they used to.

"I'm still leaving you," she said.

And just like that, it all hit him again. Just as hard as the first time, a swift backhand. Images of his kids played in his mind. Brian thought of holding each of them in the hospital on the day they were born, watching them grow and loving them more than anything in the world. And now he was going to lose them all over again. They'd live with Mom until she met another man, and then that other man would be around them more and he'd grow more comfortable with them, and they with him. And before you know it, Brian's kids would be calling another man Dad. *New Dad* would be throwing a football around in the yard with Mason and coaching his sports teams. Lacey would choose *New Dad* to walk her down the aisle on her wedding day instead of Brian, her loser father who could never sell a book.

"Then why did you say–?" he managed to escape the first part of the sentence before she detected his battered tone and cut in.

"Why did I send that text?" she finished. "Because I do need to talk to you, but about something that's important to the kids."

"Being a family is important to the kids," Brian said.

"Don't do that."

"Do what?"

"*That.* Make it seem like I'm being selfish here."

"Well..." he said, feeling the guilt in her tone and wanting to pounce on the weakness. Anything to make her stay. To make the kids stay.

"I've waited eight years for you to turn around, Brian. Don't you do that to me. Have a little compassion."

"Compassion?" he said. Heat flooded his face, but he kept calm. It'd be hypocritical of him to yell at her about hurting the kids, and then having them wake up to the sound of him yelling at their mother. "You want me to show you compassion? You're taking my kids away from me, Sarah." The heat in his face turned to water in his eyes. But no woman likes to see a man cry. And it sure as hell wouldn't help him win her back. So he swallowed hard and said, "Have some compassion for *me.* What am I going to do with myself?"

"We're still friends," she leaned in and took his hand. And he let her. "We'll always be friends. We have to be. For Lacey and Mason. They need to see that we can still be around each other. Still normal."

"Normal," he huffed. "Normal, divorced parents, huh?"

"We can still be normal," she said. "People divorce all the time. It's just what happens. People grow apart."

"We've grown apart? How?"

She paused and then said, "We want different things in life."

"No. I want *you,*" he said.

"And I want stability." Her answer came out too quickly, like it'd been in the batter's box for far too long and was finally called up to the plate.

He knew it. Had always had a feeling it would happen. There'd even been a few times where he thought she might be having an affair. And it'd crossed his mind that she wouldn't even be in it for the sex. It'd be for the perks of living a normal life. Maybe something as simple as the guy having a house. It didn't even have to be a nice house, just something with a driveway. His own driveway. She'd be able to pull up into the driveway of his house and park her car. And then she'd be able to walk across *his* walkway to get to *his* front door. No shared parking lot. No numbers on his door, or a peephole like a hotel. His. All his. That was all she'd ever wanted: a house with a yard and a driveway. That's it. She wasn't picky, wanting a pool and a fence and a dog. She just wanted a yard and a driveway. And after eight years, he still couldn't give that to her.

Brian could only nod his head at the response, and after they both gave the comment some time to sink in, Brian asked, "So what was the text about?"

"It was about us staying here. Just until school is out."

"Like, you and the kids stay here? Even while all this is going on?"

"Remember, we're still friends, Brian. We have to be. And honestly, I want us to be." She grabbed his hand again. "You're still an amazing person. This doesn't change that. You're an amazing father and you deserve to be around the kids. I want us to remain friends, I really do."

The thoughts he had of how this conversation would go couldn't have been any farther off. He went from thinking they would stay together as a family, to learning he was wrong, and now he was wrong but they're going to stay together still? Talk about a modern family.

"If the kids are staying, then yes. Absolutely yes. I can handle that."

"Are you sure?" she asked, letting go of his hand and leaning back on the couch with her legs crossed to read whatever reaction was painted across his face. At this point, even *he* had no idea what emotion his face was radiating. There'd been so many ups and downs with this day that it was hard to tell what the hell was going on. But he knew one thing: his kids were staying.

"For how long?" he asked.

"Just until school's out. Then we'll leave."

"Okay."

"It just helps. If we go stay with my sister, I'll have to drive them twenty minutes to and from school each day. They wake up early enough as it is."

"You're not taking them far, are you? When you leave?" he asked. "Like, running away with some other guy to a new state to start a new life?"

"No," she laughed. "My job is here. Granted, every company has an HR department and I can get a job anywhere, but I like where I work."

"Good," he sighed. "Because I want to be in their lives."

"You're their dad. You'll always be in their lives." She stood and thanked him for the conversation. "It's very mature of you to be doing this," she said. And then she was off into the bedroom to begin her nightly routine, alone once again.

Brian walked to the refrigerator, happy that he would be able to spend two more months under the same roof as his children. He opened a beer, grateful for the extension. But standing alone in the back corner of this party he was having was that dreary date two months from now, when school was out, and it would do nothing but inch closer.

11

He held an open book in front of him, but he wasn't reading it. Another story played in his mind. One that seemed so surreal. One that was so wonderful. One that was supposed to have a happy ending. The one where he and Sarah grew old together and they watched the kids grow up to be successful adults themselves. One where *one* of his books would eventually take off and they'd have the money to retire somewhere warm, and they'd laugh at the times they used to struggle and they'd say it was all worth it.

But Sarah had taken an eraser to that story a few nights ago when she said she wanted a divorce.

As Brian sat on the couch with the hardcover in his hand, he could only think of the rest of his family, sleeping only a few feet away, that would leave him eventually. And he thought back to the many times where he'd sulked about his life and told himself he'd hit rock bottom. He thought about the night his family died, and how he thought there could be no worse situation in the world. Had he only known...

While eighteen-year-old Brian Hart was trying to wrap his head around the death of his family, wanting the world to stop spinning so he could take a few moments to realize what was going on, everyone around him was taking big steps to move ahead in life. He was only out of school for three weeks before he figured he was ready to come back. In reality, he was never *ready.* But he needed civilization again. He needed to talk to people. See people. *Real* people. Not some shrink, or a police detective. He needed something else around him to be happening. Other conversations to be going on. Something. *Anything.* Anything besides someone asking him how he was doing and trying to convince him that life is a blessing and blah blah blah.

He remembered Dr. Fisher trying to tell him with her head tilted and empathetic expression on her face that "You are the only one who can control how this goes." Returning to school, she was referring to. "Humans are curious in nature. Children even more so." And though he wanted to tell her that seniors were eighteen years old, and therefore adults, so her theory would not apply, it turned out she was right.

There were stares as he walked through the halls of school. Some compassionate. Some awkward. And some looked fearful of him, like he was the one who'd died and now was back from the dead, dirt still glued to his decaying skin. He imagined these looks would have gone on a lot longer had it not been for Brady Ellison's decision on which college he'd attend being broadcast on every television in the school on Brian's second day back.

Brady was a big story, and once he declared he was leaving behind his school records in football and basketball and committing to playing Wide Receiver at Kansas State, the entire school erupted and there wasn't a conversation the rest of the day that didn't have his name attached.

As the school year went on, it seemed that almost once a week another student was coming in waving a college acceptance letter, excited to share where they were going. Girls would cry and hug as they thought about separating from each other for the first time since grade school. And guys would fist-bump and shake hands and talk about the potential for girls at whichever school they were discussing. News of where people were "going next year" traveled through the halls like Kardashian gossip: Ryan Norrin to Wisconsin on a lacrosse scholarship; Becky Kapritini to Syracuse, full ride for field hockey; Dillon Archer, Anthony Bestin, Mitchell McQuaid, all to Division 2 football programs; Antwon Smith to North Carolina to play basketball. And then there was Andrea Stapleton, the class valedictorian, who chose Yale over Harvard. Turns out she did just fine in life, believe it or not.

Brian had actually gotten two acceptance letters from Newton State about thirty minutes south of here, and to LaCadia University up north. But like the rest of the mail he'd gotten over the few-week span, he'd neglected to act on any of it. And even when he went home one of those days after school and looked at the acceptance letters and the paperwork that came with it, he had no desire to pursue. What would be the point? Who would help him do all the work? Who would file the paperwork for his loans? Or financial aid? Who would help him pack and drive him to school and tell him good luck and that they'd miss him? It surely wouldn't be the two aunts who stood slouching next to him at the funeral, never to be heard from again.

His next few years were spent contemplating community college while playing video games and living off of Mom's life insurance money. Dad had some also, but it all went bye-bye when he chose to drag the blade of a knife across his throat. Suicide isn't covered, apparently. And Brian can see why. So many people are worth more money dead than alive. Why not help out your family? Give them a nice head start?

Uh-uh, says the insurance company.

By the age of twenty-two, he had finally gotten his act together and signed up for community college. He spent two semesters there surrounded by eighteen-year-olds who made him feel like shit for waiting so long, and also with middle-aged men and women who made him feel like it could have been worse. But after two semesters, he was able to transfer out to Caperton University, which couldn't be more than fifteen minutes from his house. Call it what you will – homesickness, fear – but he couldn't fathom leaving. How could he leave his house? Leave behind the only thing left that reminded him of his family? Or that he was once *part* of a family?

He couldn't leave.

Looking back, he probably should have. The house was paid off and in Brian's name. Selling it would have put a fat chunk of money in his bank account. He could have gone far away to school and lived like a king. *You live and learn,* he would eventually tell himself, sick at the thought of wasted time. Although it did all work out. Because at twenty-six-years-old, he graduated from Caperton U with a degree in Business Administration. And as he tossed that tassel from one side of his cap to the other, something left him. The past, maybe. Because he felt happy. Felt free. Like he could move on now. Move away. Get a job anywhere in the world and there'd be nothing holding him back here.

Except for maybe that lovely girl Sarah that he now called his girlfriend.

In his junior year of college, he had to take Physics as one of his science classes, and it turned out to be heaven. It was full of beautiful women, which was a pleasant surprise. For two weeks he'd ohhed and ahhed at the girls walking through that classroom door until one day he saw Sarah, and had no idea how he hadn't noticed her earlier. But he'd noticed her then, and would never stop noticing her. And he never thought that the green eyes walking in the classroom door would one day discover a secret about him that he swore he'd never reveal.

12

The alarm told Brian it was 3 AM, and the buzzing sounded like nails on a chalkboard. He wasn't torn out of a pleasant dream at an awards ceremony full of his literary idols on this day. No, on this morning, he was torn from nothing but a deep, dark sleep. And all he wanted to do was close his eyes and go right back to it.

He woke, rubbing his eyes, and crawled slowly out of bed and to the bathroom without running into anything.

The bedroom would always be dark, regardless of the time of year. Daylight savings time couldn't help him this early in the morning. It was always so tempting to hit snooze, roll back over and go to sleep. He wanted to, every morning, telling himself another ten minutes wouldn't hurt. He listened to those demons at first, but soon realized how detrimental ten minutes could be when it came to a short, three-hour writing block. Once trained, he popped right up and stumbled, half-asleep, to the bathroom, where he would splash ice cold water on his face and look himself in the mirror: *You can't go back to sleep an unpublished loser. Get your ass out there and write.*

And once he was up, he was up. Energized and ready to get to writing...with the help of coffee, of course.

He moved through the kitchen to get that much-needed caffeine, wishing everything was rubber and silent and the door to the kids' shared room was soundproof. The coffee maker was always quiet, though, only releasing the sound of the hot, comforting coffee pouring into the pot. When it was finished, he took the hot mug with him down the hallway and to his desk in the bedroom.

That blinking cursor sitting atop a blank white screen haunted him again, as it did most mornings, and he stared back at it. He wanted desperately to know what was lying behind it. Wanted to know what words would come if he was just able to move that thing to the right a little bit.

He sat, and he pondered, so indecisive. He did everything he could to avoid actually writing, which he always did. There were always doubts running through his mind, and as he wrote at this moment, he felt like the writing was getting shittier and shittier with each passing sentence. And as he wondered what was the perfect thing to write, he thought back to yesterday morning when Sarah read his opening chapter. *Make it authentic,* she said. That word: *authentic.* It's all he could think about.

The first chapter of his manuscript ended with the main character grabbing the knife she'd use to walk upstairs and kill her husband. Comical, how people will think his idea for writing this book stemmed from his impending divorce. People would think the opposite to be true, of course. They would think that *he* would be the one to kill his wife since she asked for the divorce. But a month ago when he started outlining this thing, he had a good relationship with his wife, or so he thought.

The second chapter would start where Brian left off: with the main character's wet feet trekking up the stairs, the knife hanging loosely by her side. And he got this part down with ease. It was writing the stabbing scene that was causing the nervous feelings of rejection. What if it's terrible? Unauthentic? Unreal? How can this be authentic? How can a man who's never done anything more than poke another human being through a t-shirt write a gruesome scene with authenticity? The internet could help, but there were so many conflicting answers. Which one was correct?

A paragraph was written, and then a paragraph was erased. This was a shit session. Nothing was going well. The words coming onto the screen were garbage and he knew it. Some writers say the rule of a first draft is to get down as much as you can on paper and worry about editing later, but Brian could never do that. He could never write shit. He needed it to make some sort of sense. He had to walk away from his desk at the end of every session with a bit of pride. A tiny victory. Even if he only had one or two good paragraphs written, he knew he didn't just spew out anything that came across his mind.

But right now, the sentences were being forced. They were trash. Worthy of the garbage disposal in which his tiny little apartment wasn't equipped.

Walk away. He did.

He took his coffee mug with him and walked out of the room, down the hall, and into the living room where he quietly opened the blinds and stared out into the parking lot. He stared down from his second-story sliding glass door that led to his patio. Beyond the overhang was a streetlight, and beneath that streetlight, a neighbor's car. The light shone down on it like a singer on a stage.

Brian's sedan was parked on the other side of the lot. With no light. No idea bulb shining down onto it, just like there was no idea bulb shining down on him.

Sarah's ironically-similar sedan sat parked next to his in the dark. No irony there. The woman would live in the dark if she could – meant more time to sleep.

He pulled open the sliding door and walked out onto the patio, sitting on one of the two plastic chairs that were separated by a matching, white, plastic table. It was a warm and quiet early morning. His neighbors were all asleep. No birds chirping or cars driving by on the street just beyond the parking lot. At the moment, not even the crickets were chirping. It was only Brian and the night sky, both awaiting some sign of life.

He turned and looked through the glass slider behind him, and he could see the oven clock which read 3:41. Plenty of time for writing, but when there's nothing to write, the clock moves like an hourglass.

A drive always did him well. Windows down, sun shining in, sunglasses on and music blasting. For some reason, this was his haven. Where he found inspiration. Where he found that ideas came to him most and where every thought seemed like a great one. But at 3:41 in the morning, the only people on the road were drunks. And his life insurance payments weren't exactly up to date. Lord, if he thought he was letting his family down now, imagine how they'd feel if all his debt was pushed on them?

So he decided against the drive, and opted instead for

something way out of his realm: a run.

He walked back into the apartment and into his bedroom closet to see boxes stacked like bricks. Shoe boxes, small appliance boxes, any type of box that could be used for returning a purchase. He'd had these stored for years – his own little weird collection. Most people have weird habits and this was his. Brian kept almost every box with the idea that he may need it for resale, or so he told Sarah when she continually made fun of him. *We won't have this Keurig forever and the resale value will be higher if we sell it in the original box.* This was partly true, though there is one box he could never part ways with. There was too much to lose if someone were to get their hands on it. All but one of them were decoys, but inside one box was his entire life, and he'd do anything possible to ensure that life stays within its confines. He smirked at it, like some enemy kept prisoner. And he knew which box it was without even having to dig through the pile. He could get to it with his eyes closed if he needed to.

Inside one of the decoys was a pair of running shoes that still looked relatively new. There was no sign of deterioration over the years. Just a nice pair of fresh mesh and rubber waiting to go get some air.

With the shoes snug on his feet, he walked back down the hall and to the front door. But it was there that he contemplated whether or not to wake Sarah. Surely she wouldn't care too much. I mean, she *did* just ask him for a divorce. But just in case something happened – maybe one of those drunk drivers hit him as he's crossing the street – it'd be nice for someone to know his whereabouts.

Just go tell her, he thought, and didn't contemplate.

Leaning over Sarah, he gently shook her shoulder and

let her know he was going on a run, "Probably in the neighborhood across the street." He didn't expect much of a response from the woman who slept like she was in a coma, but she did stir somewhat when he told her. Probably due to the *run* part. He was never one to care about fitness.

She grunted, and then she was back asleep again.

What if I do *get hit?* he thought. *No one would find me until her alarm went off, anyway.*

Now the clock read 4:03 and the image of the hourglass and the steady flow of leaking sand played in his mind. He pictured each grain of that stuff falling from top to bottom, leading closer to the end of his writing time. But this run would be good. Healthy for his body and for his mind. Ten minutes is all he would need. Just something to clear his head. And to maybe give him some light on how to write a damn perfect murder scene.

He'd find a way. Shortly. And as he reached for the door handle, he could have never guessed how.

He walked outside and took a breath of the cool, fresh air. The world was still and the streets quiet. Brian started his run like he was alone in the world. He circled his complex and then crossed into the neighborhood of two-story homes on the other side of the main road – the type of neighborhood Sarah had wanted to live in since she met Brian. Having to look out the apartment window every day and see this neighborhood had to drive Sarah crazy. It was surprising it took her so long to finally snap and admit how much she hated her life with him.

Now here he was, following the curve of the sidewalk as it led him into the place she'd do anything to live in.

This was the life Sarah wanted. Right here. Right across

the street. Seemingly within arm's reach. Each house had privacy fences around their back yards, thick green grass in the front, and two-and three-car garages. The cars were all parked in the driveways and Brian wondered what could be so valuable inside those garages that the shiny SUVs and luxury cars had to sleep outside.

Sarah's dream home was right across the street and this run was just life's way of rubbing it in his face. It was as if life was telling him *You missed your target. Should have landed here.*

But maybe it wasn't too late. And maybe life was telling him that, too. Because two houses up on the left, there was a pickup truck running and a garage door open. More importantly, there were fishing rods hanging out of the opened tailgate.

Writing a bestseller was his entry fee here. There was no other way he'd get into a neighborhood like this. Not by working eighty hours a week at the pet store; not by quitting and starting a new career; not by continuing on the path of poverty he was already on. The only way he'd ever get into a house like these was if he had a book published. If he proved to the writing world that he was worthy, and then he'd get a book deal and it would be a bestseller. He knew it. There was no other option. This was what *had* to happen. But without an authentic murder scene, he'd never sell a book.

He thought back to his days fishing with his father.

"You see this?" his dad had said of his tackle box. "Don't ever reach into this. Lots of sharp stuff."

As a six-year-old, sharp stuff petrified him. Brian hated being stung by bees. He couldn't imagine what sort of sharp stuff could hurt him in there.

And then he would watch as his father attached the hooks to the line, and how easily the hooks pierced into the skin of the rubber lures. Brian would take a lure in one hand and squeeze it, and then squeeze his finger, wondering how easily the hook could go through his skin.

But it was the knife he remembered most vividly. The orange handle. The long, shiny blade that thinned as it got to the tip. There was a black leather holder it sat inside and the rusted button that would hold it in place, and he always felt like the simple act of removing the knife from that holder could hurt him.

"This'll cut your finger clean off," his dad said, holding up the knife with the leather still covering the blade. "You just ask me if you need anything."

And Brian would nod, telling himself he'd touch nothing besides the fishing rod after his father would hand it to him.

But that knife. The orange handle. It still shone in the images burned into his brain. *This'll cut your finger clean off.*

When his dad meant business, he had this certain look: both eyebrows raised, eyes open and staring straight into his, no blinking. That was the face he used when he explained the capabilities of the knife. But when he was done explaining what it would do, he justified having it as part of his arsenal.

"Dangerous," he said. "But every fisherman needs a good, sharp knife." He only went out three or four times a year – more a middle-class dad than a fisherman – but wore the fisherman hat the right way when he *did* go out.

Brian slowed his jog to a walk as he approached the house with the truck that had the fishing rods dangling from the tailgate. And as he approached the truck's bed, his father's truths were proven right.

The fisherman had a tackle box.

13

If he would have hurried, it all could have been over so much faster.

Brian hid by the rear tire of the truck in the driveway. His heart was racing, but there was no fear. No sense of repercussion. The only thing on his mind: authenticity.

The owner of the fishing gear was rustling around under the dangling garage light. Peering past the truck's cab, all Brian could see was a white ponytail hanging out of a neon-green baseball cap. While the man was bustling around in his garage doing who-knows-what, Brian took off his t-shirt, held it in his hands and swiped the tackle box from the bed of the truck.

What the hell are you thinking, Brian? The thought was there, but it was forced. No default voice reaching into his head and shaking some sense into him. No conscience to hold him back. For some reason, at this very moment, there was nothing more important than a successful story.

Holding the shirt over his hands to prevent fingerprints transferring, he opened the box to find it neatly organized – small hooks in sections to the left, getting larger as you look right; silver weights shaped like tiny, half-inflated balloons were in larger sections; plastic bags with lures and fake worms in others. But beneath all the small stuff was just what Brian knew would be there. Sitting alone in the bottom of the box was a thin, white handle attached to a rusting silver blade.

As his father had said: *Every fisherman needs a good, sharp knife.*

Brian wrapped the t-shirt around the handle of the blade, and then grabbed it with a white-knuckle grip. He leaned over and around the cab of the truck, looking into the garage. The man was there, digging through the riffraff on the workbench before him. The white ponytail swung back and forth with the man's frustrated head-shake.

What was he angry about, Brian thought. And what if his rage grows? What if this guy turns out to be a hot-head? Or someone whose temper breaks easily and he walks out here to find Brian going through his stuff? What if the knife ends up being yanked from his hand and plunged into his *own* flesh? What the hell would be the odds of that? He could write up a good description on *being* stabbed, but that wasn't really the detail he was looking for. He didn't want to be on the other end of the blade, looking into a palm full of blood in a panic.

Panic finally found its way into his veins. Each little noise around him triggered his senses and sent his head whirling around: leaves blowing in the light wind; an owl's hoot off in the distance; a single car passing by on the main road just a few hundred feet away. Alarms finally triggered inside him. There was finally a sense of fear. Only now did he worry about what he wanted to do to this innocent man. Just a guy getting ready for an early morning fishing trip. Probably meeting up with some buddies at the loading ramp. They'd plan on boating out a few miles and then anchoring down before throwing out their lines and cracking a couple early AM beers.

And it'd all be ruined.

The garage light turned off and then the only light seemingly in the entire world was the decorative fixture that hung between the man's two garage doors. Brian heard the smacking of the guy's flip flops against the bottoms of his feet, and the arrogant sound alone was enough to make him change his mind. Now he wanted to snap the guy's neck. Flip flops...ugh.

The smacking got louder, Brian's grip on the knife got tighter, and then it happened.

14

Sarah's eyes opened to the sight of the red light funneling from the numbers on her alarm clock. But a sigh of relief escaped through her nostrils when she saw the time: 5:05. *Thank goodness. Still an hour to sleep.*

Sarah plopped her head back down on the pillow after squinting to see the time and praying, as she did whenever awoken to a dark room, that the time displayed on the digital red numbers had not yet hit 6:00. But as she started to feel her breathing become heavier and slower as she drifted back into sleep, she noticed something was off. She noticed that Brian was not at his desk. Not only that, but the water in the bathroom was running.

The shower.

What the hell? Was this a dream?

As oxygen made its way to her brain and she began to wake up – every ounce of her body fighting it, eyelids filled with lead – she remembered him whispering to her: "I'm going for a run. Be back soon." And then the running shower water made a little more sense. The grogginess gave way and she was able to think rationally.

Still, it seemed odd that Brian would do anything to interfere with his writing time. It was amazing to Sarah that he could wake up at 3:00 in the morning, every single morning, to write. And then go to work for eight hours, every single day. It was a seven-days-a-week cycle and he never got a break, but he also never asked for one. If there was anything she admired in him, even with the divorce looming, it was his work ethic. Simply unfortunate that it never paid off. The writing life had sucked him in, chewed him up and spit him out. It'd given him nothing except stress and pipe dreams. But apparently for the three hours he was able to write each morning, he was happy. Which was why she found his morning run during his writing time a little odd.

Maybe he's just switching things up.

Regardless, she felt something in her stomach. The urge to check on him. Her soon-to-be ex-husband. Felt the need to make sure he was okay.

She crawled out of bed and dragged her feet along the carpet and to the bathroom where she could *feel* the steam leaking out from beneath the closed door.

How long has he been in there?

She wrapped her hand around the doorknob, but stopped herself before twisting. Should she be walking in on him like this? Just a few days after saying she wanted a divorce, she was going to trot in there like they were still a happily married couple?

But she had that gut feeling. The feeling that she needed to go in and check on him. That gut feeling that something was wrong. This was so far from the norm for Brian, and with the steam pouring from the gap below the door like some horror-movie mist, she had this horrible image of him lying in the tub, unconscious, his skin burning under steaming-hot water.

She had to go in.

She let her hand twist the knob and as the door opened, she was hit with a wall of steam that took her breath away. Her eyes shot open, but it was no help seeing through the white cloud in front of her. For a brief moment, she regretted not putting on her glasses when she got out of bed, though they'd have been fogged up before she even had a chance to take a step into the bathroom, anyway.

"Brian?" she called in a loud whisper, speaking only over the sound of the shower water hissing. She stood at the threshold and everything beyond was still a solid white cloud. She leaned her head around the door, looking into the bathroom that seemed too large and out of place for the small apartment. As the acting bathroom-slash-laundry-room, it had to be spacious. And in front of the washer and dryer set inside a walk-in closet stood Brian. His back was to her and the door, and his body was hunched over and shaking vigorously.

"Brian," she called again, this time a little louder.

When he turned around, his eyes popped and looked like two pixelated cue balls – without her glasses, her vision wasn't so clear. He coughed and stuttered, "Oh, sh– Sarah. Why are you up?"

She took a few seconds to wonder why he looked like a teenager who'd just gotten caught with cigarettes and then said, "Because I heard you in here." But what would he have to hide? Was he out with someone and not really taking a run? Was he shaking because he was scrubbing something from his clothes? Lipstick? Perfume? Was he seeing someone else already? It wasn't like she could get angry. After all, she told him she was ending the marriage.

The two stood there, looking at each other in silence for a few seconds that felt like a few hours. Sarah broke the awkwardness by saying, "Alright. Well, just wanted to check on you." And then she walked out, pulling the door closed behind her, feeling that this could have been the first of many conversations between the two that were going to be uncomfortable. As she walked back to the room and to the comfort of her bed, she thought of those upcoming conversations. She thought of standing in front of a judge with Brian being on the opposing team. And she hoped with everything in her that Dr. Epplestein's name would never be mentioned.

15

He wanted to burn it all off, but the water wouldn't get any hotter. His skin was red and close to blistering. But there was a chance something could have still been there, lingering. Some evidence. Some hair follicle or piece of skin or blood.

He wouldn't risk it. His skin hurt but he had to get it all off.

The realism of what happened hit him after he heard the pop – the sound of the knife pushing through the old man's skin. Maybe the guilt hit him right then because that was all he needed for his story's scene, was that description. Or maybe because at that point it was all real. He had just stabbed an innocent man. But he felt it, the guilt. It landed on him with the weight of a brick building.

And then he was crying. Him. Brian. The man *doing* the stabbing, and not the man being stabbed. The knife had been thrown into the grass and Brian was hunched over the man. After throwing the knife to the ground, he'd used the shirt wrapped around his hand to shield as much of his face as he could, but also for catching the tears rolling down his face. He might have been struck with guilt and fear, but he knew to keep his mind focused on not leaving any evidence.

"I'm sorry," Brian sobbed through the shirt to the man who was now lying on his side, moaning in pain and clutching his blood-soaked mid-section.

What the hell have I done?

I did what I had to do, the other half of his mind said. And he did. He got his story. He got his authenticity. He got the information he needed to try to keep his family intact. That old man was just in the wrong place at the wrong time. Plus, he was older. He'd lived a nice life. It wasn't like he killed some teenager. Or someone with a young kid at home.

That's justifiable, right?

Most importantly, he left no evidence behind. Sarah almost ruined that when she flung open the bathroom door. But other than that, there was nothing. There was no one that saw him out on his run and no way anyone would have been able to link him to it. He wouldn't go to jail for this. No way. He did this so he could be with his kids every night, and prison would give him no time at all. He'd be better off being a weekend dad than being an incarcerated one. That nightmare of his kids calling someone else Dad would surely turn to reality if he found himself behind bars for murder.

He wrapped the towel around his waist and wiped away the layer of condensation that grew on the mirror during his shower. Looking back at him through a fog was the same face he'd always seen. No difference. He wasn't a bad person now. Only a determined one.

He told himself he'd do it again if he had to. And he would. He'd do whatever he needed to do in order to achieve his goal.

And then suddenly he had this strange feeling of déjà vu.

16

Tiny little voices traveled down the hall. Whispers and laughs. They were trying to be quiet because they thought she was still asleep, but there was no sleeping for Sarah. Not after what she walked into. And not after realizing that her simple words caused it to happen. She may never sleep again.

The buzzing alarm startled her. Six o'clock. Time to wake up and get the kids ready. But they were already awake and doing god-knows-what with their father. Sarah wanted to lie in the bed forever.

She finally peeled herself from the mattress a moment or two later. After washing up, she walked down the hall and into the kitchen, she saw the kids at the table and Brian standing in front of the stove, spatula in his hand, like some still-shot captured on a poster. She wanted to pinch herself to see if this was a dream, but then the kids started to argue about crayons at the table and the poster was quickly torn down. Behind it was some dingy paint she'd been looking at for too long.

"Hey," she said, and all three heads turned to happily greet her. The kids' smiles turned back to whining frowns afterward, still in the debate over who should have the blue crayon. Apparently neither kid gave a damn about the other twenty-three crayons in the box.

"Hungry?" Brian asked her.

"Um...sure?"

"Don't worry," he laughed. "Not trying to win you over or anything." She looked to the kids to make sure they weren't listening. No surprise: they weren't. "I'm up," he said. "Just thought I'd help out a little."

"Okay." She wouldn't argue. Each and every morning she went through this process while Brian put some finishing touches on his writing, showered, spent five minutes with the kids and then headed off to work. It was nice to steer clear of the kitchen for once. "Did you pick out their outfits?"

"I'm a good dad today," Brian said, pointing at her with the spatula. "Not a great dad."

He wouldn't know which clothes to choose, anyway, she thought to herself.

With a freeing energy about her, she headed back to the bathroom where she washed up. Then she went into each of the kids' rooms, where covers and sheets were thrown to the side, and she imagined the joy they each must have had when they saw their dad waking them up for once.

The kids were crazy about him. Adored him. When he left for work every morning, they'd be upset, and when he got home at night, they'd be ecstatic, clawing at his legs and his hips, both wanting to be picked up and hugged and thrown around. She thought about him as a father, and how amazing he was. But when it came to anything else, he sucked the life out of it.

He had no money. He had no life. And he had no desire to entertain Sarah. All he ever wanted to do was write. He never took the time to think about how she might be feeling. Never once considered including her into his schedule. He could wake up at 3 AM every day to write, but couldn't get a babysitter for an hour or two and take his wife out to dinner once in a while? Sure, they were broke. She knew it. But he couldn't scrounge together twenty bucks to pay a babysitter for an hour while the two of them sat at a bar and had a cheap beer? Just one? Just to escape the reality of their redundant lives? Had he thought of this – thought of *her* – every once in a while, maybe the pending divorce wouldn't even be happening. Maybe she never would have needed Dr. Epplestein in the first place.

She picked out an outfit for each of the kids and laid each on their respective bed before she walked back out to the kitchen, smelling the sweet scent of the warm breakfast grow stronger and stronger as she made her way down the hall. Her husband-for-now turned after placing plates in front of the kids, and when he saw her, said, "Yours is next."

Sarah loved her children with every ounce of her being, but Lord, oh Lord, how she tried anything to drain out the sound of them chewing, slopping and sucking up their food. It was like they played a game with each other of who can eat the loudest, and no matter how many times Sarah would bark across the table for them to keep their mouths closed or to sit in their chair while they eat, they didn't listen. It was like they couldn't. Like they were physically incapable of sitting still and eating quietly, like humans. So every morning before she served them their breakfast, she turned up the volume on the TV.

Somehow, Brian had managed to have the TV off this morning. Lacey and Mason usually craved at least a few minutes of a cartoon as they put on their shoes and backpacks. But maybe the sight of their Dad doing the morning routine with them had taken their mind off of the brain-rotter.

They'd be reminded now, as Sarah reached for the thing they knew turned on their toons.

Grabbing the remote from the arm of the couch is all it took for their little heads to turn. And with a mouth full of food, Lacey, already out of her seat, yelled, "Teen Titans!"

"Sit down," Sarah snapped, pointing at her with the remote. "And how many times do I have to tell you not to talk with food in your mouth?" In one ear and out the other. But she sat, which was a small victory, though it wouldn't last long and Sarah knew it.

The screen flicked to life and before she even had a moment to browse the guide, Sarah was captured by the familiarity of what she saw on screen: a neighborhood of large houses, and in the background was a two-way street. Mercer Street. She looked to her left and out the sliding glass window leading to their patio. And beyond that patio and the parking lot below: Mercer Street. "Oh my god."

"What?" she heard Brian's panicked voice.

"Is that across the street?" she asked to herself more than in an answer to him. She walked over to the sliding doors and looked around, then opened them and stepped out into the muggy morning air, leaning over the railing as if the extra few inches would allow her telescopic vision. But as she squinted and searched through trees, she found she didn't need any advanced vision. Because she could see the reflection of glowing red and blue lights.

She stepped back in and the kids were now up and standing in front of the TV.

"Get back in your seats," she said. "Eat."

Then she found herself standing just as her kids were, eyes glued to the screen, wondering what happened over there.

The news anchor came on, and said with his deep, serious voice, "We now go to Brianna Williams, live outside Southeast Medical Center, where the victim is reported to be in critical condition."

Sarah's eyes didn't budge. *Critical condition?*

Brianna Williams said into her padded microphone, "That's right. Good morning, David. I'm standing outside of Southeast Medical Center where the victim, sixty-four-year-old Thomas McMann, is listed in critical condition after suffering a single stab wound to the stomach. Reports indicate that the suspect, who is still at large, used the victim's own fishing knife, which was stolen just prior to the attack. There are no witnesses, and police are still searching for any clues. Rock Park P.D. urges anyone with any clues to this attack to call immediately. David, back to you."

And David the Anchor's reaction was the same one Sarah felt on her face: horror. These things happen all the time. The news networks always have stories of murder and battery and robbery and all sorts of horrific things. And every time a field reporter gives the show back to the in-studio anchor, they always have the same empathetic expression on their face. But when it's in your own town – your own neighborhood – that expression hits home.

"Kids," Brian's voice came from the kitchen. "Eat before

it gets cold. You have to leave soon. Don't want to be late."

Sarah could only watch for a few more seconds before she shut off the TV. Normally, she hated to hear the slapping of food in her kids' mouths while they ate, but today that sound would be heavenly compared to any noise waves coming from the TV speakers.

She powered down the monitor and threw the remote on the couch. When she looked up, Brian was staring into her eyes, unblinking, and the chill that traveled down her spine was one she hadn't felt before.

17

Brian was always envious when he'd see writing better than his. Or an *idea* better than his, for that matter. *How the hell did they think of that?* he always thought, wondering what he could do to get his brain to think the same way. And any time he found himself wrapped up in a great novel, the thoughts were much more common.

How the hell does the writer seem to write with such ease? Like the words just roll off of their fingertips. Do they even stress at all about their work?

His phone sat on the table next to his vending machine cheeseburger. As he grabbed the rubbery burger with his left hand, he swiped his phone to turn the page on his Kindle app with his right. He had eighteen minutes left of break time. Eighteen minutes left of peace. Just him, the humming of the air conditioner, and an empty room in which to be left alone.

This rarely ever happened. Typically his alone time was intercepted by the high school kids sitting and scrolling through their social media feeds, or watching videos with their volume turned up to *Can you hear this, too?*. So it was nice to have the alone time. It was just a shame that it came on a day like today, where every word he read was forgotten almost as fast as he read it, and all he could think about was the morning. Did that really happen? Did he really kill a man?

No, he didn't. The news network this morning said he was in critical condition. So where did that leave Brian? What happened if he got caught. *If? Come on Brian. Everyone gets caught.* Would he be tried for attempted murder? That helped, right? If it was only attempted, he'd get out of prison a little sooner. But what if the cops wouldn't catch him, and then this guy survived? Would Brian have to go back after him? Finish what he started so the guy couldn't turn him in?

Christ, he really was thinking like a killer.

His taste buds were tricked by the abundance of ketchup dumped on the microwaved beef, or whatever it really was. But the burger wasn't bad, and he took another bite as he once again slid his finger across his phone screen to turn the page, thinking to himself that he had no idea what he just read.

Sarah used to make him lunch. For a while, she did it with enthusiasm, feeling like a good wife. And she was. Every night after dinner, she'd pack him up some leftovers and put it into his lunch box with silverware and napkins. Or if there were no leftovers from that night's dinner, he'd get a sandwich with some chips in a separate bag. Either way, he was fed. And he did nothing in return besides waste his life away at this pet store. But it was all just temporary. That was what he told himself and Sarah, and it was what Sarah told herself...at first.

She continued to make his lunch for him as the temporary job turned into a permanent job, and then a career. But there wasn't much love in it anymore. She wouldn't tell him what she'd packed right after she'd packed it, looking for a well-deserved pat on the back. Sometimes she would forget the napkins or the silverware, or would forget altogether to do anything for him.

They sure had come a long way.

Brian swiped across the screen again and then leaned over to take another bite. Just as he did, the door behind him whipped open with such force that it swung around and hit the wall.

"Hey. I need you to come out here, Bud." Eric.

Bud? Brian didn't even turn around. If he turned around right then, it'd be to throw something at the smug bastard. The only things in reach were either his burger or his phone. So it'd be his phone that went flying. And he'd be glad to see it shatter. Break apart on the dickhead's face. Then he might have even gotten up, grabbed a shard from the floor, and started swiping it at his neck. Fucking prick. *Bud?* For real? Remember where you are, douchebag. You manage a fucking pet store, which means you get to boss around high school kids. And get your little dick hard when the sixteen-year-olds working the register find it *sexy* that you have some authority. Give it two years and then ask them where they stand on your "position".

"Hey, Brian?" Eric said with obvious annoyance that he had to repeat himself.

Yes. That's *my name. Not Bud. Or Sport. Remember, you weasel, that I'm older than you.*

Brian turned around to see Eric standing in the

doorway, one hand on his hip and the other leaning against the door frame. "What's up?"

"I need you to come out here. Tommy and Stephen can't operate this forklift and I need some pallets moved. We have a shipment coming in."

"Now?" he asked, wanting to hold up his burger but feeling pretty embarrassed about having his lunch dispensed from the machine in the corner of the room.

"Yeah. Shipment is on its way."

"Another shipment?"

"The Lauderworth store had some inventory issues. Ordered too much. I told them we can take it."

We can, huh? Did you even look at the warehouse? It's jam-packed.

"Neither of them can operate it?" Brian asked. "It's just a forklift."

"They didn't take the safety course," he said in a lower tone, growing more annoyed with the questions he needed to answer. It was so clear in his face that he wanted to put his foot down and demand Brian go into the warehouse *Right now*. And it made Brian a little happy inside to see him growing irritable.

He's going to be a miserable father, Brian thought.

"Alright," Brian said. "Give me a minute."

"Shipment will be here in twenty." Eric's way of saying Brian didn't have a minute, and to get his ass out there.

Then Eric was gone. And when he walked away, he left the door open rather than shutting it to give Brian back his peace and quiet. Instead, the break room door remained open for all to look in and see him as they walked on by, customers and fellow employees both.

Man, it'd be nice to bash that fucker's head in.

18

It was a redundant job, operating that forklift. But it was a peaceful job. When the thing was running, no one would talk to him. There was no side chatter for the eight hours there, bullshitting about nonsense or women or politics. The only thing to do was think, and think he did. This is where he usually brainstormed his ideas. But as his day came winding down, he grew angry at the fact that he couldn't think about anything but Eric's comments earlier.

That fucking prick, he thought. Always getting into his head.

He carried on with his day behind the wheel of the forklift, removing pallets from the shelving. Tommy and Stephen would tear into the plastic wrap to get to what they were told they needed. And when they were done, they'd wrap up the remaining items on the pallet and Brian would put it right back into its original slot.

Tough work.

It was the in-between time that he usually did his thinking. His brainstorming. On this day, it was just a slideshow of the past and a glimpse of the future. That poor old man, horrified, and the pop of his skin as his own fishing knife entered his body. And Brian sat, comfortable in his climate-controlled warehouse and padded chair. Prison still didn't even seem realistic.

He couldn't go to prison. Come on. This was Brian Hart. The same Brian Hart that was scared of his own shadow. Still is. Every time someone around him laughed: *They're laughing at me.* Every time someone stared: *Why are they staring? What's on my face?* Every time a girl would look his way: Nothing but flushness in his face and a look in the opposite direction.

This is the person who stabbed a man?

What had his life become? Seventeen years ago, his world was turned upside down as he sat on the bumper of an ambulance with a warm blanket around him. He stared on into the night as the limp bodies of his mother and sister were carefully pried from the overturned car and taken away. He was the victim then. Battered. Shaken.

Seventeen years ago that happened. And look at him now. What a difference.

19

There's some new sense that courses through your veins when you see those red and blue lights flaring in the night sky. It creates a total body uneasiness. And it doesn't matter which side of the line you're on.

It was the worst night of Brian's life, the night his mom and sister died. Dad walked away, but by the time Brian arrived on scene, he'd fainted or passed out or something like that and had been taken to the hospital in a separate ambulance.

He remembered the chaos. The commotion. The emotion. Cops yelling at spectators to stand back and the paramedics working vigorously. He remembered the blood, and the glass, and the wheels of the car pointing up to the sky. The car itself looked like a dog on its back. He remembered this because he saw it every night in his dreams.

One of the EMTs had him wrapped in a blanket, sitting on the bumper of their ambulance, treating him as if he was one of the injured in the crash. But he wasn't. He was just one of the passers-by, on his way home from a late shift at work when he recognized the car on the side of the highway.

The car ended up flipping and slamming into a telephone pole. The aftermath made it look like someone swung the wooden pole into the side of it like a baseball swing. And the worst part was that his mom and sister were still in there, trapped.

There were spotlights shining everywhere as firemen used the jaws of life to get the two women out. But spotlights shining on a dark crime scene make it harder to see from afar. It was all a blur. A bright blur. But through the flashlights, spotlights, and collage of red and blue lights swirling around in the air, Brian watched as each one of their lifeless bodies was taken from the car.

He could still see them if he closed his eyes.

The paramedic had asked him a time or two if he wanted to leave, but he insisted on staying. If this was the last time he'd see his family before the organs were plucked from them and replaced with cotton and marbles and whatever other kinds of filler Morticians used to present bodies in a casket, he wanted to be there.

The movements of the first responders became slower and slower, and as Brian looked around, conversations that had begun on the topic of curiosity had now turned to different topics as a whole. Sort of the same way a funeral works, where the people who show up and grieve earliest find ways to talk about other things later in the service. The newcomers to the party will look over, appalled. *How can you be smiling at a time like this?*

Brian watched as two stretchers were brought over too slowly and set beside the car. There was a First Aid kit sitting on each one and he figured it must have just been protocol. They were dead. They'd been dead for a while.

Chaos around the car had continued to die down. He figured they must have found a way to get the bodies out. For a second he had a sliver of hope, and he could feel his slouching back straighten a little as he concentrated on everything going on. But then he saw what he knew he'd see: two bodies taken out, one by one. Both with pale skin. One a bit larger than the other – Mom was always getting on Christina about her weight but Christina didn't seem to care. "I don't want to be some stick runway model," Christina would always say.

Brian knew it: they were dead. As soon as each body was pulled from the wreck, they were put into body bags.

Two stretchers with black body bags were taken to two separate ambulances, and the two separate ambulances took off from the scene about a minute apart, no doubt on their way to the same destination.

It was hard to know what to do at this point, but he started mumbling something to the paramedic beside him. Something about a part of him wanting to cry. A part of him wanting to scream. A part of him wanting to lie down in a ball and sleep until this whole thing passed – until the grief was over.

"Let's get you out of here?" she said to him, rubbing his back. Had he not been in the current situation, he might have hit on her. She was cute. A young blonde with blue eyes, maybe doing this part-time while going to nursing school. As an eighteen-year-old, single man, it wouldn't have hurt anybody to ask her out. But as an eighteen-year-old who'd just lost his mother and sister, it may come off as a little tasteless. So he simply nodded and followed her to the passenger side of the ambulance, where she opened the door for him.

She was about to shut the door after he got in, but held the door open instead and looked curiously at him. She had one of those side head-nods dogs do when they're confused. It was like some thought had just hit her and she had to think for a second before opening her mouth. And then she did, asking, "Hey, where's your car?"

"Not here," he said nonchalantly, grabbing the seat belt and pulling it over his body.

"Then how'd you get here?"

20

They were all buried on the same day, Mom, Dad, and Christina were. Dad killed himself less than twenty-four hours after the accident and maybe that was why – he wanted to feel like he went down with them.

Brian could remember starting off so many sessions with Dr. Fisher using those exact words. No matter his mood or where the story went from there, everything always seemed to stem from that Thursday morning, four days after the crash. On that morning, three open caskets were situated in the front of the church and the line of criers and huggers wept on their knees in front of each one.

Mom was an only child and both of her parents had died, so the only people who stood beside Brian in the precession line were Dad's two divorced sisters. They wept just as hard as anyone in the room, and he'd hoped for their sake it was because they hated the color black that everyone was wearing. The two of them sure weren't crying over the bodies in the casket. They couldn't have been. Because they didn't care enough to visit them when they were alive, so why would they be upset over their death?

Brian had more hugs that day than he ever had in his life, and then Round 2 of the hugs came when the burial services were over with at the cemetery. But of all the people who used his shoulder as a landing pad for tears, there were only a few who crossed paths with him again, and none were on purpose.

That night, when his family was in the ground for good, he went back to the empty house his parents used to live in, wondering what he'd do now. He walked to the bay window in the kitchen and stared out into the dying grass and eerily silent yard for quite some time, never removing the long pea coat he wore during the day. He remembered watching the birds as they flew in and out of the trees in the back yard. He wondered if they were a family. And if they were, were they a happy one? Did they argue, the Mom and Dad? Did they fight? Were the kids smart? Did they go to school? Did *they* fight?

But eventually the questions in his head ended, and so did the day. The birds nestled in for the night, all in one small, happy nest. Whereas Brian was alone in the two-story nest with nothing but memories and pictures to remind him of everything. The death and loneliness were still so fresh in the house that even the food his mother had bought at the grocery store just a few days ago was still in the refrigerator. Hell, his Dad's fingerprints were probably still on the carton of orange juice.

Not once did Brian turn on the TV that night. Nor did he open that stocked refrigerator. Or go upstairs and past the bedroom doors that wouldn't be opened again until someone new lived in the house. Instead, with the coat still on his back and the Oxfords still on his feet, he laid himself on the couch and stared up at the ceiling until sleep took him away for the night.

That night he dreamt of nothing. He figured he would have had nightmares of his mother and sister in their final moments, screaming and clawing for something to hold on to. Or his father, weeping the following morning as he pulled the blade of the butcher knife across his throat, unable to cope with what had happened the night before.

But none of that occurred. His sleep was calm. It was a sea of quiet, still blackness.

21

Sarah sat in the stiff leather seat that never felt comfortable. This never felt like a safe place. Not like her father made it seem when he first started paying for these therapy sessions. Then again, Sarah wasn't the average patient, and her father hadn't the slightest clue what she managed to get herself into.

With other patients, Dr. Epplestein probably had some writing pad on his lap, jotting down notes that he may or may not have added to their charts. But with Sarah, he always held this binder on his lap. It was a maroon, bulky thing, full of what Sarah knew were trends about her husband.

"So you really think he did this?" he asked.

Sarah didn't even have to swing her eyes from the bright white ceiling and over to the old man. She knew what he was doing. She knew he was smirking. Or smiling. Trying to hide the excitement his little game was bringing him.

"I know he did," she said. "I watched him scrub the blood from his clothes."

"What makes you think it wasn't Brian's blood? Maybe he bit his lip? Tripped while running?"

She thought again about what she was doing here, just as she had since the beginning. Even before this game started, she wondered how she ended up in this spot.

Sarah had an amazing life. She had a life that she swore she'd replicate when she was older. Both her parents worked, and they worked hard. Her dad worked three jobs when they were growing up and her mother went to school full-time when Sarah and Bethany were teenagers. It was no easy feat to work full-time, go to school full-time, and come home to two adolescent girls ripping out each other's hair over a tank top.

All that hard work her parents had put in and where did it land her? Here. With a psychologist, because she couldn't open herself up to them and reveal how much she hated how her life turned out. She loved Brian more than anything, but she should have taken the route Bethany took. Bethany entered relationships purely for the money. That was it. And now look at her. Stay-at-home wife with no kids and a filthy-rich husband. They travel, they drink, they laugh, and what do Brian and Sarah do? They struggle. They get through each day but it's a little more difficult with each sunset.

Sarah was still defensive of everything said about Brian. Mostly because they were best friends. For all the financial struggles and bullshit societal wants they could never afford, she still loved him. There was a time when he used to make her laugh, and although those days are gone – carried away by the strong winds of stress – he still made their kids laugh. And to Sarah, there was nothing in the world more precious than the laughter of her children.

"Your positive this stabbing was something done by him? You weren't just dreaming it? Lost in a deep sleep and thinking it was him?"

That made her move in that leather recliner. Finally. No more looking straight up at the ceiling, motionless like some sort of corpse. She finally swung her head to the side and asked in a shouting whisper, "Are you fucking kidding me? I know what I saw." She sat up and said, "I know exactly what I saw. And what I saw was my husband scrubbing something from his clothes. I couldn't see any goddamn blood but I know what happened."

He just nodded and wrote in his binder. The prick. He was jotting down his notes for his study. The damn study.

"I know what you're doing," Sarah said. She turned up her nose and said, "You don't give a shit about me. You don't give a shit about my family. All you care about is this stupid little book you're trying to write." She slapped the binder shut on his lap and stood.

He stood to match her quicker than she would have expected, but he was no threat. He was a man in slacks and slip-on shoes and possibly zero muscle in his entire, scrawny body. But when he stood, he said, "You knew exactly what it was that you were getting into when you agreed to this little ordeal." He looked down and did this swirling thing with his hand as if the *ordeal* were right there in front of them. "I'm taking notes because they are important to my research."

"Well your research," she said, swirling her hand around in the same manner, "is tearing my family apart."

There was a brief pause and the two seemed to take a step back. Dr. Epplestein said to her, "I would like to remind you, Sarah, that you voluntarily joined this study. I in no way demanded or insisted you partake. I simply gave you an option and you chose to do so."

So snooty, she thought. So arrogant and impersonal. How was this man a psychologist? How was he qualified to tell people how to think?

"I did choose to join," she said. "But I was desperate. You offered me *money*, Dr. Epplestein, and I happen to be a mother of two young children who have barely any of it."

"I know that, which is why I found you to be a perfect fit for this study. Your husband is not a test dummy, if that's what you're beginning to think. He is simply helping my colleague and me to realize the capability of a new study. And we want to help you by setting you up financially."

"No," she said. "No. I'm done. I'm not getting sucked into the money scheme you'll throw at me again." She made her way towards the door and that's when he said the phrase that set her off.

"I can take all the money back, you know. And I will if you don't cooperate."

"Take it back?" She marched her way back deeper into the office. "Take it back?" She yelled louder. "Please fucking do, Dr. fucking Epplestein. Please take it all back. Take the money. Take your stupid research. And while you're at it, take back the fact that you made my husband stab a man with your stupid fucking antics."

"Sarah!" he yells, but it's a calming yell.

Don't you do it, asshole. Don't you try to be the nice-guy shrink now. I'm done with you.

He dropped his binder on the seat behind him and put his hands on her shoulders. And she needed it. Oh, how long had it been since she and Brian had been able to hold each other and promise good things. How long had it been since Brian grabbed her and pulled her in and made promises of his writing career. It actually felt good for those hands of Dr. Epplestein to be pushing down on her shoulders as if the petty force would calm her.

"Sarah," he repeated. "Everything is going to be alright." He leaned down to look into her eyes that were hitting the floor but she wouldn't let his meet hers. "Everything will be okay. Trust me. This is all part of something that's so much greater than you and me. We're onto something amazing here."

Sarah finally let her head and eyes lift and she looked her shrink directly in the eye when she said, "Take back the money. I'm done with this."

22

It was 3:30 AM again, and Brian was at his desk in his room, coffee getting cold by his side. Sarah's head was buried under the covers, but even if she was up yelling at him, he wouldn't have noticed. On this morning, he wrote like the words had been burning inside him, waiting to come out.

He had his story now.

His authenticity.

Francesca muddled up the hardwood stairway in the dark, leaving tracks of water and mud that sloshed beneath her every step. The knife hung loosely in her right hand, swinging beside her hip. Her bedroom was at the top of the stairs, and her eyes never wavered from the closed door.

Outside, the rain came down hard, crashing into the roof and siding like hundreds and thousands of little warning bells attempting to wake Lucas from his peaceful dream. He was surely off somewhere else, probably tropical, and probably with her.

   He'll be yanked back soon.
   He'll pay.

Even the story felt better. Felt right. As the words came out, there was no reconsidering. No regret. No anger or thought that this story could have been so much better.

Rainwater rolled down her skin and the wet clothes suctioned against her, showing the curves of her body that she assumed Lucas now found undesirable. For three long months, she sat quietly and watched him sneak around behind her back. Tried to confront him. Tried to reason with him. But he just lied. Smiled, kissed her, told her he loved her, and then walked out of the house to his whore.

   Francesca reached the bedroom door and gently swung it open. It creaked ever-so-slightly as it came to a stop. And when she saw him lying on his side under those clean white sheets – the sheets that she washed so often recently to get her *scent out of* their *bed – she envisioned the beauty of his pain.*

Brian wanted so badly to get to the good part: the stabbing. He hoped the story in his head would come out as clearly on the word processor in front of him – the processor that no longer remained idle but must now have wanted a break to catch its breath after a long run. But he couldn't rush the scene. No reason to. Suspense was everything. So he carried on with the dramatic buildup.

She felt a tickle run across her forehead from a running droplet and wiped it with the back of the knife. The feel of cold metal on her forehead sent a chill down through her body and it felt so good. Orgasmic.

When her hand came back down, she looked into the blade of the shining object and the engraving in the steel made her laugh: The Pintler Family, *it said. It was a gift from the real estate agent when they'd bought the home, ready to start a family. That was eleven months before this very day.* Not here, *she thought.* Maybe some other woman will be lucky enough to start a family in this house. But I sure as hell won't.

A crackle of thunder shuddered the house and she stared at the bed, ready to pounce on any sign of movement. But there was nothing. Of course not. He just crawled into bed an hour before, claiming he was out with the boys to celebrate Jordan's new business venture. Bunch of rich boys with their God complex, talking about their next million-dollar deal and flashing their money around the bar – a luring scent for slutty little whores like her.

Not anymore.

She inched toward him, and then climbed overtop him and onto the bed. Images of their wedding day played in her head but she quickly shook them off. No need for reminiscing. Or feeling any regret.

Lucas surely hadn't.

He stirred, opened his eyes and smiled at her.

"Hey, baby," he said, the stench of beer spilling from his mouth.

She smiled as she straddled him and looked down into his eyes. She dragged the blade of the knife down his rib cage, but he couldn't feel it through the sheet. Dumb shit probably thought it was just her fingernails.

He grabbed her by the waist and then his eyes opened completely when he realized she was soaking wet. He was awake now. "The hell?" he asked. "Why are you all wet?" He looked at his hands and then on the sheet beside him. Everything was wet and he was just now taking notice.

That's when she did it.

She brought her bent elbow up by her side and then plunged the knife downward and into his stomach, right beneath his rib cage. She felt the pop of the knife going in. And just as the sound of the knife piercing his skin filled her ears, so did his echoing cry.

Scream all you want, *she thought.* No one will hear a thing in this storm.

There it was. His *pop*. The authenticity. Anyone reading this now who'd stabbed someone knew the truth. Could relate. Or they'd at least know it was written properly. Brian almost felt like he could go hand out this book at local prisons and he'd get positive feedback from everyone doing time for stabbing someone.

The words carried on. And the story became better. There was no writer's block this morning. And it felt great.

Lucas threw Francesca off of him, but as her body separated from his, so did the knife. Blood now pooled out from the open wound and through his fingertips as he pushed hard with both hands to try the stop the bleeding. When it didn't work, he grabbed the bedsheet and pressed it against the opening.

"You bitch!" he screamed at Francesca as she remained on the floor where he threw her. His eyes grew wide with rage and he leaped from the bed. He dropped the sheet

and the blood ran hot again, streaming down his stomach and staining his boxer briefs.

Lucas hovered over her, lifted his right hand and slammed his fist down into her face. Once. Twice. Three times. She felt like a brick had just fallen on the side of her head. The pain was excruciating and the ringing in her ears was deafening. And then his fist came down again, but this time the blow felt much weaker. She looked up and saw the color leaving his face and his body. His eyes grew wide with fear. He looked down at his stomach and the blood that now soaked his briefs. And then he rolled off of her and slid backward, sitting up and leaning against the bed. He grabbed at his stomach and asked with barely any strength, "Why?"

"You know why," she said through a swelling and bloody mouth.

All he could do was look down at his wound. And his head never came back up.

Brian ended his chapter there, happy, thinking once again that *This is the one!* It was only 4:45 now and Sarah and the kids wouldn't need to wake up for over an hour. And since he was on a roll, there was no point in stopping now. Best to utilize all the time he could. Every word written was one word closer to getting out from behind that forklift for good.

So he carried on.

In the next chapter, Francesca dragged Lucas's lifeless body down the stairs, not caring at all about the smearing trail of blood on the hardwood. She dragged him out to the yard and into the woods behind their house where she'd dug a shallow grave for the shallow man. And when she came back in, she showered and put on her pajamas.

Then she picked up the phone.

"9-1-1, what's your emergency?"

"My husband," Francesca said. "He's... He hit me." She reached for the left side of her face. The swelling had caused her eye to close and her cheek was sensitive to the touch. "And then he left."

23

The chair creaked as Brian leaned back from the computer for the first time since he sat down. He cracked his knuckles and smiled. A smile. Man, how long had it been since he felt this satisfied with a writing session? He couldn't remember.

He looked at the red numbers illuminating from the digital clock beside his wife's head: 5:41. After *that* writing session, it was perfectly fine to call it quits. He would go make breakfast again and wake the kids for school. Hell, it even crossed his mind to lean over the bed and kiss Sarah.

This was a good day.

All he could think about as he closed his laptop and turned off the overhead lamp was that this had happened so often recently, leaving the writing desk early. But typically it was for negative reasons.

Not on this day.

He took his coffee mug to the sink, rinsed, and made himself another, as if more caffeine would keep this good mood train rolling.

No stops. This mood is too damn good. Keep those wheels spinning.

He walked into the bedroom doorway of the kids' room and stared in at the two innocent bodies sleeping in their beds. His prizes. Regardless of how he or his writing turn out, those two kids always put a smile on his face. If not for him, the divorce would surely have happened long ago. And Brian? He'd probably be on suicide watch by now. All the rejection letters he'd received in his life and attempts to succeed with his writing were tough. They were emotionally-draining. And the only reason he was able to get over them was because he had his kids. His family. They offset the bad.

He slowly pushed himself off the door frame and walked back to the bedroom. *Time to get his clothes ready for work.* He tip-toed down the hall, as he did every morning, out of courtesy for Sarah's scarce time remaining to sleep. He thought about what he could do to be as quiet as possible – avoid the squeaky hinges on the closet door, use cell phone flashlight instead of turning on any lights – but when he reached the door, he realized he didn't need to worry.

Sarah was awake. Standing up and putting on her glasses. The red tint of the alarm clock numbers reflected off of her side, and then he looked at the numbers themselves: 5:49.

"Hey," he said.

"Hey," she looked over at him, lifting her chin to be able to see him through the glasses that sagged slightly on her nose.

"You're up early," he said.

"Yeah. I couldn't sleep."

That's what she always said when she didn't sleep like she was in a coma throughout the night. She'd toss once in eight hours and declare she couldn't sleep.

"Oh. Was I loud?" he asked.

"No. Not at all. How did writing go?"

"Good," he said, and walked over to sit on the bed.

"That's good." She looked over at him with a smile, and then went to wash up.

Brian remained seated on the edge of the mattress. He looked into his coffee and took a sip from time to time, dreading the thought of walking over to that closet and putting on his khaki pants and that stupid red shirt. The morning's writing session might be the first step in a new direction for his life. Sad, it could have cost a man his life. And then he wondered about the old man, and if he'd died yet. Brian didn't want to have to sneak into the hospital to finish him off, so he wished he was already dead.

"Hey." Sarah's voice yanked him from his psychotic train of thought. She was back now, glasses off and contacts in. "You alright?"

"Yeah," he said. "Fine."

"Okay. You were deep in thought there for a second."

"Just thinking about the book," he said, standing from the bed and walking to the closet.

"So what was today's chapter about?"

She knows.

"Today's?" he asked from inside the closet. "Just introducing the detective that'll be chasing my main character around."

"Oh. That was easy then, huh?"

"I guess." He left the closet with his work clothes draped over his forearm. "Hey, where's the iron?"

She smiled. "You iron your work clothes now? Since when?"

"I don't know." He looked down at his clothes, then lifted his forearm and said, "They look kind of wrinkled. Don't want to upset the big guy."

She took a few steps toward him, slowing the closer she got. "I want to tell you something."

Brian felt his face grow flush. She was going to tell him that she knew. That she wasn't asleep the morning he went for his run. That she knew how long he was gone and when she walked into the steaming bathroom, she saw him scrubbing the blood off of his shirt. She saw him dump bleach onto the thing and scrub like he wanted the cotton to up and disintegrate right before his eyes.

"It's sort of a confession," she said.

A confession. That's a good word for it. *I confess that I know the truth.*

Sarah inched in closer to Brian and placed a hand on his shoulder. "That authenticity thing I said to you the other day? I'm sorry about that. It was rude of me. What I should have said was that I think it's a good idea, and left it at that."

"Well–" Brian began.

"Hold on. Let me finish."

It's a good thing she cut him off because he had no idea what would have come from his mouth anyway. There was nothing on his mind, so the words would have come right from the tip of his tongue, which could have gotten him into some serious trouble.

"I think you're a great writer. I really do. I mean, look at Dark Marker. You self-published that and still managed to get, what, twenty-one five-star reviews?"

"Four *and* five," he said and then shut his mouth because he felt the boasting had taken over his modesty.

"Still. You did great. Without even having an agent or a publisher. You did that all with your writing." She took a breath and said, "I guess I was just...I don't know...in a bad mood. And I took it out on you. I'm sorry."

"Wow. Thank you, first of all, for apologizing. But it's really fine."

"It isn't. It was rude."

"Alright," he said. "I'll take it as constructive criticism and we'll leave it at that." He smiled at her, and when she returned the smile, he realized how much one can learn from a person they've known for more than eight years. You learn their habits, and their flaws, and their desires. But one thing you learn about them is their smile. And Brian knew very well that Sarah had one for when she was faking something. Or lying. And the smile he saw on her face right then was that smile.

She knew.

24

"I told him everything."

In reality, she hadn't. She merely threw him a clue and hoped to hell he could dissect it. But he didn't. Brian took her words for what they sounded to be: a simple apology.

"You what?" Dr. Epplestein's voice came through the speaker on her phone. "Sarah, tell me you're joking."

Sarah felt special. Dr. Epplestein was always available to speak with her. It didn't matter if he was in another appointment or on a lunch break or even at home late in the evening. Ever since Sarah agreed to this little project of his, she'd received special treatment.

"I'm not joking."

It took Sarah less than five minutes after seeing the kids off to school to make this phone call. The thoughts ran through her head all night that this was all her fault. Sure, Brian made a false promise that he'd be able to provide a better life for this family and sure, Sarah could have found another way to find supplemental income rather than to sell her husband's living brain as some sort of social experiment. But she didn't. She'd gotten herself into this position with her actions and now she was ready to fix it.

"What did you tell him?" Sarah could envision him gripping at the bridge of his nose. Somehow she could hear the stress in his voice.

"Everything. I apologized to him for what I'd done."

"Sarah," he said, his voice still relatively calm at this point. "I'm really hoping you haven't told him everything. I know how you must feel, but I assure you this is research. We are simply taking a study that has been done – and proven! – and we are building upon it."

"And how does that benefit my husband?" She stood from the couch where she sat in her quiet apartment. "Huh? How does your research help him?"

"Has his writing gotten better? Is he happier?"

"Oh, don't give me that horseshit excuse, doctor. You know damn well that this is sick. You've got some little game going and my husband is your guinea pig."

"How do you think research is conducted, Sarah? This is what happens. Subjects are volunteered and then they are supplemented with money in exchange for their participation."

"What research that you know of that has been conducted could lead the *subject* to a life sentence in prison?"

"Please, Sarah. I assure you that this research will be valuable. And with the money, you will be able to provide your family – your children – with the lifestyle you've always wanted them to have. Now if you please, I must be getting ready for my nine o'clock appointment."

"I want out. I don't want to be a part of this anymore."

The calm doctor on the other end of the line surely wearing one of his many pairs of corduroy pants and moccasins suddenly lost his calm demeanor.

"No!" he demanded. "Sarah, I have supplemented you with a great deal of money in exchange for your participation in this experiment. You have voluntarily agreed to this. I assure you now, as I have in the past, that your husband will not be caught. We will do everything in our power to protect him and his freedom, but you must not inform him of what is going on. The more you tell him and the more roadblocks you put up, the longer this entire process will take. Would you like to drag this out longer than it has to be?"

"I don't want to drag it out for one more second. I'm done. And I believe I'm done seeing you as a doctor, also."

"Your father will stop seeing bills come and he will wonder. Would you like your father to think this has all been a waste of time? That he's spent these thousands of dollars–"

"How dare you!"

"–for you to come here for nothing? Thousands of dollars later and you're still living with the man he wants you to leave? Still in that apartment?"

"I won't be sucked into your grasp, Dr. Epplestein. You're not my boss. You're my shrink. You need to listen to me vent and that is all."

"Sarah," he seemed calm again. "I assure you I am no bully. I think you know me well enough. I promise you I have good intentions with this research. You came to me with a problem, remember? And I believe I've found a solution. A solution to your love life, to your financial problems, and to your husband's inability to have a breakthrough in his writing."

"And what if I want out? Doctor-patient confidentiality, Doctor. You can't tell anyone what's been going on."

"In the event that someone else's life may be in danger, I most certainly can. But I don't want to. Sarah, I simply want to continue with my research."

She was quiet for a moment. Lost. Everything she said, he had some sort of response. A comeback. It worried her. That she was stuck. But more importantly, she wondered why *he* was so stuck. So caught up on this. "Why do this? Why are you so adamant about this?"

"I'm a psychologist, Sarah. There's a reason I chose Psychology as a profession and not Psychiatry. I don't believe in medications. I don't believe that depressed people need to be pumped with pills. I am a firm believer that any cure for any state of mind can be obtained without drugging someone. A colleague and I have already published several e-books on the matter. We have treated PTSD and clinical depression and night terrors, all without throwing money at the pharmaceutical industry. We want to prove that *anything* is possible through our words and our actions. And, unfortunate and sick as this may sound, we need to prove the opposite, as well. We have proven that we can bring out the good with this mindset of *no pills*, but we also want to prove that the opposite is possible. And we're so close, Sarah. I promise you, we're so close."

"I love him," she said. Tears welled in her eyes. She thought back to the good times, before money became a sword that would slice the inseparable pair apart. When they had fun and the pipe dream of Brian becoming a famous writer was still attainable. "Even after all we've been through, I still love him."

"And you love your family, I'm aware of this. Which is why you are participating in this research. We are giving you a great deal of money to help us here, and has the money helped?"

"It has." It was hard to admit, but it was so helpful. The calls from debt collectors had begun to dwindle, though she worried that Brian would soon begin to realize and wonder why.

"We need your help here, Sarah. Will you remain on board with us?"

She felt like one of those drugged patients he mentioned in the conversation. Only her drug didn't come in a pill bottle. It came in the form of a stack of money that she took with her each week as she left his office.

There was silence on the end of her line.

"Sarah?" Dr. Epplestein asked.

She remained quiet, but not for long. He'd lured her back in. He threw out the bait and she was hesitant at first, swimming around to check it out. But ultimately, she did what she knew she would do. She chomped down on the bait and sank her mouth right into his hook. From there, all he had to do was reel her in.

"Fine," she said.

25

The phone conversation ended with Dr. Epplestein being reassured. Sarah, on the other hand, was not. She hated herself for caving to the doctor's words all the time. He made everything sound okay. So normal. But it wasn't.

Brian had stabbed the old man across the street while he was out for his run and Sarah knew it. There was no denying it now. Her words and Dr. Epplestein's sick little game crawled into his innocent brain and corrupted the easy-going writer who wouldn't hurt a fly.

What would become of all this? She was just promised over the phone that everything would be alright. That Brian would be protected. But how? How the hell would they protect him?

She stood in front of the TV, remote in hand, wondering what the hell happened to the man across the street. It'd been forty-eight hours. How have there been no updates? Or no leads? Or sketches?

But a knock on the door no more than five minutes later

gripped her by her shirt and ripped her into the reality she knew was coming.

Where are you now, Dr. Epplestein?

This was the knock she'd been expecting. The one she'd been dreading hearing for two days now. The one that told her something she already knew.

Sarah didn't immediately answer. Instead, she remained still, as if movement could trigger the person's knowing she was inside. Stillness, on the other hand, and they'd leave. Like playing dead in the presence of a bear.

The knock came again, and it wasn't a hard knock, or an authoritative one. It was not a knock that demanded an answer. So she told herself it must be a neighbor. Or maybe it was someone from property management. Were they late on their rent again? Who was she kidding? They were always late. She wished at that moment that they'd just put the notice in the door knocker and leave like they normally do.

And then a third knock came, followed by "Rock Park P.D.," and she realized there'd be no notice left in her door knocker. No need to look through the peephole to examine. This person was perfectly fine identifying themselves.

Better go put on a bra, she thought. Getting taken out of an apartment building and put in the back of a cop car with no bra on wasn't exactly where she wanted to be in this stage of her life.

"Mornin', ma'am," a tall, lanky cop said. He had brown skin and freckles on his nose and cheeks. "My name is Officer Willis. I'm sorry to bother you this morning. As I'm sure you're aware, there was an incident on Tuesday morning in the neighborhood across the street." He pointed over in the direction of the adjacent neighborhood.

"I heard," Sarah said.

"Well the victim passed away in the hospital early this morning."

Sarah froze. If the man standing before her knew her for any more than the three or four seconds that he had, he would have been able to see it written all over her face: guilt. She felt like she was wobbling but somehow managed to stay upright.

"We're walking around this morning to see if anyone has heard anything, or might be able to give us some information about the other morning." He paused, then said, "May I please have your name, ma'am?"

"Sure," she said. "It's Sarah."

"And your last name, Sarah?" he asked as he wrote into his tiny notepad.

"Wellington." Her maiden name. Why did she give her maiden name? She looked at the officer and forced herself to breathe.

"Okay, Miss Wellington. Were you home early Tuesday morning?"

"I was asleep."

He looked up at her and smiled, a defeated smile. "Yeah, that seems to be the most common answer I've been getting." Sarah smiled back at him, hoping that would be all he said, but it wasn't. "You live alone, Miss Wellington?"

"With my family," she said.

"You have children?"

"I do."

"And how old are your children?"

"They're seven and four." She watched a smile come

across the officer's face when he wrote it in his notes. *Cute and innocent*, he must have been thinking.

"Husband?"

"Yes."

"Your husband, what's his name?"

"Brian."

"Brian Wellington," the officer mumbled, writing the name into his pad. And for some reason, she didn't correct him. Why? What was she doing? With each passing second, she felt like she was digging herself deeper into a hole. But she couldn't fix it now. Speaking up now would have seemed way too obvious that she was hiding something.

"And your husband, is he home?"

"He's at work."

"You mind me asking where he works, Mrs. Wellington?"

"He works at Eats N' Treats. It's a pet store not far from here."

"Sure, I know where that is. And what hours does he typically work?"

"Nine-to-five." Not true. He left the house at seven every morning.

Officer Willis looked up from his notepad, again with a smile. "He was asleep too, I'm assuming?"

No. He was awake. And in the shower. Which he never did at that time. And before he got into the shower, he was scrubbing something off of the clothes he was wearing when he went for a run. And he looked frantic. Like something was wrong. Like something bad had happened. Like he'd just stabbed a man and gotten blood on his shirt and ran back to the house to scrub off the stain from his clothes and the blood from his body and pretend like the whole thing never happened. And he did it because I told him his story was shit. That it wasn't authentic. That his fourteen years of writing meant nothing if this story was another flop. And Dr. Epplestein made me put these terrible, subtle words into his head. And that's why he did it. Let me put my hands out and just take me in. Lock me up. I'm so done with all this.

"He was," she lied, forcing a smile to match the officer's.

"Alright," Officer Willis said. He flipped his notepad closed and pushed the pen into the metal rings. "If you can think of anything at all, please give a call to the department."

It was there. On the tip of her tongue. Everything she knew. Everything she wanted to say but couldn't. The tug-o-war played out in her head and at that very moment it was leaning toward jail time for her. What would happen then? What if hiding the truth meant jail time for *her* down the road? She could be charged with conspiracy or obstruction or accessory to crime or whatever the legal lingo was for it. Whatever it was, if she could be arrested for it, it defied everything she was trying to do, which was to protect Lacey and Mason's way of life. They needed to live a normal life, and having one or both of their parents behind bars wasn't normal.

She almost wished she hated Brian. Wished he was some deadbeat like so many other fathers out there so she could let those words go. Those words that hung sealed behind her lips and that could bust open the entire case this officer was looking to uncover. But he wasn't. He was a good person. A kind person. He'd just been manipulated, is all.

Was that true? Or was she just as crazy as he was?

"I will," she said to the officer.

"Thank you, ma'am." He gave her a head-nod and walked away.

Sarah shut the door and pulled the chain lock into place. She leaned her back on the door and felt like nothing in her body was functioning. She had no feeling in any extremity. She slid down the door, replaying the conversation in overdrive. She said what she said. She lied. And there was no going back now. No rewind button. Her words to Officer Willis were her words.

What had she done?

A three-beat knock jolted her body upright and she was standing again. Following the knock, she heard, "Rock Park PD." But the knock didn't shake her door, and the voice was low and muffled.

Officer Willis had moved to the next door.

26

"You two have to help Mommy clean the kitchen, and then we'll do the pumpkin, alright?"

Brian walked in the door from work with a large pumpkin beneath his arm. Lacey and Mason draped themselves all over their dad the second he walked through the door, just as they always had, and Brian somehow managed to prevent the thing from falling out of his arms and exploding on the doormat.

"Alright, alright!" Brian said through the growing smile on his face. The sight of his kids sprinting to him never got old. Nor did the sound of their yells for his attention. He never felt he deserved the amount of love they gave him, but he ingested every second of it.

"Daddy's home!" the two kept yelling in unison. They only stopped when told by their mother in the kitchen to go wash up for dinner. And then they were off, racing down the hall to see who could claim the bathroom sink first.

"Should I even ask?" The words came out of Sarah's

mouth as she pointed to the large, orange ball under Brian's arm.

"If you care to know," he said. But by the time he responded, she was already back by the stove and working on dinner. It didn't seem like she cared much.

Brian set the pumpkin down on the counter and went through his normal after-work routine. And as soon as he was done, he heard the stampede of his two offspring coming down the hall for dinner.

"You washed your hands?" Sarah asked. Even when the kids answered that they had, she asked again to confirm. Always had to.

After dinner, the kids did as they said they would. They helped to clean, clearing the table and helping place the dirty dishes in the dishwasher. Five minutes into cleaning, Brian had already counted three times they asked if they were done. And as Lacey, Mason, and Sarah were doing their thing, Brian was covering the table with newspaper to prepare for the mess of tearing apart the pumpkin.

It came again: "Can we be done?" And Sarah let out a defeated Yes.

"Come on, kids," Brian said, plopping the pumpkin down onto the table. He was always aware that his thermostat of temperament had a much shorter needle than Sarah's. He went from calm to fuming with the flip of a switch. Sarah, on the other hand, had a slow rise to her frustration. And when he saw the mercury in her thermometer rise, he called the kids over to the table.

Brian saw the pumpkin as a prop, whereas the kids saw it as a toy. Either way, they both wanted to tear into it.

"Where do we start?" asked Mason.

"The top!" Lacey yelled from somewhere deep in her

gut.

She was right. And with the two kids having their knees where their butts should go, and their elbows where their plates should go, hovering close as if this couldn't start soon enough, Brian took the knife in his hand and pressed it up against the skin of the pumpkin. "Okay, kids," he said. "We're going to take our time with this. Cut through it nice and slow."

"No! No!" Lacey thought it was some sick joke Dad was playing. "Do it fast! Let's get the seeds!"

Mason mimicked her every word.

To have a recorder would be nice. Something he could speak into to translate the feeling of what he was about to do. But with the kids and Sarah in the same room, it wasn't possible.

Kids, Daddy has to talk about how stabbing this pumpkin feels because he wants to write a book about stabbing a person and can't admit that he's already done it for real.

They were seven and four, Lacey and Mason. For both of them, those words coming from their father's mouth could have been the first time they'd ever heard of stabbing someone. *You can stab someone with a knife?* It would be embedded in their brains forever. And who knows what could have happened after that. They could have become serial killers with those words burned into their brains.

He kept his dialogue internal and pushed the tip of the blade into the skin of the soon-to-be Jack-o-lantern. He let out a gasp when he felt the pop – the same pop he'd felt when he stabbed the old man. It was there. And now could be used for description in his writing. Or an excuse.

Sarah may have known what he did, but she'd never

admit it. With what he's doing now, right in front of her, they can both have a story to go off of. If anyone asked, this was where he did his research: in his own kitchen. With his wife and kids by his side, he found the prose for his novel.

Because Brian knew the police would come. There would soon come a day where he'd have to explain himself. He'd have to have an alibi.

And if the police hadn't already come, they'd surely be on their way.

But Sarah would have told him.

Right?

27

Did Dr. Epplestein's words really do this? Was this whole Misinformation Effect a real thing? Could these stupid little words and phrases Sarah was saying into Brian's ear really lead him to do what he's doing? Lead him to kill?

She knew what he'd done the other morning, but was it because of some words said to him? These *trigger words*? There was no way. As Sarah stood over the sink, finishing the cleaning that the kids found to be such hell, she listened in to what was going on at the dinner table.

All the kids wanted him to do was rip the thing open. They wanted him to smash the pumpkin on the linoleum floor if that's what got the seeds out fastest. But he took his time. Stared intently into the thing as if dissecting it. And she knew why. He'd stabbed the man across the street and came up with some half-assed attempt to cover it up.

How did you write that stabbing scene so well, Mr. Hart?

What the hell happened to her life? As she washed the plain, white dishes in her cheap, rental sink, she thought back to what she always did when she had these reminiscing moments: she thought about her dad.

Her parents never approved of Brian and they let her know from the moment the two began to get serious. While her friends were intrigued by his aspirations to become a writer, her parents weren't. Her mother was especially crude towards the idea. *There's something just not right about him*, she'd tell Sarah, going on to say she saw something untrustworthy in his eyes. And as a young and naïve woman, Sarah listened to the wrong crowd.

There are many memories that make a person cringe. Everyone has at least one moment in life where they look back and wonder what the hell they were thinking. Meeting Brian was most certainly *not* one of those moments. She still loves him today just as much as she did back then. But pushing off her parents' opinions as hearsay is something she wished she would have never done. Parental advice is never something one takes seriously until they are themselves a parent. And then the favor of eyerolls is returned. Sarah knew that she'd soon see those eyerolls from her own children when she tried to give them advice.

"Talk to someone," her dad had said on more than one occasion. "Because I know you won't talk to me."

It was true. She didn't want to admit she was wrong to not listen to them. She didn't want to admit that Brian's writing career would never flourish and that her investment in him was a bust. That they'd never have the life Sarah wanted. And although she and her friends used to hang on every one of Brian's promises to make it as a professional author no matter what it took, that his words no longer held any value. That his attempt was a swing and a miss.

She could say none of these things to her parents and she didn't know why. They may have let out that parental *I told you so* too many times, but don't all parents? If Sarah had sat down and talked to them and spilled everything, they would have probably just given her a hug and told her everything would be okay. But she still couldn't manage to do it. She couldn't find the courage to let them know she was wrong.

Instead of allowing her parents to hear her cries of regret, she kept it bottled up. She held in these emotions for so long that her parents had begun to drop the whole subject. Once the kids came and nothing changed between Sarah and Brian, Sarah's parents figured their daughter was stuck in one of those lifelong relationships of mediocrity. All the Princess birthday parties and tiaras and nightgowns were no more.

Her mother shifted her attention to Lacey and Mason, as did her father. But Sarah's father never completely let go of the sadness he could clearly see in his daughter's heart. And since she wouldn't let him be the ear to listen to what she had to say, he insisted on her going to see a doctor. A shrink.

Sarah's dad wasn't a business executive or someone who gained a nice inheritance. He was the son of two casino workers and was himself a mid-level employee at a software company. So his dollars didn't come rolling into his bank account with ease. He earned them.

Her father never picked a favorite, though he joked about doing so. Sarah and her younger sister Bethany would pretend to fight for his Number One Daughter role, but it was all fun and games. Neither was favored and both knew it. They had an amazing father and cherished his every breath. Sarah knew that what her dad did for her would be something he'd do for Bethany, also. In a heartbeat. But Bethany was never in the situation Sarah was in.

Since Sarah refused to talk to her parents, her father had sought out a therapist and scheduled an introductory consultation. "It's a psychologist," he told her when he first brought the idea her way. "I don't know what the difference is with all the head doctors," he said with a smirk, "but if you don't want a psychologist, let me know and I'll cancel the appointment."

She didn't know the difference either, so she didn't cancel the appointment. Instead, she anxiously awaited the consultation date. And when it came, she dressed in clothes she'd normally wear to a job interview. In subsequent appointments, she wouldn't dress nearly as nice. But for that first meeting, the butterflies in her stomach took over.

"Welcome," he'd said. The first impression of the shrink was that he was welcoming. Experienced. Your stereotypical shrink: an old, thin, man with a balding head of gray hair and glasses clutching to the bridge of his nose. He was easy to open up to and never cut into her story until she was ready to let him in. Her first impression of the man was that he was so kind that she felt she could hug him. And that's why it was such a shock to see him turn into a pushy salesman at the mention of his plan for her.

The whole idea sounded like a game. Like the session was a set-up. A joke played on her by her father. Maybe because he hadn't seen her smile in so long that he figured he'd play a prank. But it was no prank. Dr. Epplestein's suggestion to use Brian as a test subject was as real as the man informing her of the offer.

"I don't think so," she'd said to him at the moment. What she wanted to say was *Hell no! What the hell is wrong with you?* But she was never one to be rude. And in the moment, the possibility of this being some prank was still alive and swirling around in her head.

But then greed kicked in. Or maybe it was *need*. But when Dr. Epplestein told Sarah that she would be paid weekly for agreeing to this, all other thoughts faded. "Money? How much?"

"At the moment, one-thousand per week." Sold. He had her right then and there. Hook through her cheek, reeled into the boat, picture taken with his hand through her gill. But he kept going and she let him. "If we get the results we think we can achieve, the research will make a lot of money and we will be able to provide you with more."

The money. The thousand dollars per week that Dr. Epplestein found to be so mediocre would do wonders for Sarah. For her kids. Even for Brian, though he wouldn't know about it. Sarah was able to get caught up on the rent, the bills, and load up the kids' school lunch accounts. Life wasn't as stressful as Brian thought it to be so he kept going about his life as though it was.

Finances were finally in order, but at what cost. At what *real* cost? Brian had killed a man. It was no longer a stabbing. The cop that came knocking at the door this morning made it clear that Thomas McMann was now dead and that this case was a homicide investigation. The main suspect was right in front of her, dissecting a pumpkin with his kids in order to come up with some bullshit backstory as to how he was able to so vividly describe a murder scene.

Sarah felt as though her decision to say yes to her shrink's experiment was more detrimental to her family than Brian's decision to kill a man.

28

Brian drove to work in his Honda Civic that he'd had since he was twenty-two. When his family passed, he inherited over a quarter of a million dollars – $150,000 from Mom's life insurance policy and $112,000 in equity his parents had in the house when he decided to sell it. But unlike many young adults in his financial situation, he spent it scarcely. A Honda Civic was known to run forever and that's exactly what he wanted it to do. Thirteen years later, the thing still ran smoothly.

He pulled into the parking lot of Eats 'N Treats and drove around to the back near the loading ramp – employee parking. The front of the store was lively, with illuminated letters spelling out the business's name, sliding glass doors with windows surrounding. And in those windows were posters for products and this week's sales. But the back? Nothing fancy whatsoever. Just a loading ramp and a large garage door that shut when they weren't loading, or when the weather was shit.

If it wasn't for Eric popping a vessel in his shiny, bald

head, Brian would park in the front every day. But the front "is for my paying customers," he'd always say.

Alright, *that* was a joke. Everything in the store for Eric was *my my my*, but he never went as far as to say the customers were his. Surprisingly.

He would park in the front if he could because the giant, green dumpster in the back attracted seagulls like a box full of Playboys attracted an eleven-year-old boy in the eighties. The only difference was that the damn seagulls were shitting all over their box of magazines, and all around it. No matter how far Brian parked from the damn thing, he'd leave every day with shit on his car.

Park in the back he did, as an obedient little employee. With coffee in hand, he walked in the employee entrance and through the concrete warehouse full of metal and wood shelving, full from floor to the ceiling with bags and packages that would soon be sent home with some house pet. At first it would amaze Brian to see how much stuff was in here, yet how much would still come in on order trucks every day. He thought the store was making billions the way product would turn over in the place.

It was only 7:35 and the break room was empty, just the way Brian liked it. Especially first thing in the morning.

Brian hated the place and everyone around him knew it. So he liked to be alone in the break room for a few minutes when he could, where he'd sit, open up the e-reader app on his phone, and get in ten minutes or so of quiet reading time while sipping on his coffee. Then it was usually Eric that showed up first, barging into the break room like it was three PM and he'd been up for hours. Maybe that was because he *had* been up for three hours, and he made it known that he just finished up a two-hour gym "sesh" followed by eating a dozen eggs for breakfast. Brian once joked with him that he should put his mouth straight to the chicken's ass, but Eric didn't find it very funny. Sort of a running theme.

Seven forty-five came, and then 7:50, and then 7:55, and no sign of Eric yet. Some of the other day shift employees – mostly retirees – came through with their small snack bags and placed them into the refrigerator. For the most part, they'd only work four-hour shifts, but they still took a small break. Force of habit, maybe. Or maybe they wanted the feeling back of working full-time, so they looked forward to their thirty minutes of peace like every other working person in the world. Or maybe they just flat out didn't give a damn about being fired so they thought *To hell with you, I'm taking a break right now.*

When 8:00 hit and there was still no sign of Eric, there was this uncontrollable wave of happiness that came over Brian, and for some reason he didn't feel guilty about the thoughts running through his mind. Those of Eric's little sports car wrapped around a tree somewhere out on the highway with Eric trapped inside screaming and pleading for help. He'd try to wave his arms out the window but they were too short and stocky to move.

Josie walked through the door to the break room at 8:01 looking frantic. She was a sweet old lady with a hearing aid and she wouldn't hurt a fly if it came, laid itself out in front of her and flipped her off. Not that she'd be able to anyway, as she was about as small as a child, with bones probably so brittle that she'd break her arm in the process. But she was one of the sweetest women Brian had ever met.

"Morning, Josie."

"Hey there, Brian," she said with a smile, but her wide eyes searched the small room. "Where's Eric?" she whispered?

"Not here yet, I guess." *Dead. Moved. Gay. Who knows?*

"No?"

Brian shook his head. "Nope."

"Oh, thank heavens." Her relieved expression was followed by something a teenager might say. "I didn't want to get into trouble for coming in late."

Brian looked at the digital clock hanging on the wall beside the vending machines and said, "Josie, it's only 8:01."

"Oh, I know. But you know that Eric. He's a young man that likes things done on time."

Brian nodded with a smile. And if it wasn't for the door swinging open right at that moment, he might have told Josie where he thought Eric might have been.

"Morning," Eric said, looking back and forth between the two.

But it was only a formality, and Brian knew it. It was only a matter of time before–

"Josie, I need you up front."

There it was. Before Brian could even finish his thought, Eric began his demands. "Store's open. And Brian, Tommy called out. I need you to pack orders. Lists are on my desk."

Fucking Tommy. Called out so often it was a real wonder he still had a job. And Stephen went to the local community college and had classes until two. Or maybe three. But until then, it was just Brian, packing and unpacking, loading and unloading.

Josie said nothing. She smiled and walked by the two

men and out to her register.

Eric put his oversized lunch bag into the bottom shelf of the refrigerator – an area that had been deemed his, for the obnoxious size of the lunch box he brought in. Maybe he brought the weights with him in there.

"I'll go get those lists. Wait here," Eric said, and he pointed as if telling Brian, *don't move*. The guy had been here for thirty seconds and already Brian hoped he'd slip and break his neck.

Out of spite, and really, really hoping to get a rise out of Eric – *Didn't I tell you to stay there?* – Brian walked to the other side of the room to wait. But when Eric came back, he said nothing. Simply walked over to Brian with some papers in his hands.

Damn. He tried.

"Okay, look." Eric held the papers head-level, which is Brian's chest level, and had the audacity to explain to his fellow college graduate how a packing list works. "And these numbers here? They're the amount. So you just run your finger across the page to see which item they line up with. You see what I'm saying?" He looked up at Brian.

Brian shook his head, wondering if Eric knew that he'd worked here for seven years and had, believe it or not, seen a packing list before.

"So look," Eric said. "Right here, right? Puppy Chow Complete, twenty-pound bag." He dragged his finger across the page, still holding it head-level and tilting his chin to look up at the thing. "Need three of those." He looked over at Brian.

"Got it," Brian said.

"Next one." He looked back at the paper.

Is this dude fucking for real? Heat rose in Brian's face

now. Eric was fucking with him. He had to be.

"Puppy Chow Complete Chicken," he looked back at Brian. "That's different. You know that, right?"

"Different name, different product. Yeah, I think I can handle that."

Eric's mouth hung open as if he was going to carry on with his lesson regardless of what Brian said, but the comment instead pissed him off. *Point for Brian.* He closed his mouth and sighed from his nostrils. "Alright, wise-ass," he said, pushing the papers into Brian's chest. "Here you go." He walked toward the break room door saying, "Don't come asking me any questions. You had your chance to learn."

The skin on Brian's face should have melted, he was so hot with rage. And his mind suddenly drifted to his novel. And Francesca, his main character. How she'd just murdered her cheating husband by stabbing him to death. Maybe now she'd move on to the mistress. Maybe she'd kill *her*. But how? Brian thought of the possibility of using some sort of slow death. Strangulation, maybe. Yeah, that would work. Francesca would certainly love to look directly into the eyes of her husband's lover as the life slowly left her body.

Strangulation.

But it had to be authentic.

29

Sarah was there, but she wasn't there. Her body may have been in the swivel chair and her face looking into the monitor, but she was off. Elsewhere. In her mind, she was lying on her back in that leather chair, looking up at the crisp white ceiling of Dr. Epplestein's office.

"I just don't see how doing this is going to help him."

"Not him," Dr. Epplestein had said, leaning towards her as he always did when emphasizing his points. "His writing. And when you help his writing, you're helping yourself."

"You're telling me to ask him for a divorce." She sat up when she said this. And at that very moment, she wanted to walk out of his office.

But she was in too deep. She couldn't give it up. Couldn't walk away.

A loud ding alerted Sarah that a text had come through. She looked down at the phone on her desk and saw it was from Brian. Well, from Brian, lips emoji, heart emoji. In order to keep with her storyline, she'd want to drop the emoji suffix. They were, after all, getting divorced. Weren't they?

The Human Resources department at EmerGent Engineering was secluded from the rest of the sea of cubicles. In her third tour with the company, Sarah shared an office with Tina in the back of an L-shaped section of the building. While EmerGent Engineering was gracious enough to take her back after both pregnancies, they weren't gracious enough to throw any perks her way, say, with an office of her own.

Both times leaving felt eerily similar. Sarah would go on maternity leave, and maternity leave would turn into a two-year holdout – oh, stay-at-home mom life sounded so heavenly – to her being back on their doorstep crying that Brian's income wasn't nearly enough.

Tina, her office-mate, was a twenty-three-year-old going into her second year with the company. She was a talker, and when she heard the dinging alert go off on Sarah's phone, her voice was tossed across the office.

"Oooh!" she howled. "Setting up a date night already, are we?"

The girl's outlook on life was always positive, and Sarah certainly couldn't fault her for that. She was twenty-three. Young. Single. Living in an apartment with another roommate who was apparently gone at her boyfriend's all the time. So she was basically on her own.

Sarah never considered herself to be envious of anyone, but she was maybe just a little jealous of Tina. She was a gorgeous young woman with light brown skin and bright blue eyes. And she dressed so cute for work every day, just to come sit in an office with Sarah, answering phone calls and emails from disgruntled employees.

Sarah used to be like that. Used to care. Used to feel sexy. But after two kids and an uphill battle with life, she felt more like a forty-year-old woman, beaten and tired. It was rare that she put on anything more than mascara in the mornings nowadays.

"Not quite," she said in response to the comment.

She opened Brian's text message which read, *Going out for drinks after work. With Eric, believe it or not. He had a bad day and asked me to go to happy hour.*

Okay was her response, because she had to pretend she really didn't care what he did. But with Eric? That did strike her as a bit odd. He hated Eric. With a passion. When Eric first started working at Eats-N-Treats, Brian would come home with steam shooting from his ears and would talk to Sarah for an hour about how much he despised him. Wanted to *bash his fucking head in* to be exact, on more than one occasion. And now they were friends?

"You know, I can babysit if you need," Tina said from her chair. She swung her chair to face Sarah and exposed her crossed legs that ended with red heels.

"Thank you," Sarah said, respectfully declining and trying to hide the far-from-sexy flats that she wore on her feet. Not because she didn't want a night out, but because they wouldn't be able to afford it anyway.

Sarah couldn't remember the last time she and Brian went out together. Alone. Like they used to do. And they used to have so much fun. If she could afford a babysitter now, she'd sit at a bar and have a drink. Or a bookstore with a cup of coffee and a book. Something to break the same, everyday routine.

"The offer always stands," Tina said, smiling at Sarah with her perfectly straight, white teeth.

Sarah thought to herself that Tina must have plenty of time to work on herself. *Keep it that way for as long as you can*, she wanted to tell her. *It'll all be gone one day. And you'll be miserable and tired and maybe even alone.* Instead, she smiled back and said, "You're sweet. Thank you. I'll talk to my husband."

My husband. Because she hasn't told anyone at the office yet about her pending divorce. Should she? Will she? Or will this nightmare all end when she goes to visit Dr. Epplestein next?

When Tina switched her attention back to her computer monitor, Sarah looked in her phone and reread the text from that husband. And a feeling of fear came over her. Something wasn't right.

She called him, but got no answer. Of course he wouldn't answer. She waited a few minutes to see if he'd call back, but got nothing. So she sent a text:

Please call me back. Thomas McMann died in the hospital. She wanted to add *That poor old man from across the street that you stabbed because of me*, but, of course, she didn't.

He had to know. Texting that created a paper trail, but he had to know. What if he was planning on doing something bad to Eric because he thought he hadn't killed yet? By god, Dr. Epplestein's words were starting to get to Sarah, too. Was this really what she thought he was going to do?

The answer that jumped into her head scared the shit out of her.

She tried calling again. No answer.

"Please pick up, Brian," she whispered with her eyes closed.

30

Sarah was tossing and turning all night. There was no way he was at the bar with Eric. Where was he? What was he doing? She looked over at the clock and saw that it was six minutes until midnight.

Brian was out there. He was out there and up to no good. He was going to kill again. She knew it. And it was her fault. The feeling was eating away at her gut. It felt like someone was grabbing her stomach with both hands and twisting.

She couldn't fall back asleep as hard as she tried. She tried throwing the pillow over her head. Tried thinking of anything else, remembering back to when she was a kid and swore monsters lurked under her bed.

As a child, when Sarah would have nightmares or would think of some monsters or ghosts, her mother would come comfort her and tell her "When you close your eyes, think of something fun. Like Disney World." So as a kid, when she'd close her eyes on a bad night, she would take herself to Disney World. To Magic Kingdom, dressed like a

Princess. Epcot, riding the rides. Mickey. Minnie. The whole deal. And the next thing she knew, her mother would be waking her up in the morning and she'd do anything to get back into that dream.

The effort was there on this night, but there was no payoff. On this night, lying in her dark bedroom in an even darker apartment, instead of Disney, she thought of a beach in the Maldives, or somewhere in the Caribbean. And she wasn't dressed like a princess this time, but in a tiny, white bikini. She was no longer carrying around the few extra post-childbirth pounds, and instead had the body of her nineteen-year-old self, resembling one of the women in the Sandals commercials.

Just as she was being handed a fruity drink by a waiter beachside, looking out into the teal water, she heard a crackling sound. Her eyes shot open. It wasn't her mother waking her, but the sound of the deadbolt down the hallway being unlocked. The fruity drink was gone. The beach was gone. Her smile was gone. *Wait for me*, she thought of the dream she tried to chase. *Please wait for me.*

Sarah heard the footsteps coming down the hall, but remained beneath the covers. She wanted him to think she was asleep. *I didn't hear anything, Brian. Don't know what you've been up to.* That was the game she was playing, right Dr. Epplestein? On any other night she would be asleep, so it wasn't a stretch for him to believe she really was.

What she was hoping was that the footsteps continued all the way down the hall and into the bedroom. If he went right into the bathroom and turned on the shower, she would lose her mind. Because it would mean something was definitely wrong. And then, her walking in on him last time while he was scrubbing away at something meant that the something was that poor old man's blood from across the street. And it also meant that Brian was going into the shower right away because he'd brought the blood of another injured or dead person back into the apartment. The same apartment where his children slept. And if that was the case, it meant he was a murderer. That there wasn't just one single event. He'd be a multiple offender.

Suddenly the complaint of insomnia wasn't the worst thing on Sarah's mind.

But he didn't stop in the bathroom. He came right into the bedroom. Sarah's head was still under the covers so her eyes were open, but her body remained still as a statue. She remained this way while she listened to him as he undressed in the dark, and then he was out and into the bathroom and turning on the water. With his clothes in here, she didn't seem so worried about the shower now.

After a few minutes of the bathroom door being shut with the water running behind it, Sarah removed the covers. She grabbed her cell phone from the nightstand beside her. Can't turn on the bedroom light now, she thought. Her luck, he'd come walking out of the bathroom as she was draped over his clothes, examining them. *I'm looking for lipstick on your collar* could be an excuse, but not after what had gone on the past few days. He'd know. Surely, he'd know.

In the dark, she walked over to the hamper and then turned on the flashlight from her cell. His clothes sat right on top. Nothing hidden. He didn't try to shove them under the pile. She picked them up and swiped her light over every square inch like a blacklight on a crime scene. But she found nothing. She swore to herself that she was missing something and began to double-check. Then she heard the shower water cut off.

What an idiot, she thought to herself. Now he'd definitely hear her get back into bed. The creaking of the old, whining springs would be an alarm to him and he'd know what was going on.

She tip-toed back to the side of the bed where she tried to get under the covers in one swift motion to drown the noise, like swinging open a door with squeaky hinges at lightning speed. But it didn't work. The bed still let out a moan and then a clap as the headboard smacked the wall. She pulled the covers back over her head and tried to replicate the exact way she was laying when he'd first come in.

He heard. He had to have heard. He knew.

She laid there in fear as the bathroom door opened and he came back into the room.

His steps slowed once in the room. Why did they slow? What was he doing? She asked herself these questions, but in her head, she knew what he was doing. He was looking right down on her, looming over her, inching closer. He knew. He was just plotting what to do with her. How to kill her. To make sure she could never tell a soul what she knew. About this. About the other night. About anything. She'd plea. If she felt him move one step closer, she'd plea. *I swear to God I won't say anything. I won't. I promise. Just don't kill me. The kids need me. Need us.*

But it wasn't even his fault, was it? No. It wasn't. He was in the middle of some sick little game.

Tell him already, Sarah. Just tell him already.

A low, groaning sound made her flinch and a little scream escaped her mouth. And that was when she felt his hand on her ankle and her heart stopped.

"Sorry," he whispered. "It's just the drawer."

The dresser drawer opening. That was the sound. The groan. Her heart began to beat again but at a thousand beats per second.

His hand came off of her ankle and then he was pulling clothes out and putting them on. And within seconds, he was crawling into bed next to her. He moved in close, wrapped his arm around her like some drunk boyfriend, and kissed her neck. It felt amazing, both the kiss and being held. She couldn't remember the last time he'd held her or kissed her. But the greatest part about the kiss was the stench of beer that came off his breath. The smell itself was strong and godawful, but it meant he really was at the bar. It meant he wasn't out murdering people all night like a character in a video game. Her mind was stirring, going crazy as she thought about all the negative scenarios. But in the end, he was just sitting at a bar. With a guy he used to hate, but maybe now liked.

Relief came over her like a wave, and in no time, she was back asleep, on the beach with the fruity drink and the teal water and white sand all around her.

At 6:00, Sarah's alarm went off. Her hand came out from under the blanket with the speed of a bullet ejected from a pistol's chamber. *Right for the snooze button,* Brian thought. *How many times would she slap at it this morning?*

Brian was at his desk, slouching in his battered, wooden chair. He was holding the weight of his head on his hand, elbow on the desk. The sight of Sarah made him contemplate crawling back under the covers with her. But that wouldn't have been smart. It took just short of a mechanical hand coming down from the ceiling and prying her up to get the woman out of bed.

After two more segments of buzzing, she was up. She sat on the edge of the bed and put on her glasses.

"Hey," she said to him.

He looked over and even in the dimly-lit room, he could see that she was leaning towards falling back onto the pillow.

"Everything okay? What's up?" she asked.

"Nothing. Tired," he said with a pause between the two words. "Haven't even really written anything."

"You hung over?"

"Hate to admit it," he said, "but yeah. No tolerance anymore."

"How much did you drink?" she asked with a surprising smile, like a college buddy laughing at their roommate who'd puked the night before.

"Not much."

"You didn't smell like *Not much* when you got home."

"No?"

Sarah was up. She moved past him, and that was her answer. *You reeked of booze.* It had been a long time since she told him that. And then she was out the bedroom door and towards the bathroom, off to do her morning thing.

Brian looked down at his illuminated screen and saw his word count for the day: 184. Not even close to his daily goal of 1,500. As was the case nearly every day, he came up short on his expectations. The story was there, all of it in an outline and in his head, but the words could never come out. They were sitting in the back of his mind, clinging to the sides of his skull as the creativity winds tried to suck them out of his head.

He rubbed at his temples trying to suppress the pain between them. He only had three beers the night before. How was the pain so bad? How was it that any time he went out to drink, he was hung over? But when he sat at home and had the same amount, nothing? He remembered back when he and Sarah first started dating and they'd go out all the time. And the same thing happened. Always hung over. But they could sit on the couch and go through two bottles of wine and he'd feel great in the morning.

He closed his laptop screen, feeling like staring at the brightness for three hours might have had something to do with the headache. It was time to get ready for work, anyway.

When he shut the laptop, he shut it softly, as always, because if something were to happen to that laptop he'd have absolutely nothing. No writing format. He'd start writing freehand, sending in legal pads to agencies and seeing the laughing faces of the recipients in their high-rise New York offices as they opened the envelope.

His walk-in closet looked color-coordinated, but it wasn't. It just looked that way because work clothes were the only ones he had. Other than some old faded t-shirts and shorts, the red shirts and khaki pants lined his side of the closet like some department store rack. But he never complained. After all, where the hell was he going other than work?

As he pulled one of the shirts over his head and slid on his khaki pants, he thought about his clothes from the night before. Thought about coming into the bedroom, stripping them off and dropping them into the hamper. Right on top. Like some used condom wrapper for his wife to find. But worse.

He had to remove them. Throw them right into the washer or shove them to the bottom of the plastic crate.

Too late. As he came walking out into the room, Sarah was walking back in from the hall. To move them now would be to give himself up. Stick out his wrists, turn his head to the side, and wait to feel the cold steel of the handcuffs.

"Bar outfit?" she asked. Her glasses were gone, replaced with contact lenses.

"What?"

She pointed at his chest. "You wore that outfit to the bar?" She got a chuckle out of it that sounded like some bratty teenaged girl bullying another about a horrible choice of outfit.

"Yeah, I know," he said with a dumb smile. *Just don't pick up the laundry basket.*

"You won't even stop and get milk in that thing when I ask you to."

"It's embarrassing."

"Apparently not *that* embarrassing."

"It was just some dive. But you're right. Not going to impress anyone wearing this thing."

"I'm not saying impress, I'm just saying–"

"Well I am. I mean, I'm single now, right? I need to start dressing the part again."

"You're not single yet. Don't go bringing another woman's perfume into this bed. That's all I ask."

He did a good job of redirecting her mind from his work clothes, but doing so drove heat to his face. Don't go bringing another woman's perfume into this bed? Who the hell was *she*? He couldn't imagine why she'd even care. She was leaving him anyway. Packing up and taking the kids. What did it matter if he had the smell of another woman on him?

That wouldn't happen, though – him with the scent of another woman. Unless she was paid for. Look at him. Sure, he had a full head of hair and a fair, smooth complexion, but blinding anyone who could have looked at the positives was a bright red shirt with big, white, ironed-on letters: Eats-N-Treats. Women his age weren't looking for that. Clearly, as Sarah had shown. They were looking for suit and tie. Financial stability. Things he couldn't offer. Not yet, anyway. But soon. This next book was going to be the one that landed him on bestseller lists.

Sarah grabbed her phone from the nightstand, sat on the bed, looked at the time and let out a long sigh. After a short silence, she whispered, "Brian, did you hear what happened?"

"What happened?"

"To the old man across the street. Thomas McMann."

He shook his head.

"He died yesterday. His family took him off life support. A cop came knocking at the door yesterday morning."

"A cop?" he asked, trying to relax every muscle in his face. "Why a cop?"

"He was questioning people. Everyone in the area, I guess. Looking for leads."

Don't look right at her. But you can't look away, either. Shit. Stop overthinking. But he couldn't.

"Yeah?" he said. And then after a long pause, he looked down at the bright red shirt covering his torso and turned the conversation's steering wheel completely to the left: "You know me pretty well: I hate this outfit. I wouldn't normally wear it out in public."

"It's alright. You had fun."

"I did," he smiled.

Oh, he did.

32

"It's Friday," Sarah said. She pulled the cover off of Mason and he stretched to where his belly hung out from his Ninja Turtle pajamas. "No school tomorrow. You can sleep in." She sat beside him and rubbed his chest as he moaned in disapproval.

As Mason moped out of his bed, Sarah walked over to the closet to choose outfits for both kids. She pulled the handles to the folding closet doors and exposed the segregation of colors: pink and purple clothes on the right, blue and green on the left. She took clothes from each side and placed them on the kids' beds.

"Don't forget," she said. "I need to sign your planners before you leave." And when neither responded: "Okay?"

"Okay," Lacey managed to mumble. Such a difference, these kids were in the morning. But she couldn't blame them. She was the same way.

The kids slowly came into consciousness and got dressed, which meant it was on to Step Two of Sarah's every morning routine: breakfast. But before she could place a check mark in the Step One box, Lacey called to her.

"Mom."

"Yeah?"

"I wore this shirt on Monday."

"You did?"

"Yeah."

"Are you sure?"

"Yeah," Lacey said, somehow more alert with the flip of an annoyed switch. "I'm sure."

A *why-I-oughta* hand begged to be raised, but she didn't allow it. When Sarah was a kid, her ass was met with a belt on more occasions than she cared to think about, but in today's world she'd probably end up in the electric chair for the same act. So she settled for gritting her teeth and telling Lacey to pick out her own damn shirt.

Lacey walked over and flipped through hangers like she was at a shopping mall. She found the shirt she'd wear for the day and pulled it from its hanger. Sarah watched a preview of what Lacey's teenaged years would be like and cringed.

"Better?" Sarah asked, and Lacey nodded. "So tell me again why I pick out your clothes in the mornings when you're perfectly capable of doing so yourself?"

Lacey shrugged. "I like when you do it."

"Well guess what? I like when *you* do it. And I'm the boss." Not sure if she got the hint, but she would.

Sarah went out to the kitchen, leaving Lacey to wonder if she'd really have to pick out her own clothes from now on. Oh, the horror. She began making breakfast for the kids and then when they were dressed and at the kitchen table eating, she turned on the TV. The day the kids started chewing like normal human beings would be an amazing day for Sarah. Until then, she'd have the TV on to drown out the sound of their chomping.

She peeked her head down the hallway to see if Brian was still in the room. The news was on, and though she typically wouldn't think twice about watching the news, recently it'd been a little different. She wanted to see what was going on. Wanted to actually watch it, rather than just have it on in the background. She wanted to see if anything happened overnight. Brian told Sarah he was at the bar and he certainly smelled like it. Everything in his story lined up, but she was still skeptical. After all, this wasn't the same Brian from a few weeks ago.

The kids ate their breakfast, spilling most of it on the table. And when Brian came out, they celebrated like he was their own personal form of entertainment: *Yay! Dad's awake!* They never had a clue that he was up hours before them. For kids, the world only exists when they're awake and participating.

"Ready for the day!" he responded, walking to the table and putting a hand on each one's shoulder. "What did Mom make for you? Eggs? Yum!"

"With cheese, too!" Mason yelled loud enough for a neighbor to respond. How was it that the two slugs from a few minutes ago were now somehow balls of energy?

Brian grabbed his lunch box and told his kids to have a good day, as he always did. The man who hated his job still found a way to put on a happy face when walking out each morning.

Before he left, he looked at the TV and then to Sarah and said, "Been watching a lot of the news lately. Don't let the kids watch that trash. All negative." And when she said nothing, he said, "What ever happened to cartoons?"

"You're right," she said, and she meant it. She didn't want her kids watching the news. Stories of murder, theft, deception, and now one of those was directed at their own father. She flipped to the cartoons and threw the remote onto the couch.

Once Brian left, she helped the kids with their backpacks and shoes and then walked down the steps with them. Mason's backpack was the size of his body, making her nervous as he trotted down the steps. "Hold onto the handrail," she reminded him every morning. And bless his little heart, he tried. But he also wanted to try to keep up with his sister, who was two-stepping it down to get to her friends.

Sarah hung by the bottom of the steps as the kids ran to the bus stop the next building over. She never really had the desire for early-morning conversation with the neighbors. Some people were morning people and she most certainly was not. She wasn't one of the parents standing by their child, coffee cup in hand, ready to take on the day. At this time of day, her eyes were still uncrossing.

The bus came and swallowed the kids, taking the noise they were making with it. When Sarah was back in the apartment, happy to avoid conversation for yet another day, she grabbed the remote and turned the TV back to the news. This was her *me* time. Her social media time, usually. *What's everyone up to?* But she took her daily twenty minutes of lounging and social networking on this day to listen to the anchors talk about mostly depressing stories.

And then it came. The story she knew she'd see. A

snapshot of a smiling Thomas McMann sat in the top corner of the screen. One his family must have submitted to the station. One of a much happier day. A day where he had no idea that his life would be cut short by the blade of his own fishing knife.

The anchorman, David Kensley, shook his head and took the time to allow the camera to see his one, long, slow blink as he reported the news of Thomas McMann's passing. "Rock Park P.D. asks for anyone's help in this matter. Please call the RPPD tip line if you have any information."

Sarah's insides churned. She became lightheaded. This was all real. This really happened. It seemed every hour of every day, something was jumping in front of her to remind her of what was going on.

She hit the power button and walked back into the bedroom to get ready for work. She turned on some music on her phone to try to clear her mind – forget about this all, if even only for a short time. And it worked. For a bit. She stood in front of the bathroom mirror putting on her mascara and filling in her eyebrows, thinking to herself that her office-mate Tina would surely show her up today, as she did every day.

When she walked into the closet to pick out her clothes, the first thing she noticed were Brian's khaki pants and work shirt hanging over the side of the mounding laundry crate. She thought about what could be on those clothes. There was no way Brian was out drinking last night. No way he was just hanging out with the man he hated. Something happened and he was using Eric as a decoy. The man had no other friends, so who else could he lie about being with?

Whatever happened, it was her fault. And she had to carry on with trying to cover it up. She picked up the crate from its handles, walked to the bathroom and threw it all into the washer. Brian's outfit from yesterday was drowned in the water and soap, along with whatever was left on it.

33

There were two cop cars parked by the front door of the pet store when Brian pulled into the parking lot. A young man in a uniform said something with a smile to the young lady in a matching uniform, and then both of them laughed before sipping on their coffee. The only thing they didn't do in unison was shoo away a mother and son walking across the parking lot toward the store. The young lady was the one who took care of that.

Brian drove around to the employee entrance in the back, hoping to get a glimpse inside an opened loading dock door, but had no such luck. The oversized garage door was pulled closed and he was about to find out why.

The gas pedal grazing the bottom of his shoe was his escape. *Just hit it,* he thought. *You don't even have to stomp on it. Just extend that foot the slightest bit and cruise on by the store. No one is looking. No one is suspecting. No one knows what happened.*

But he didn't.

Instead, he turned into a parking spot far from the

dumpster, as he tried to every morning (those damn shitting seagulls). He grabbed his lunch box from the passenger seat and slowly got out of the car, locking the door behind him and lumbering across the parking lot toward what was his usual cage for the next eight hours. He was miserable, just as if nothing out of the ordinary had happened. And just as if nothing had happened, he swiped his badge on the pad beside the door and waited to hear the click of the lock disabling itself.

Then he opened the door into hell.

He was hit with a sea of black and yellow as he stepped through the threshold. Another uniformed officer was standing with his back facing the door, but quickly turned around when he saw Brian. "You work here, Sir?" the baby-faced cop asked.

"I do."

"What's in the bag?" he glanced at the soft-pack lunch bag hanging from Brian's shoulder.

"My lunch."

"You mind if I check?"

"Sure." Brian handed it over.

The officer quickly unzipped the top and looked inside. Then he handed it back to Brian unzipped. "Here."

What a dick move. Surely the authoritative hard-on displayed by a rookie cop. Brian considered tossing the contents at the cop, melting ice and all.

"You mind coming with me?" the cop asked, but it wasn't really a question.

Brian followed him through the empty and quiet warehouse. Gray floors were shining and clean. Shelves tidy and organized. The room was ready to be woken for a normal day's work, but it would need to wait a little while longer.

They stopped when they reached the silver double-doors leading to the front of the store. The cop leaned into one and signaled for Brian to walk through. "Go right in there," he said, pointing to the break room door just a few feet down the wall.

Brian could feel the cop staring at him as he walked. He felt like a woman in a short dress and heels walking down the city sidewalk, the cop a male construction worker sitting atop a steel beam, letting out a catcall.

Once Brian hit the doorway to the break room, he turned to see the cop still staring. He pointed a curved finger at Brian, telling him with the motion to get inside the room. And then he was gone, back into the warehouse, the aluminum door swinging behind him.

"Your name?" Brian was asked by yet another teenager in a policeman's uniform, only this one was bulky and seemed even more pissed off. Maybe he wanted to make Detective and it was taking too long. Or what he really wanted was to be in the FBI. But he was stuck here, taking names like a restaurant hostess.

"Brian Hart."

The cop wrote in his notepad, pointed to a seat lining the wall, and told Brian to sit there.

The break room had been gutted, internally speaking. Three of the four circular tables had been closed and leaned up against the wall beside the vending machines. And the chairs that surrounded those tables – made of something that should never claim comfort – had all been pushed against the opposite walls. It no longer felt like a break room, but like a high school cafeteria being cleared out for an assembly. And Brian felt odd having the strap of his lunch bag still draped over his shoulder.

But he sat. In silence. As told. And awaited what he could have avoided by pressing the gas pedal rather than pulling into the parking spot out back.

In the chair next to him was a girl named Nicole, who'd been at Eats-N-Treats for almost three years now, starting in high school and working a few hours here and there now that she was in college. Her dark hair hung to the side of her darker face, and she looked as though she was no longer able to move the muscles in her body.

The poor thing. She'd always been bright. She was never one of the girls hanging out with the stock boys in the back, doing the flirting-just-for-the-fun-of-flirting-yet-it'll-never-lead-anywhere thing. Never showed up late or snuck out back for a bowl hit. And now she was sitting in the presence of all this chaos.

Brian looked over at Nicole but she didn't look back. Not even a look out of the corner of her eye. It wasn't until he spoke that she finally looked over.

"Hey," Brian said. "What happened?"

She looked at him, eyes glazed over as if she hadn't blinked in an hour. "You didn't hear?" she asked. "Eric." She paused. "He's been murdered."

"What?" To Brian it almost sounded like a laugh, and he glanced around the room expecting to see incriminating eyes on him. But there were none.

"Yeah," Nicole said. "It's crazy. Yesterday he was here, and now he's gone." She turned and looked forward again, into seemingly nothing, just as she had been before Brian interrupted her thought. "Right here in Rock Park. Murder. And then that stabbing." She turned back toward him with the same lagging gesture and asked, "You heard about that, right? That old guy getting stabbed in his driveway?"

Brian nodded. Yes. As a matter of fact, he *had* heard.

"I heard he died," she said. "Heard he finally died in the hospital. He was in critical condition and now he's dead." Her head drifted forward and it was starting to seem through the conversation like a magnet was drawing her head straight. Or some force was pulling her back into whatever daydream she was having. "Right here in Rock Park," she repeated herself. "Two murderers right in this town." She looked back at him. Her turn was quicker this time, but still slow by any limber human's standards. "Crazy to think how close these psychotic people can be, isn't it? Bad people are so close to us. All around us."

"It sure is," Brian said, sitting just inches from her.

Brian felt like an early morning commuter waiting for the bus as he sat patiently, legs crossed, fingers interlocked on his lap, head leaning against the glossy cinderblock wall. He remained this way while several co-workers were interviewed, and then the angry, bulky cop walked back over to him.

"Brian Hart?"

"That's me," he said, pushing his head away from the wall.

"The detective will speak with you now," he said as he turned his body and nodded in the detective's direction.

After sitting there for so long, with so much time to think, he finally allowed himself to worry. What if he acted too nervous? What if he wasn't nervous *enough*? What if his eyes gave it all away? Or he started shaking his leg? Or biting his nails?

Why the hell didn't he just hit the gas pedal and drive right on by this place when he had the chance?

Brian stood from his chair and grabbed the strap of his

lunch bag: "Take this?" he asked.

The cop shrugged his shoulders and shook his head. "Sure, why not."

Surely they didn't care if he had his lunch bag next to him. It was just some leftover chicken and rice. Had they not gone through his bag when he first walked in, maybe they'd be skeptical. But he wasn't asking because he felt comfort in having his damn lunch bag with him. He was asking because he wanted to put it in the refrigerator like he'd do every day. No sense in letting perfectly good food go to waste.

He lifted the bag from the strap and walked over to another blue, plastic chair sitting alone in front of the round, cafeteria table, and he sat. He was now eye-to-eye with the detective who would ask him some questions, and felt as though he'd walked himself right onto Death Row.

The setup had him facing the corner of the room like a child in time out, only there was a table and the detective between him and the corner. And as the detective sat there, looking down and rustling through the endless scattered papers and manila folders before her, Brian's mind raced.

"Brian Hart?" she asked, not looking up. She had that tough tone that most black women have, but her look didn't fit her tone. She was pretty. She took care of herself and it showed – hair, makeup, nice white smile.

"That's me," he said, raising his hand.

She smiled a bit, but only glanced at him for a brief second before looking back down into her paperwork. "My name is Detective Jones," she said.

"Nice to meet you, Detective Jones."

"You know why we're here, Mr. Hart?"

"I heard," he said. He instinctively looked back to Nicole to tell the detective who'd told him about it, but was met by the wall of black uniforms standing between him and the line of employees waiting patiently. He turned back, shook his head: "Crazy."

"Yeah," she said, looking at him now. "Crazy."

A long pause ensued as she studied his face. Unsure of what to do, he finally asked, "Did they find out what happened?"

"They?" she asked. "*We*, Mr. Hart. *We* don't know anything for sure yet, but we know a lot. We have a team of forensic scientists at the scene now. So far they have fingerprints and footprints that they've found and sent in; just waiting to hear back with the results."

"Good," Brian said. No sweat. No flushness. Who *was* he?

"It is," she said, leaning back in her blue, plastic chair. It was the type she probably hadn't sat in since elementary school but Eats-N-Treats employees lounged in every day. "So we'll find whoever did this pretty quickly. But we still have to go through protocol. And I'll have to ask you a few questions."

He nodded. "Sure."

"Can you tell me where you were last night, Mr. Hart?"

"I can. I was home last night." It began. He could envision the doors of the prison opening and some guards escorting him through. He saw himself in a prison jumpsuit, shuffling along with his ankles in shackles.

"Can you tell me what time you got home?" She was looking down now, writing into a legal pad.

"Right after work." *Shuffle along there, prisoner.*

"So you worked yesterday?"

"I did."

"Until what time?"

"Five o'clock."

"And then you went straight home?" She was looking up now, right into his eyes, giving the overused pen a break.

"Straight home," he said. But he was transitioning into a play on words. *I never said I went straight home; My answer was straight home.*

"And then what, Mr. Hart? Did you stay home for the remainder of the evening?"

"I did. I had dinner with my family and then watched TV for a little bit and then went to bed."

"What did you watch?" she fired back quickly.

"The news," he responded, trying to hold back the relieved smile. *Where did that come from? Quick response, Brian. You: One. Detective Jones: Zero.*

"What was on the news last night?"

"Murder."

"That's it? Just murder?"

"Basically. That's all that's ever on the news anymore, isn't it?" He smiled and looked to her for an agreeing one, but received none.

"You seem awful joyous about that," she said, and then leaned down to write something in the legal pad. And as she did, Brian saw himself shuffling down the prison walkway again. He heard the entrance door slam shut behind him, locking him in his new home. No more kids. They'd be calling someone else Dad.

"My kids," he said. "They were jumping all over me. Always are. I don't really remember what was on because I was playing with my kids."

"How old are your kids?" she asked, looking up again.

"Seven and four."

She smiled. "You have a wife?"

"I do." *For now.*

"Can she confirm your whereabouts yesterday evening?"

"She can." His new prison-mates hooted and hollered at the new piece of meat as the guards walked him down the path to his new cell.

Detective Jones wrote down some more on her notepad. Brian tried to look, but her handwriting was too sloppy to try to decode.

"Thank you, Mr. Hart," she said, and this triggered an officer standing beside her to lean in and tell him to go back to his seat now.

He did, standing and grabbing the lunch bag once more, imagining the horrendous smell building within as the food slowly began to grow bacteria and go bad. The second he walked out of the store, he'd toss the food out of the container and into the dumpster in the parking lot. He envisioned the seagulls he'd hated so much finally being pleased with him. For seven years he hadn't fed them a thing, knowing they'd just keep coming back. Today was their lucky day. They could eat his food and then shit on his car and he'd be fine with it. This could be one of the final times he'd be able to bitch about it.

Once back in his plastic seat against the wall, he realized the room was less cluttered than before, and he assumed someone from District had come and finally spoken to everyone, allowing them to leave – including Nicole, who was no longer there. While many were curious as to what happened to Eric, some were curious as to their pay for the day if the store was going to remain closed.

"You don't have to wait anymore," the bulky cop walked over to Brian and said, just as Brian had taken his seat. "One of your bosses is out there. He wants to talk to everyone."

"Then what?"

He shrugged. "Not sure. He'll tell you."

Brian walked into the hallway to find several employees already there – Nicole included – huddled around the District Manager, hanging on his every word.

"It'll have to remain closed during the investigation, I'm told," Matt Hornqvist said to his followers – his cult, it would seem to anyone on the outside looking in.

"Are we still gon' get paid?" Tanesha, one of the clerks, asked. Brian remembered running into her several months back when they were on break together. They talked about their kids and exchanged pictures. It's normally awkward when people show you pictures of their kids – *come on, push out a smile* – but hers really were adorable.

"For today, yes," Matt said. "Unfortunately, we can't guarantee anything beyond that." He had to raise his voice over several groans and grunts when he said, "We're taking this day by day and we'll let you know everything we can just as soon as we get some more information. But for now, go home, be with your families during this time, and you'll hear from me soon."

The people around him disbursed and walked back through the warehouse and out the employee door. Brian followed the crowd and when he stepped outside to see the sun again, he imagined stepping out of prison when he would finally be released. Sure, he was walking away a free man now, but everyone gets caught.

He walked over to the dumpster and opened his lunch

bag. He dumped the contents of the plastic container into the opened lid and then looked up at the gulls circling around, moving in closer, waiting for the human to get the hell out of the way so they could feast. And with a smile, he did. *Eat up, you sons of bitches.*

Brian followed the line of cars out of the parking lot, each going their own separate way to the places they called home. Soon Brian would get a phone call. Or a knock on the door. And some uniform would ask him where he *really* was on that night.

35

Alicia Jones was the only female detective in the Rock Park Police Department. It wasn't for lack of females within the force, just that the others had no desire to be detectives. They wanted to be out on the street. In uniform. On the front lines with the others. Maybe it was some show of feminism or pride. *We can do anything men can do.* But Alicia didn't allow herself to get caught up in the political bullshit that surrounded her precinct. She did what made her happy, and working behind the scenes to investigate crimes was what made her happy.

She didn't start out in the homicide unit when she first made detective. After three years as an Officer, pushing and hinting to those at the top that her goal here was to make detective, she'd gotten it. And of course some of the male officers whispered to each other that she must've been sleeping with someone in order to get the promotion so quickly.

Perkins was the worst. He was a little Irish prick and had that attitude to match. Maybe he felt he had some making up to do for his lack of height. He was shorter than Alicia who only stood at five-foot-six. Or maybe the fact that his wife walked out on him to be with his cousin a few years back led him to resent all women. Whatever the reason, he was an angry little shit.

He was a detective himself, but it hadn't been long before Alicia. Though both the same rank, he felt he had this seniority over her. He seemed to have it out for everyone in the unit, but Alicia more than anyone else. Maybe he thought she was an easy target. Whatever the reason, she never let it get to her. In her mind, he was trying to break her. *See, she can't handle being detective.* And she wasn't about to let him win at the petty little game, if in fact that was his game. So she nodded at his asinine actions and comments and went about her day.

Her first attachment was to the Domestic Violence unit, where her feminist counterparts would have had a stroke within the first hour had they stood beside her. Men beating their wives for not heating up their dinner fast enough. Men beating their girlfriends for things their kids were doing wrong. Men beating their wife, girlfriend, whatever terminology they were using, simply because they felt like beating the shit out of them. But these weren't the reasons the feminists would have the stroke. It was the opposite cases that would send them into a frenzy.

If Domestic Violence taught Alicia anything, it's that cell phones are the main culprit for many fights. She can remember clearly her first case where the woman was convicted of battery and attempted murder. And it was all because of a cell phone.

The convicted woman and her boyfriend were having dinner in their apartment and he got up to go to the bathroom. That's when she grabbed his phone and started looking through it. She found some pictures of another girl in there and lost her shit. She grabbed one of the kitchen chairs – a wooden, sturdy thing – from its back, picked it up and swung it at her boyfriend when he came back into the kitchen. He yelled, she yelled back, and then she grabbed a knife, chased him back into the bathroom and stabbed him in his side. She was a mess when the police arrived, crying and saying how sorry she was and that she didn't know what got into her.

Her boyfriend lived. The girl actually dropped the knife after she pulled it out of him and tried to help put pressure on the wound. But he was yelling so loudly for her to get the hell away that she finally did. Ran out into the living room and called the police using the same phone that started the whole ordeal.

She landed in jail, of course. Got three years for assault with a deadly weapon. Had she not been compliant and plead guilty, she would have been tried for attempted murder.

Just a normal girl. Alicia can remember interviewing her and she was so down to Earth. Knew she'd ruined her life and couldn't escape the idea that some guy she'd been dating for ten months turned out to be the reason for her demise. All because she thought she loved him.

Alicia told the girl she should write a book while in jail. Might sell. But she never did.

Her assignment to the Homicide unit came nine months later. Jittery, she showed up to her first crime scene of a drug deal gone bad. Guy shot in the head. A pool of blood staining the sidewalk. Body still lying there underneath a black tarp. One minute alive and breathing, the next, just a lump of bones and meat left to be examined for clues.

For nine months, she'd spent her mornings arriving on murder scenes. And this morning was no different.

Victim's name was Eric Millford. Twenty-six years old. Found dead in his driveway by his neighbor on the way out the door for work. No blood. Strangulation seemed to be the route – bulging eyes and swollen lips. Still not a site for sensitive eyes, but much better than the more gruesome ones she'd come across since being assigned to the Homicide Unit.

If you'd asked Alicia to describe the layout of the office at the police station, she could have gone into great detail and been correct about it all. Even before stepping one foot into this place. That's just how generic a setup the Rock Park PD had.

Offices lined the walls, blocked off from the guts with wooden doors and plated windows with the stereotypical mini blinds. Within those guts of the place, two rows of cubicles running parallel to each other. At the ends of these rows were two identical work stations: printer, fax, copy machine. Alicia stood in front of the printer closest to her cubicle.

The captain's office was right behind her. Set up so he could see the whole room, most likely. But he wasn't the type to breathe down anyone's neck. Most of the time he was dealing with people breathing down *his* neck – the press, mostly – leaving him no time to breathe down anyone else's.

"Detective Jones," he called through the open door to her. "When you get a minute," he said, waving her in.

Pages pushed out of the printer rapidly and

continuously as the background checks printed from her computer and into the pile before her. When they were all out, she took them and placed them into a manila folder.

"Good morning, Sir," she said as she walked through his doorway. She tucked the manila folder under her arm as she did so.

"What've we got?" he asked.

Captain Furlong was just what you'd envision when you see a police captain: he was an old but rough-looking guy. He looked like an ex-marine. *Was*, in fact, an ex-marine, and the haircut showed it. What was left of his gray hair was short and spiked straight up in the front. And on the sides, nothing but shiny, bald skin. The times had changed, but his looks hadn't.

"Still a lot to go through," Detective Jones answered, patting the folder tucked against her side. "Just got back from Wave One of interviews."

"And?" He asked, standing behind the metal desk in his office.

"What about the house?"

"Forensics has been on the scene all morning. Still no word on anything new. Looks like an attack. Didn't look like anything was in disarray in the surrounding areas. Perp could have known the victim. Or it could have been a sneak attack, being it was nighttime. I'm hoping forensics gives me something good. I'll let you know when I hear back."

"Okay. Good work, Detective."

"Thank you."

He took a step to the side, looking as if he was moving to another pile of neatly-stacked papers on his desk. But then he abruptly stopped just as Alicia was about to get away.

"Any new developments on that McMann case?"

That dreaded McMann case. Where no one seemed to have seen anything. There were no witnesses, no cameras, no footprints or fingerprints, no hair samples or marks of any kind under the victim's fingernails. Nothing.

"Heard he passed," Captain Furlong said.

"I heard."

"Any updates?"

"Working on it."

The captain nodded, sending her back through the walkway separating cubicles from offices, peasants from important people. And it was in her cubicle that she started looking through the reports of squeaky-clean high school students whose boss was just murdered. This would hopefully be the closest they got to death or murder. They were all working part-time at the ages of sixteen and seventeen, which was a foot in the right direction. While others their age were out causing mischief or sitting glued to a TV screen, these ones were practicing responsibility.

She smelled her first scent of blood when coming across the file for Thomas Brandon, one of the warehouse employees. Alicia reviewed his file: nineteen-year-old white male; clean driving record; one misdemeanor on his criminal record – looked like he had a Possession case dropped down. As it should have been, she thought. It was only marijuana. No reason to send some kid's life spiraling downward by slamming him with criminal charges over a little bit of weed.

She wasn't supposed to have that mindset, but she did.

Nothing on Thomas's record that would suggest murder, though. And nothing from his interview notes to suggest he'd have any grudges against his boss.

Continuing to flip through the pages upon pages of black lettering on white paper, she eventually found herself staring at a familiar face. The age on his report was much higher than anyone else's at the place, and his image stood out amongst the rest. She could picture his demeanor and the way he stumbled toward the table with strap of his lunchbox thrown over his shoulder. He looked like a man who'd been up all night.

If she could manage to be honest with herself for a second, she'd admit that she'd hit a wall here. Again. Just like the McMann case. Unless forensics came back with something positive for her, she was going to be battling a steep uphill climb again.

Brian Hart might have been the oldest of the employees there, but his single-page record showed he hadn't been a badass during his lifetime. He had a few address changes listed and that was it. Nothing. So maybe those bloodshot eyes and blank stare weren't from a lack of sleep because he was out killing his boss in the night. Maybe they were there from the pain of his life. Maybe he hates coming to this job so much that the life is sucked out of him each and every morning when his alarm clock goes off. There are so many people like that in the world, and Alicia was grateful not to be one of them.

She was about to flip the page on this guy Brian – next page, fingers crossed – when something caught her eye.

His address.

He lived in the neighborhood across the street from Thomas McMann.

36

The apartment was empty. And quiet. Brian wasn't used to this. Not used to being alone. He worked at the pet store seven days a week. Even on Sundays, when there was no delivery truck coming to pour its guts into the warehouse, Brian was still there, organizing, stocking. "Pet food doesn't sleep and neither does Eats-N-Treats," Eric always said.

No, he didn't. But even then, with Eric in a body bag, it felt right to crack jokes at his expense.

When Brian first started working at the pet store, he tried to freelance as a writer on the weekends, but it never worked out. People were insane. They wanted to pay ten dollars to write a research paper for them. And that fee included doing the research, writing, and rewriting. Another ad he saw once was for someone in need of a writer for a book. *I've got this great idea for a novel, but I'm not a writer.* And you know how much this person was willing to dish out? Fifty dollars. He almost rolled out of his chair laughing when he saw it. *Fifty bucks to spend six months writing your book? And then you get all the royalties and the credit? Sure! I'll have it back to you in six months. What's that average out to per hour?*

Freelancing was going nowhere. So he was able to convince his then-manager, Darren Anderson, to let him pick up hours on the weekend. And Darren allowed it. Because he wasn't an asshole. Like Eric is. Or *was.* Things didn't start going downhill until Darren retired.

Brian walked into the apartment, dropped his lunch bag on the counter and walked slowly through the quiet hall and into the bedroom so he could change into something that didn't remind him of his miserable existence in the working world.

Once in his sweatpants and t-shirt, he walked out to the living room and turned on the television. For a second, he considered opening a beer. Why the hell not, right? Sure, it wasn't even eleven o'clock, but he had one day off. Not one day this week or even this month. He had *one* day off in Lord knows how long. He wanted to take advantage of it. Not waste it. So he went into the fridge, cracked a beer, and told himself with a smile not to feel any remorse. It wasn't like anyone was going to see him anyway. Sarah didn't get done work until three and the kids...

The kids. He'd be able to pick them up from school. For once, they wouldn't have to go to after school care. They could come right home. And how happy would they be to see Dad coming to pick them up? Not too happy if he smelled like beer. The teachers wouldn't be, at least.

He lifted the twelve-ounce can and looked at it: *Ah, one beer won't hurt.* He had at least four hours until he had to think about picking them up anyway. Which made him think: what time did they get done school?

He could send Sarah a text, but then she'd wonder why the hell he was home, and asking. Better just to look it up himself. On the internet.

The closed laptop that sat on his desk spoke to him as soon as he walked into the bedroom and glanced down at it. The little green light beside the charger let him know, *Hey, bud. I'm ready for you.*

He probably should have written. Right then. He bitched and moaned about life so much and how badly he wanted to be a writer... well now was the perfect opportunity to increase that word count. Every word punched into that computer brought him one step closer to being published, he kept telling himself. He grabbed the laptop, but only because he needed it for the internet – that thing he told himself to steer clear of every morning during his writing sessions.

Keep all distractions far, far away.

Beer in one hand, laptop in the other, Brian walked back to the couch. He opened the laptop, illuminating the bright white screen with little black letters he'd last seen before the wife and kids rose and ripped through his bubble of alone time. Behind the white laptop screen was the larger TV screen he'd turned on when he first walked in.

The kids. They weren't done school until 2:24. Plenty of time.

He closed the laptop and dropped it on the cushion beside him, ignoring the screaming little voices in his head telling him how irresponsible he was. That he must write or face the regret that would come in a few hours, when he'd tell himself he was a piece of shit for not utilizing perfectly good writing time.

We told you so, the little voices would say.

But he didn't listen. Instead, he kicked his feet up onto the ottoman, crossed ankle over ankle, pointed the remote towards the TV and started flipping through channels, sipping on the cold beer almost subconsciously.

Brian flipped through channels and told himself with a head nod that women must watch a ton of daytime TV. It was nothing but talk show after talk show after talk show, all of them with commercials slotted in for cleaning products and in every commercial the kids were spilling shit all over the house. Yet after the lady in the commercial would wipe up the spill, the whole house somehow looked immaculate. It'd be nice if life was like that. Make a mess of your life? Here. Clean it right up. Fresh slate.

Flipping through the channels to rid himself of the redundancy, he came across something that looked familiar. It was a news station. Or just a news hour slotted into a station. Either way, it didn't matter. What mattered was the building behind the woman with a microphone in her hand.

Southeast Medical Center. The hospital where the old man was housed until he lost his life.

The woman nodded her head and pushed the mic closer to her mouth. Brian put his feet down, leaned up from the couch and inched toward the screen.

"Thank you, Rachael. I'm standing here outside Southeast Medical Center where Thomas McMann of Rock Park was pulled off of life support by his family yesterday. The police still have no leads pointing toward a suspect yet and the family has just stepped in, offering a $25,000 reward to anyone who has information leading to the suspect's arrest."

And then the camera cut to a prerecorded message from

a middle-aged woman, heavy with glasses and short gray hair. She was standing behind a podium when she declared, "My husband was a good man and whoever did this – whatever coward did this to an innocent man – needs to be brought to justice. My family and I don't want any other family to go through what we've had to go through over these past few days, and will continue to go through for the rest of our lives." She lowered her head and wiped a tear from behind her glasses. "Our family will never be the same." Some younger people moved in and put their hands on her shoulders. Her children, most likely.

The remote remained in his one hand, beer in the other. Neither fell to the floor. But it seemed like they should have. He couldn't move a muscle in his body. He was weightless. Nothing there. No breathing. No movement.

The reporter continued: "RPPD is urging anyone with details to please contact the police department as soon as possible."

Her anchor thanked her, and then the reporter was off the screen. The anchor, then, was off to her next story.

How else was he supposed to research? How else was he supposed to write? With some authenticity. How? He had to do this. Had to get the facts straight. Because he had to be published.

He walked to the kitchen and placed the half-full beer can in the sink, remembering that he'd soon be the main suspect in two murder cases. And day drinking wasn't how he wanted to spend his dwindling free time.

Staring across the countertop that separated the kitchen from the living room in his small apartment, Brian watched as the news carried on, as does life. And he couldn't help but feel a sense of relief. Sure, the old man had died, but it would have ended up much worse if he lived and Brian had to track him down to finish the job. Stabbing the man for the sake of research was one thing, but hunting down a survivor and finishing him off was ruthless.

Before the first beer was cracked open, the plan was to have a few more in succession. That plan was out the window and instead, he grabbed a glass from the cabinet and filled it from the faucet.

He went back to the couch, sat, and watched the same news anchor show similar emotion on a different story, sending the camera to a different field reporter in a different location.

Power Off.

He couldn't watch this shit anymore. Couldn't agonize over it any longer. Couldn't tear himself in two wondering which way he should feel. It was done. He did what he had to do in order to be a better writer. If some unlucky old man and some douchebag pet store manager had to be on the receiving end for his story to be better, then so be it. Life would go on. People die every day. And people also worked hard at their professions every day. It was a cut-throat world. Survival of the fittest. Only the best writers made it to the top and only those willing to do anything to improve their craft would be crowned one of the best.

The best would also write. Plain and simple. He needed to get his words down into his processor. That's the only way he'd improve. So he grabbed his laptop from the couch cushion beside him, opened it, and started writing.

But he'd be interrupted by one constant thought: *I*

should pack.

Something was telling him to pack. To get the hell out of the empty apartment. Get the hell out of Rock Park. He was a sitting duck and they'd surely find him. The police would come get him and take him to his new home: prison.

This would have been a great day to sit back and write without interruption. Home from work seven hours earlier than usual without kids jumping on him and no wife jumping down his throat. But he just couldn't do it. The laptop was in his lap, but he knew before he even had the slightest inclination to begin that he wouldn't be able to concentrate. There were too many thoughts racing through his mind. Too many scenarios playing out. Each one of them ending with him being handcuffed and taken away in the back of a cop car. The worst image playing its reel in his mind was the one where his kids were standing in the parking lot of the apartment complex, crying, wondering why Daddy was going away. And Sarah, humiliated, looking at him as though she wished he would disappear from their lives for good.

But he could avoid all of that. If he just left. Packed his shit and hit the road. His kids would be crushed, but he could still call them. And if there ever came a time where he couldn't call them, well then maybe it was for the better. It would save them from the scene they might have witnessed if he was to stick around.

He closed his laptop and set it on the cushion beside him. And then as if there was some gravitational pull, he was up off the couch and walking back to the bedroom.

This wasn't for good, he told himself. It wasn't like he was up and leaving his family. His kids. He was just going for a long ride. A route no one around here could know. A route that would keep him from going to prison. Because he *was* going to prison. One way or another. He knew it. Had known it since he felt the pop of that fishing knife pierce the skin of old Mr. McMann.

He grabbed an old duffel bag from the bottom of the closet, where Sarah's shoes were mixed with Sarah's clothes that have fallen off of hangers, mixed with Sarah's numerous wristlets and purses that have amounted over the years. "We wouldn't have money problems if you'd sell your shit," he'd joke with her many years ago, when the jokes still created laughs.

He looked down at his neatly-stacked pile of boxes and froze – *to bring it or not to bring it.* But then he reminded himself again that this wasn't permanent. He was only leaving for a little while. He would never leave his kids forever and he'd do whatever he needed to in order to come back here for them.

Plastic clinked together and hangers swayed from the wire racks like kids on a swingset as he pulled down some shirts to take with him. For a second, he thought about taking all of his work shirts and tossing them out the car window on his drive. One by one. Maybe while driving down the highway. Look out the rear-view mirror and watch as the cars behind him ran them over, squeezing out the years of anguish and misery as they did.

But he decided to leave them. If him going on the run wasn't a tell-tale sign of guilt, the riddance of what he wore into that hellhole for the last seven years would be the equivalent of him marching right up the steps of the municipal building with his hands out.

The bag was filled with everything he needed, and he

threw it over his shoulder and walked down the hallway and into the kitchen to grab a few more things for the road: water bottles, some granola bars, and a can of honey roasted peanuts that he knew would sit in the cupboard for years if he wasn't there to eat them.

He took his laptop from the couch cushion and curled it under his arm, then swept the area for anything else he might have needed to bring with him. He found nothing, but in his searching, he looked down the hallway and decided to walk down once more. He knew he shouldn't have, because it would only make him sad, and because he knew what he wanted to walk down there for. He wanted to go into the kids' bedroom. To look around. See where they'd lay their heads tonight, upset that their father wasn't there to tuck them in. And then they'd wonder where he was again in the morning, and then after school, and then after dinner. How long would this last? How long would he have to be away? How long until this all blew over? Or would it *never* blow over? If it never blew over, would they understand why their dad did what he did? Would they understand that he did it for them? So that they could have a better life?

He never wanted to kill anyone. Never wanted to hurt anyone. Never *wanted* to, but it turned out he *had* to. He'd devoted his entire life to writing. To being an author. He'd turned down decent jobs and an opportunity to pursue a different career path because he knew what he wanted. What he *had* to have. He had to be a published author. A bestselling author. Had to make his children proud of him. And make sure they never had to worry about finances like he eventually had. His kids had to be able to rely on him when they got older and never worry that Dad doesn't have the money to help them. And he didn't want them to have to rely solely on his life insurance money.

He knew it would break him emotionally, but he walked down that hall anyway. And when he got to the kids' bedroom door, the duffel bag on his shoulder wanted to slide off. Brian wanted to lie down in each of their beds. Wanted to smell them. Really, he wanted to go to the school and pick them up and hold them. Forever.

He remembered lying in bed with each of his kids when they were younger, and afraid of being on their own. He'd hold them as they'd stare up at the ceiling and he couldn't fight the urge to kiss their cheeks continuously. To kiss their soft cheeks and rub their soft arms, and envy that the only fear they had was of some monster they may have seen on today's cartoons. He wanted to tell them that Daddy saw monsters at night, too, but they came in the form of Final Notice envelopes that had come in today's mail and rejection letters that he kept in his inbox. And they crept up on him when he closed his eyes at night.

Instead, he held it all in. Pretended the world was a glorious place and not some stressful tight-rope walk with high winds. He would hold the kids until they fell asleep, calm and feeling safe that Daddy was there with them in case any of those cartoon monsters decided to come out.

Would they understand why he left? Or would the memories of those nights in the bed together fade away with their little minds and morph into some hatred for him?

This isn't permanent, he said to himself. *So stop acting like it is.*

Tears welled in his eyes. This would be the first night he didn't spend with his children since they were born. Both of them. This was one of the reasons he never took one of those corporate jobs. He never wanted to lay his head on his pillow without kissing his children goodnight. And the corporate, airport and hotel life wouldn't allow that.

He turned and walked down the hall towards the door. He had to leave. Now. Stop overthinking. Stop contemplating. He was being selfish now, thinking of himself and his desire to want to snuggle up next to his kids and never move again. But he was doing this for them. It had always been about them.

Brian walked out of the apartment and locked the door behind him, then hurried down the stairs and to his car. He threw the duffel bag across the center console and into the passenger seat before turning the key over to fire up the engine. One last time, he looked up at the apartment building and pictured the kids waiting by the door with smiles planted on their faces. Those smiles would be ripped off when he pulled away.

Tears no longer welled his eyes but ran down his cheeks in streams. His vision was blurred but he knew he must leave before he could think any longer. Maybe if he was away from the apartment and the thought of the kids, he wouldn't think so much about them. He'd think of other things. Maybe drive a little distance and pull over to write.

He backed the car out of the parking spot, then put it in drive and started drifting down the asphalt. He passed the next building and came up to where the bus picked up the kids in the morning. He could see them, getting on the bus, screaming and yelling with all the other kids. There was no bus there, of course, and what he envisioned might not even have been what they did, because he'd never seen his kids get on or off of the bus because he had always been at work.

Snap out of it, he told himself. It was better that way. For the kids.

As he rounded the first curve before the stop sign at the complex's exit, a car was approaching from the opposite direction. He wiped at his watery eyes so the blurred vision didn't send him into the oncoming car. And after a quick wipe and a few short blinks, his vision became clear again. But he felt like he must have still been envisioning things, just as he envisioned his kids running to the bus. That wasn't real and this couldn't be either.

The car drove right on past him, but Brian still wasn't breathing. He remained as still as he could while looking out his side-view mirror, then rolling his head to look out the rear-view one. That passing car continued driving. And that recognizable woman's face driving it:

Detective Jones. The detective who did the interviews this morning.

When he got to the community exit, he paused. He was no longer upset about leaving. No longer felt the guilt of not being there to greet his kids after work. Because he now knew he wouldn't have been there anyway. He'd be leaving in the back of the detective's car.

37

"I need coffee. You want one?"

Sarah rose from behind her desk as her co-worker, Tina, said with her cheerful smile, "No thanks. Still have this from earlier." She lifted her Wawa coffee mug.

"Wawa needs to set up a booth in here," Sarah joked, but not really joking.

It wasn't great coffee, but the coffee in the kitchen was free. And all Sarah really needed was the caffeine, so the free stuff did the trick.

Every company has a Human Resources Department, but few in the area had one quite like EmerGent Engineering Company. Emergent Engineering Company, or "E-co," as they call it around the office, has an 18-person HR department, which is much larger than other companies with 200 employees.

E-co really wanted its employees to know they had a place to turn, should they need it.

"Be right back," Sarah said as she walked past the row of filing cabinets lining the wall on her way out the door. She traced the L-shaped layout on her way to the door that would take her out of the Human Resources Department and into the sea of cubicles filled with tiny bald heads and funnels of light thrown onto shiny foreheads.

Some in HR joked that stepping out of the secure department was like throwing yourself to the wolves. The general employees would stop you to ask questions like they were waving down the mailman to ask the whereabouts of their package.

Any word on the Christmas party this year? Are we having a Secret Santa?

You know, the bathrooms are kind of dirty. Who do we talk to about that? You?

This is bullshit. I forgot to take my Tupperware out of the fridge and the cleaning crew threw it away.

Most of the questions and comments that came her way really were that dumb. *Yes to all* would be an answer she thought she'd like to give collectively. It'd be nice if there was a button to push. A *Make Them Smile and then Disappear* button.

There were more important things going on inside the office than which dips would be available in the fruit tray during this Friday's free monthly lunch. It was just that a majority of the work populous wasn't aware of anything else. Like Ted Nashton's sexual harassment case. Or Sammy Vertunsky's slip-and-fall in the parking lot during an ice storm a few months back that was costing the company a decent amount on legal fees, but they couldn't fire him. Oh no, for if they fire him, they get sued for so much more.

Sarah made it to the kitchen without being stopped, for once, but it was the kitchen where the small talk usually occurred. And it was rare to find the kitchen vacant.

Of course, this time was no different. Once she turned the corner to the kitchen, the frame of a human was standing there and she could only imagine the conversation about to take place.

But she sighed an inner sigh of relief when she saw it was only Byron.

"How are you, Sarah," Byron Cardinal said as Sarah walked into the kitchen. Byron had been at E-co for nearly twenty-five years, and managed to know all but maybe twenty-or-so of the employees' names.

"I'm good, Byron. How are you?"

"Oh I'm good, dear," he said with a smile, looking at her through his thick-rimmed glasses. "Just doing what I do every day, and getting some tea to help me through it." He chuckled at his own little joke and then told Sarah to enjoy the rest of her day as he headed out.

"You too, Byron."

She remembered meeting Byron's wife, Darla, for the first time during a Christmas party in her first year with the company and thinking to herself that if she and Brian could be anything like Byron and Darla, they'd turn out just fine. But that was years before.

Sarah walked through the lion's den and back to the HR department. She badged in, walked past the offices of the Senior Executives, and to her office in the back corner. She'd made this walk many times in her three stints here at E-Co and every time she wondered why the four Senior Executives would want to be closest to the door, where foot traffic was the highest. You'd think executives would want to be left alone to do their own thing, which was usually a lot less than what they expect of the rest. Sarah wasn't spiteful at the thought. Three of the four weren't HR Officers when she first started, but they worked their way up.

She walked across the industrial carpet than lined the office where she and Tina resided between the hours of 8:30 AM and 4:30 PM. A *real* eight hours. Paid half-hour for lunch, none of that clock-out while you eat bullshit. E-Co was one of the few companies around that still offered that. Paid lunch and an overstaffed HR department to take care of the employees. CEO Dan Carpenter might have been a multimillionaire, but he was still humble and decent. The money hadn't buried its way into his heart and turned it to ice just yet.

When she turned into the office doorway, she saw her empty desk, and then the one sitting right beside it, where Tina stared intently into her computer screen. Always hard at work. She'd be an executive in no time.

Tina glanced up at her. "Hey, what happened?"

"Nothing," Sarah said. "Got away scot-free. Only Byron Cardinal down there. Sweetest old man ever–"

"No," Tina cut off Sarah as she was placing her paper cup onto her desk. "I mean what happened with Brian's boss?"

"His boss?"

"Yeah," Tina turned her monitor as far as it would go. "Says here he was murdered last night."

She could feel the vomit as it worked its way up, warm and acidic. So she kept her mouth closed and stared, trying her hardest not to let the lightheadedness send her to the floor.

Not exactly a surprised reaction, one might think.

"Can you email me that link?" Sarah asked without looking over, thinking all she'd have to do would be to log onto the local news channel's website to see the nightmare article.

"Sure," Tina said, more than likely thinking the same thing.

Tina remained quiet on the other side of the room while Sarah read through the short article that summed up by saying Eric's death was assumed at the moment to be a murder and that no suspect was in custody yet.

"Have you talked to Brian today?" Tina asked as if she knew the very moment Sarah was finished reading.

"Why?" Sarah snapped.

Eyes a little wide now and in a more retreated state, she said, "It's...his boss." Then she shook her head: "I'm sorry. This must be a lot for you to take in." She swung her chair forward and apologized once again, almost under her breath this time. "I'm sorry."

The range of thought traveled from one direction to the other in a span of just a few seconds. So many stories played in her head: Brian murdered his boss; Brian was at the bar so there's no way he murdered his boss; Brian and his boss were at the bar and someone must have killed Eric after. Maybe he got wrapped up with another man's wife at the bar and that man found out.

"No." Sarah shook her head to clear the thoughts. "Don't say sorry," she said to Tina. "You're right. I should call him."

And she did. She stepped out into the hall to call him but there was no answer, and she almost felt relieved. What would she have said anyway? She wouldn't have come out and asked if he'd done it. She'd pretend, just as she'd done before.

Did Brian really just kill his boss?

"What did he say?" Tina asked her as she walked back into the office.

"No answer."

"Oh. Does he usually have his phone on him?"

"All the time." It came out of her mouth before she could even think. And she regretted saying it immediately, though it soon dawned on her that the concern coming from the statement could render her more of a distraught victim than a negligent conspirator.

A nurturing look came over Tina's face. One that showed regret and compassion intertwined. A look that said she shouldn't have brought it up but that she was there with a shoulder to lean on in case Sarah needed it. "I'm sure everything's fine."

"Yeah," Sarah said, trying to pull herself out of the world of thought she'd been floating off to.

"Maybe the police are there and they can't have their phones or something," Tina said.

Police. The word triggered a memory: the young officer knocking door to door, looking for clues as to who stabbed the man across the street. The officer was looking for Brian and didn't even know it. And now there were police involved again. At the very moment Sarah was thinking about it, Brian could have been right in front of them. Or talking to them. She could see them asking him questions and him lying right to their faces – the suspect in two open cases sitting in their laps and they don't even know.

"Maybe," she said.

Sarah sat back down at her desk, and she must have unknowingly been staring off into space because the next thing she heard was "You should go."

"Huh?" She looked over at Tina.

"You should go. I'm sure they wouldn't mind." She gestured her head in the direction of the Senior Executives' offices.

She didn't want to. What was she going to say to Brian if she saw him? Was she going to ask him what happened? Or, being more blunt, ask him if he killed Eric? Would she pin it on him, or would she have a backbone and admit what she'd been doing all along?

The answer: none of the above. She tucked her tail between her legs and waited for it to ride out, just as she'd done up to this point.

But for the sake of not giving away her secrets, and for sparing Brian the immediate blame, she left. Because staying at the office and working while this was going on would throw up red flags all over the place.

No one at the office knew she and Brian were on the brink of divorce. So it wouldn't look right if she showed so little emotion for the situation at hand.

"I'll take care of everything," Tina said. "It doesn't matter how long you're gone; I'll take care of things here."

Sarah stood and threw her purse over her shoulder with all the signature signs of determination. "I'll text you," she said as she walked out from behind her desk.

"Okay. Hey, Sarah?" Tina called before Sarah hit the doorway. "Tell Brian I said I'm sorry for his loss."

Sorry for his loss. "Sure. I'll tell him."

38

Sarah walked through the carpeted halls of the building and up to the door with the frosted piece of center glass with Dr. Epplestein's name taped across it. She yanked the door open, but her frustration was muted by the air shocks sending the door slowly shut behind her.

"Mrs. Hart," Alex was flustered, eyes wide as she stood behind her elegant receptionist desk. "Is everything alright?"

"No. I need to speak with Dr. Epplestein. Now."

"Mrs. Hart, you can't show up like this. He has a schedule to keep."

"I don't care. I need to see him." She walked right over to the double-doors that led to his office. Both were closed and she reached for both handles.

"Mrs. Hart, please."

But it was too late. Sarah had swung open both doors. These doors were not constricted by air shocks like the front entrance. Instead, they both flew open and the handles connected with the wall. Both Dr. Epplestein and

193

his patient jerked their attention toward the noise. And standing in the large opening was a determined Sarah Hart.

"I need to speak with you," Sarah said, pointing at her doctor.

"Sarah," he said with as much shock as his receptionist had shown a few seconds prior. "I'm sorry but I'm in a meeting right now."

"I don't care. This is urgent."

"Uh," he stood and looked with an open mouth at his intruder. But then he looked down at his patient and said to the young man, "I'm sorry. This is important... I'm going to have to reschedule. I'm very sorry." The young man began to stand and the doctor followed up with, "I'll cover all costs for this session and next. I'm very sorry."

"It's alright," the young man said. He stood and walked out with his head down feeling out of place. Sarah wanted to apologize to him, but she was afraid to open her mouth. There was so much on the tip of her tongue and she was worried that one single word could trigger the faucet and this young patient of his would hear the entire, unbelievable story.

Once the patient walked out of the office – hanging his head in embarrassment – Dr. Epplestein felt the time was right to ask Sarah to elaborate on her presence.

And that's when Sarah let it all out.

"I'm done. *We're* done. This whole thing is ridiculous. And there's no way in hell that this can be legal. How the hell can you live with yourself? How can you sit back and go through your life like nothing is wrong?"

"Sarah."

"My husband is killing people! And it's your fault! And

then you have the audacity to sit here and tell me that it'll all be okay? That when my husband gets caught – not *if*, but *when* – that you'll be able to 'take care of it'?"

"Sarah."

"How? How the hell do you expect to get my husband out of multiple murder charges?"

"Sarah, please. Come into my office and we can talk more." He managed to pull one of the double doors shut, but Sarah remained in the way of the other, unmoving. She could barely hear a word he was saying she was so hot with rage.

"Did you know that his entire family died, Dr. Epplestein? Did you? Or did you even care to know more about my husband before you started this sick little game of yours?"

His expression switched. He was no longer trying to lure Sarah into his office to close the door and try to muffle the sounds of her screaming from neighboring offices. "I did not," he said.

"His entire family died in a car accident when he was eighteen. Well, just his mom and sister, actually. His father killed himself afterward because he couldn't take the responsibility of knowing he was driving the car that killed them both. Did you know that?" Before he had a chance to answer, she continued. "Of course not. Of course you didn't know. Why? Because you never asked. You saw a test dummy, that's all. You saw a susceptible woman in a financial crisis and you exploited it."

"I'm sorry to hear that, Sarah, but if you'll come into my office, I'd like to hear more."

Sarah could care less about what he wanted. "Why? So you can convince me that what we're doing is something spectacular? Something magnificent? You think you're going to get some Nobel Prize with your name on it and there won't be any mention of my husband. He'll be rotting away in a prison cell while you get praise for brainwashing him."

That was the breaking point for Dr. Epplestein.

"What we are doing here is conducting research," he said in defense of her accusations. "This is groundbreaking research that you agreed to, may I remind you. I never forced anything on you or your husband. This was a mere opportunity and you accepted the opportunity to join."

"You exploited my situation."

"I made an offer," he said in a lower tone.

"Yeah? Well I'm done. My husband will surely be spending the rest of his life in prison because of you and I'll be damned if I watch you reap the rewards of his actions."

Sarah turned and headed for the exit. The heat had left her. The anger and the hate were gone, poured out onto the floor of Dr. Epplestein's office.

"I beg you to not walk out like this, Sarah," the doctor said. And anger filled his voice again when she didn't stop. "This won't make things better for you." She kept walking. "You're already in too deep. I will not defend your husband!" She ignored him and kept walking. "I'll sue you! I'll recoup every damn cent I ever gave you!"

He was irate now. As irate as a fragile old man in corduroy pants and a sweater-vest could be. Sarah knew there was nothing left to say. To turn and say one more word to him would only open up the possibility of her being lured into his trap again. So when she reached for the door to exit his office, she had no hesitation. She turned the handle and walked out.

As she stepped into the hallway and the door started slowly closing behind her, she heard Dr. Epplestein's voice one last time.

"Alex, get on the phone and call..."

But then his voice faded and she couldn't hear who he wanted his receptionist to call. Sarah thought to herself that she hoped he was calling the police. Because if they came to her, she'd tell them everything.

Building 500, apartment number 502.

Detective Jones drove slowly through the parking lot, looking out her window. She spotted big, white-painted numbers pasted to the blue building on her left: 700. The number 600 hung from the next identical building. Same thing with the next, number 500. She pulled into a parking space, threw the gear shifter of the Crown Vic towards the roof, and looked to her right: "Ready?"

The detectives in her precinct always worked alone and that's the way Alicia preferred it. But it was a requirement to bring along another detective when going out for a questioning or a potential arrest. When this was the case, her first choice was always to go to Detective Russel.

"I'm ready." Those were Detective Russell's first words during the ride, which is the main reason Alicia prefers him over any other detective.

They exited the cruiser, climbed the wooden stairway to the second floor of building 500 and stopped in front of door 502. With one hand, she unsnapped the button of her holster, and with the other, knocked with authority. She gave a head-nod to Russell who stood against the painted, wooden siding beside the door with his hand on his holstered weapon.

These were always nervous moments for Alicia, not knowing what was waiting on the other side of that door. Or who. Or what that *who* was doing, and what intention they had. She kept thinking this Brian Hart guy could be standing on his end of the door, looking through the peephole with a loaded shotgun in his hand, smile across his face, ready to blow a cop's head off for the fun of it. But that was why her holster was now unsnapped. And her hand on the pistol's grip.

Never be the first to fire was cop's code. Shout, Show, Shove, Shoot was the four-step process in military-speak, and Captain Furlong carried that over from his Marine life and into his life here. *Fuck that.*

After three knocking attempts and proclamations of her name and rank to an unresponsive rectangle of metal, she assumed no one was home. It had only been a few hours since the initial interviews of the employees were conducted and all sent home for the day. She couldn't imagine where he would be. Unless he was one of those daytime boozers, the *give me any reason to start drinking and I will* types and he was sitting at a hole-in-the-wall right now.

With no answer at the door and no search warrant that would give her permission to kick in the door, she and Russel could do nothing. With Russel behind her, she descended the staircase after snapping her holster button back into place. Alicia looked out into the parking lot, wishing Brian Hart's police record listed what type of car he drove. In a relatively empty parking lot, that might be all the information she'd need to determine if he was here or not.

A wave of defeat came over her when she reached for the door handle of her unmarked cruiser. Surely she thought she'd have some more questions answered. Or better, a suspect in custody. Instead, she got into the car and called in a warrant.

"Okay, give me about twenty minutes," the voice on the other end said.

"Roger."

In the meantime, she looked over to Russel and said, "Let's check out the clubhouse. They have to have a key, right?"

She pulled up to an inviting clubhouse and into a spot marked "Future Resident". Neither detective would be a future resident. Alicia had locked herself into the devil's contract three years back and still had twenty-seven years to go until she could live mortgage-free. But that was too far into the future to even consider dreaming about.

The paved path to the front door was lined with large river rock and colorful plants and even a small fountain that Detective Jones could see little fish swimming around in. She wasn't thinking of moving here, so she felt safe admiring the landscape of the walkway without feeling like it was a trap to suck her into a lease agreement.

"Good morning!" a young woman sitting at one of two desks in an open lobby said. She was a pretty young thing, thin, blonde hair, and soft skin. Another marketing ploy. *I'm your friend. Move in here because I like to hang by the pool sometimes. Hey, maybe I'll see you around!*

"Good morning. My name is Detective Jones and this is

Detective Russell," she pointed behind her, and for a quick second wondered what was going through the man's mind. "We're with the Rock Park PD."

The girl's smile disappeared. "Oh," she said. "Is everything okay?"

"It is. For now. But I have a warrant to search a property and I need to get the key for access. Do you have a spare key to apartment 502?"

"I–" she stuttered. "I'm going to have to get my manager. Hold on one second, please."

"Sure."

The girl walked down the small hallway with a single open door on the side, and when she returned, a middle-aged woman was with her.

"Good morning, Detectives," the middle-aged woman extended her hand for Alicia and then for Detective Russell. "My name is Felicia Ester. I'm the property manager here at Heather Ridge."

"Good morning," Alicia said.

"Can we..." Felicia motioned behind her. "You mind if we take this in my office?" Her eyes said what she meant: *The site of cops or detectives might scare away a real Future Resident.*

"Sure," Alicia said.

The detectives followed the woman back into her office where she gestured for them to take a seat opposite her at the desk. The manager wasn't nearly as young and pretty as the girl working the front desk, but she tried her hardest to be.

"So, a warrant?" Felicia asked as she took her seat, looking back and forth between Alicia and Detective Russell while speaking.

"Yes, Ma'am."

"For 502?"

"That's correct."

"May I..." Felicia paused, and Detective Jones knew exactly what she was going to ask. The answer was No, but she let the property manager finish the question anyway. "May I ask why?"

"At the moment, I can't tell you anything. If we find something through this warrant, and information is available to be released to the public, you'll know before anyone else does; you have my word on that."

"I appreciate that," she said, looking a bit annoyed that Alicia wouldn't tell her anything at the moment. The response angered Alicia. The woman was just being nosey. "It's just that people will be calling up here and asking what the cops were doing here, that's all. It'd just be nice if I could put them at ease. Let them know everything is just fine."

"And you'll be able to do that. Just as soon as we get definitive information."

Felicia's only response was a nod and, "I guess you're right."

"So... the key?"

"Oh yeah. Sure." She stood and walked around her desk. "Let me go talk to maintenance," she said before walking out of the room.

Detective Jones looked over to Russell and received nothing but a simple head-nod. One other reason she chose to bring him along on her rides: he never stepped on her toes.

They sat quietly and each examined Felicia's office as they waited. Pictures of the property manager and what seemed to be her two teenaged daughters were placed on her desk and the bookshelf that sat along the far wall. *Funny,* she thought. *The woman has a bookshelf to hold pictures and novelties, but not a single piece of literature.*

"Alright, so I have the key." Felicia walked back into her office.

"Great."

"Do you have a copy of the warrant? I can't legally give it to you without it," she said out of the side if her mouth.

Bitch. "I'm waiting for a judge's signature."

"What does that mean?"

She had the smarts to ask for the warrant, but didn't know how a warrant actually worked?

Detective Jones explained to her that she didn't have the warrant now because she needed a judge to sign it. At that point, she could either go get the warrant, or, if Felicia really wanted to be stubborn here, she could have it faxed. Of course, she had to be as courteous as possible, so she left out the part about her being stubborn.

"But if I have the key now," Detective Jones said, "I can start solving this case right away." Good choice of words, she thought to herself.

"I'm sorry, Detective. I'm just not legally allowed without the warrant. That's someone's house," she tried to justify, with a finger pointed in some random direction. "I can't go giving away the key. As much as I want to help, I just can't."

After a half-assed handshake and a fake smile through gritted teeth, Alicia Jones found herself back in her unmarked squad car, driving toward the complex's exit. Russell sat in silence. No judgmental observations or *What I would have done* comments.

Before leaving, she decided to take one more quick drive by Building 500. Maybe someone came home. Maybe Brian would be there this time. Waiting. Ready to confess and surrender.

She reached 500 and slowed the car to an almost unmoving roll. She looked to her side and out the window and sucked in a deep breath of air when she saw that there *was* someone there. From the open center alley, she could see a woman at the top of the wooden steps, standing in front of the door, looking hesitant to open it.

Was she witnessing a B&E or was this Brian Hart's wife? Must be his wife, she thought. Girl looks to be in her late twenties, beautiful brown hair hanging down the middle of her back. Dressed up like she should be at work. Doesn't fit the type of a burglar.

And then the door opened and the woman stepped in.

"Holy shit," Russell said.

"Let's go."

40

He could still be here, Sarah thought to herself. His car wasn't in the parking lot, but maybe he ditched his car. Or parked in front of another building and walked. Car or no car, he could still be there. Bunkering down. Hiding out from the police. She knew he did it. Knew he killed Eric. And she knew he stabbed that old man across the street, too. If he was here, she needed to confront him. Talk to him about it. If there's a more nerve-racking buildup to a conversation than that of *I want a divorce*, telling him *I'm the reason for it all* would be right up there.

She turned the knob and opened the apartment door, able to exhale when there was no immediate sign of Brian.

The midday silence was eerie. Aside from the mornings after the kids went to school and she took twenty minutes to herself to snoop around online and see what everyone else was up to, the apartment always had some sort of noise. The kids, the TV, the arguing with Brian that had seemed to stop since the day she told him she wanted a divorce.

She shut the door behind her and put the chain into the lock. "Brian?" she called for him.

No answer.

The living room, the kitchen, the hallway, the bathroom, the kids' room...she looked, but he wasn't in any. There was only one other place he could be: in his room at his desk. But he wasn't. She'd tiptoed down the hall and peaked her head in past the door jamb to find an empty desk.

His laptop was gone, which meant *he* was gone. He had to be. He took his laptop with him everywhere except to work.

This was her fault. He left because of *her*. Killed because of *her*.

Three loud bangs on the apartment door came echoing down the hall. She jumped and a small scream escaped her mouth. Who in the hell could that be?

She knew who it was.

And why the hell were they knocking like that?

Because they were trained to knock like that. With authority.

Walking down the hallway felt like walking into a twilight zone. Everything around Sarah seemed to spin.

This was happening. She knew from the start it would happen. She'd ruined it. Her life. *His* life. The *kids'* lives. All because she couldn't put her foot down and stand up for herself. Couldn't say No to Dr. Epplestein.

Sarah grabbed the door handle. She knew there was a cop on the other side. She knew they'd be looking for Brian. Knew they were inching closer to putting together the pieces of the puzzle. They'd ask her where he was and she couldn't lie. Why lie, anyway? What was the point?

He'd end up in prison. She couldn't protect him. She couldn't shield him forever just because she wanted her kids to have their father around. It was useless.

She twisted the handle and pulled back on the door to reveal what she knew to be true.

"Hello, Ma'am." The woman at the door was wearing a suit, not a uniform. She was a light-skinned black woman, short but stocky in the shoulders. Behind her was a man dressed in a similar suit and his hands were intertwined at his waist. "My name is Detective Jones, and this," she pointed behind her, "is Detective Russell. Is Brian Hart here?"

"No," Sarah said. "I don't know where he is."

"You mind if we step inside for a moment, Ma'am?"

"Sure," she said, stepping aside to give the detectives a path to enter. And after they were in, Sarah closed the door.

"Thank you."

"No problem. Excuse the house," she said. "I just walked in." But the detectives seemed to ignore the comment, and instead began to look around the apartment as if searching for something they may have forgotten.

"You said you don't know where your husband is, Mrs. Hart?"

"I don't. I just came home and he was gone."

"Where were you coming from?" Detective Jones asked. As she did, she pulled a small notebook with a pen from her pocket. "You mind?" she asked, holding up the two.

"Not at all," Sarah said. "And I was coming from work. I left early."

"Why did you leave early?"

"I heard about Brian's boss. Horrible," she shook her

head.

"What did you hear?"

"That he was killed." And then without a breath in between: "Please. Have a seat." She pointed to the couch with an overturned palm.

"Thank you," Detective Jones said as she walked over and sat down. Her partner opened his mouth for the first time and thanked Sarah as he sat.

"Can I get either of you something to drink?"

"No, thank you."

"You sure? I'm going to grab a bottle of water if you don't mind."

"Sure, go ahead," Detective Jones said, but then she stood and followed Sarah into the kitchen and continued to watch her as she reached into the refrigerator for the bottle. At first Sarah wondered if somehow this woman thought No means Yes and she offered her a bottle after taking one out for herself. The Detective shook her head and then followed Sarah back out to the couch where Detective Russell remained seated.

"I just have to make sure," Detective Jones said once they were back on the couch.

And then it hit Sarah. This woman was a cop. Interviewing the wife of a murderer. And by this point she must have known that Brian was the murderer they were looking for, or at least she was *close* to knowing. So Sarah's reasoning to walk out into the kitchen could have been for a gun.

I'm going to get a bottle of water. How nerve-racking is that simple comment to hear for a police detective? Take it too literally and you could have some psycho come walking back around into the living room with a rifle.

What a crazy, dangerous way to make a living.

"I'm sorry," Sarah said. "That didn't even hit me until right now."

"No worries." And then she looked down into her little notepad to see where she left off and asked Sarah if she was home last night.

"I was."

"Were you home all day?"

"Not all day. I went to work, picked up the kids, then came home."

"And what about your husband?"

"He usually gets home a few minutes after I do. Sometimes a little later; he works overtime any day he can." She tried looking back and forth between the detectives as she spoke. Whichever one she was speaking to, she could feel the other's eyes on her.

The moment was coming. The moment where this Detective asked a question about Brian and where he was last night and Sarah would give an answer that threw him right under the bus.

"And last night? What time did your husband get home?"

She shook her head. "Oh, I don't remember."

"You don't remember?"

"No." She looked up, as if trying to recount an event that never happened. "I can't ... I can't remember."

"Can you tell me what you *do* remember?"

Sarah remembered lying in bed and thinking about Brian. About where he was and what he was doing. Whether he was really sitting on a barstool in a dingy dive bar beside a man he'd hated for so long, or whether he was driving a knife through another man's flesh and watching the life leave his eyes, reaffirming what she knew about him. She remembered lying under the covers, eyes wide open, staring into a dark ceiling and wondering where her life was set to go from here. If she was losing her mind and overreacting to what she thought was true, or needed to listen to what her mind was telling her and get herself and the kids the hell out of there.

"I remember lying in bed," she started. "I remember lying there in the dark and wondering what Brian was doing. Where he was." She looked at Detective Jones and found piercing eyes staring back at her, soaking in every word. "We're in the process of getting a divorce, Detective.

"Brian and I have been having our differences. And long story short, I told him just a few days ago that I wanted a divorce. But we're staying here, the kids and I are, until the school year ends. I remember having to move in the middle of the year when I was in sixth grade, and it was horrible. Kids were mean. I hated school. Told my parents every morning for at least a month that I felt sick. Didn't want to go. And they knew what was really going on, but there wasn't anything they could do. They needed to work. I needed to go to school. It was as simple as that. And I don't want that for my kids. They're young still, but I don't want them to have to go through that. So Brian agreed that we'd stay here until the school year is over and then we would go forward with ... well, whatever it is that we have to go through.

"So you see, Detective, I don't really know what Brian was doing. And I don't care anymore. I'm not allowed to. But all I could think about as the hours passed was that he might be lying in another woman's bed. For the first time in who knows how long, he might be with another woman.

That was all I could think about."

This was a lie.

"Well I'm sorry to hear about your situation, Mrs. Hart," the Detective said with much less empathy than Sarah had hoped for. "But is there anywhere else he could have been? I know where your mind may have taken you, but is there anything else you think could have happened?"

"I'm not sure, Detective. For all I know, he could have been anywhere. All I know is that he wasn't in our bed when I was."

She took notes in her pad, and finally showed a bit of compassion when she asked, "Were you able to fall asleep at all last night?"

"I was," she nodded with her entire upper body swaying on the couch. "Eventually."

"And when you woke up in the morning, was Brian there?"

"He was."

"Do you remember him coming in? You were asleep, but did you wake up? Look at the clock?"

"I remember him coming in. I don't know what time it was."

"You didn't look at the clock?"

"No."

"Can you tell me what you did look at, Mrs. Hart?"

"What I looked at?"

"Yes. What did you look at? You were thinking of him possibly out with another woman ... did you look for lipstick? Smell for perfume? Alcohol?"

"I looked. I mean, as much as I could. My contacts were out and the room was dark. He ..." With everything in her she wished she could have had at least a minute to think over each of these answers. She couldn't bear the thought of one word leaving her mouth being the sole cause for Brian's incrimination. At the same time, she couldn't show any hesitation. "He did smell like he'd had a drink. A beer or two. But he usually has one or two when he gets home from work, so I was assuming he'd grabbed one out of the fridge when he got home."

Detective Jones took some notes in her notepad and then looked up again. "And when you woke up in the morning, you say he was there with you?"

"Well not in the bed with me; he was at his desk."

"His desk?"

"He's a writer. Novelist. Well, he's been trying to be." Sarah told the Detective about the plan for the temporary pet store job that turned into a career, then all but came out and said that this was the main reason for their divorce.

"You mind if I take a look around, Mrs. Hart?"

"Around the apartment?" Sarah looked around and felt her stomach drop farther than it had when she'd opened the door to find two detectives glaring at her. "Now?"

"If you're okay with it."

"Sure," Sarah said as she stood. "Please excuse the mess, though."

The detectives stood and Sarah waved them to follow. They walked down the hallway, both looking around, and made stops in the kids' room and the bathroom. Detective Russell was trailing Detective Jones, and only the former seemed interested in what they were seeing.

Sarah walked them down to the end of the hallway and into her bedroom, where Detective Jones verified with wide eyes scanning the room that this was where she really wanted to be.

"You mind?" she asked Sarah.

"No. Go right ahead."

Detective Russell remained in the doorway while his counterpart walked into the closet and looked around. It looked like any normal closet. It was a mess. There were clothes half-hanging on hangers, clothes on the floor, and Brian's infamous box collection. Detective Jones gave it an awkward glance and Sarah described to her Brian's inability to part ways with boxes. "He thinks he might one day need to return everything he buys," she shrugged.

"I see."

"He took some clothes with him," Sarah said. "So I guess he really did leave." She said it more to herself than to the detective.

"His laptop is gone, too," Sarah said when Detective Jones stepped out from the closet doorway. "That's probably more of a sign than the clothes."

The Detective walked over to the desk and examined. The closet, the desk, the entire fucking apartment. She wanted to see it all.

Sarah was sitting there sweating out every ounce of guilt, the truth hanging on the edge of her tongue, and all the while Dr. Epplestein was probably sitting in his office, legs crossed on his leather lounge chair, listening to some other poor, gullible person and wondering how he could tap into their lives and hold something over their head.

Don't blame him, she thought. *It's all your fault.*

"Anything else unusual?" Detective Jones asked.

"Not really. I mean, I was only home for a minute or two before I heard your knock, so I didn't have much time to look around. But the clothes and the laptop... those are the only things he'd take, anyway."

"Alright." She nodded and took one more mental swipe of the room, then looked to her fellow detective for any advice. He answered with a simple head nod.

Sarah guided the detectives down the hall and back out to the living room. "Can I offer either of you a water for the road?"

"You know what? Sure. I'll take one," Detective Jones said.

"No, thank you," Detective Russell spoke for only the second time.

Sarah walked into the kitchen and Detective Jones followed, just as she had done last time. *Is she still wondering if I'm reaching for a gun? It'd be a little late now.* But as the refrigerator door shut behind her and she stood to hand the bottle to the detective, she saw the reasoning for her coming in here.

"Thank you," Detective Jones said, accepting the bottle from Sarah during her swipe of the kitchen. She was looking at cabinet doors, appliances, backsplash, like she was taking pictures and storing them in her memory. For what, Sarah couldn't really comprehend. But the next spot she looked was in the kitchen sink. And instead of taking a mental note, she reached in and lifted up a beer can. "This you?" she asked.

"It's not." Would never be. Not at eleven in the morning. But it made her think. When was the beer there? Was it Brian's from last night? Did he come home smelling like beer? Or did he open this before coming into bed, like she pretended to believe when Detective Jones asked her before? Is that where the smell came from? Was Sarah assuming again? Assuming that her husband killed someone and then coming up with a story in her head that matched? Was she leading this detective to believe Brian killed Eric and was now on the run when in reality he could have nothing to do with it?

You really are the demonic one here, Sarah. Digging your innocent husband's grave.

"Still cold," Detective Jones said.

The comment seemed to comfort Sarah. *Still cold. It wasn't from last night.*

"One more question, Mrs. Hart. What kind of car does your husband drive?"

"Um...a Honda Civic."

"What color?"

"Silver."

"And do you know what year?"

"Goodness. I don't know. It's pretty old. Ten years old maybe?"

"Thank you, Mrs. Hart." Detective Jones extended a hand to shake, and Sarah grabbed it.

"What now?" Sarah asked.

"Now we issue a warrant for your husband's arrest."

41

Brian knew what they'd say: that this book was an autobiography of his life. But it wasn't, damnit. This was a fiction novel done right. With thorough research. Didn't these people get it? In order to be a great writer, you've got to do your research. And if a few people had to die because of it, well then so be it. Test mice die every day. Guinea pigs, monkeys, frogs, fish, birds. Hell, even dogs and cats. They're all sacrificed each and every day for the sake of research. So why is it that Brian's research was such a horrible thing? Are human lives any more important than any of the others?

Apparently so. Because he'd seen about twenty cop cars go flying by with their lights flashing and sirens blazing.

He looked periodically into his rearview mirror and out the sides of his car, half-expecting some patrolman on foot to be the one to find him, leaves crunching under his feet as he walked out through the woods. That'd be some shit. On a normal day, he'd be more likely to see a grizzly bear in these woods than he would be a trooper on foot. *But watch*, he thought to himself as he sat in his sedan, looking at the surrounding trees. *Today will be the day.*

Brian worked as a go-fer for an exterminator when he was in high school. A house owned by one customer was a mansion set back in the woods about a mile off the main road, everything covered by pine trees that acted as umbrellas from the sun. All day, everyday, nothing but shade. It'd been fifteen years since he came down this driveway in a pickup truck to spray for mosquitos, ticks, spiders, and whatever else lived in these trees. But on this day, he came down the driveway again, this time in a Civic.

This was his hideout, about halfway down the old man's driveway. Parked, anxiously looking from side to side.

He told himself he'd never live in a place like this. After working with the exterminator and seeing the differences in living atmospheres, he told himself he wanted sunshine. The thought of walking around his house in the damp soil and cool shade even though the sun had been burning bright for days – moss and mold growing on the aluminum siding – wasn't appealing to him. He wanted openness. And sunlight. And he promised himself he'd have that. Promised Sarah, too, but there wasn't much behind those words.

This was his hiding place of choice not only because of its seclusion, but because the end of the driveway was a mere hundred-or-so feet from the highway entrance. He'd take off like a bat out of hell if he'd heard even the faintest of sirens...or the crunching of leaves. Hell, the owner of the house might have even been the one to come investigating the silver sedan in his driveway.

He reached over to grab his laptop sitting on the passenger seat. His freedom was a ticking clock and he had to get this story down before he lost the chance. Writing pads and paper would certainly be of abundance in his prison cell, but the court system surely wouldn't grant a murderer access to files on his computer, would they?

He could see himself pleading: *Please, I can't write my story without my notes.*

They'd tell him to go right to hell.

He had the murder scenes down. Those chapters were complete. His main character, Francesca, had murdered her cheating husband while he was asleep. She walked up the stairs with the knife in her hand, straddled the lying bastard and plunged the knife into him. Brian read back on this chapter and he could see the bulging eyes of Thomas McMann as Brian drove the fishing knife into his stomach. Those eyes were now cold and dead, just like the eyes of Francesca's husband.

The scene read so wonderfully. But now it was time to write the strangulation scene. Eric was the test dummy for this in real life, but what about Francesca's life? Who would she strangle? Who would she kill next? The whore who opened her legs to a married man? A neighbor who may have seen too much? A police officer who shows up to the scene after Francesca called 9-1-1 to report the murder of her husband. *It was self-defense. He struck me. See what he did to my face?* Or maybe it would be the detective who solved the crime and came to arrest her?

Brian realized that strangling Eric had now thrown a wrench into his story's outline. He hadn't planned for anything more than a wife killing her cheating husband and then going on the run. But if he didn't strangle someone in the book, then why kill Eric? He *was* a prick and the world *would be* a better place without the bald, roided-out freak, but that still wasn't reason enough to kill him.

No time for debate. He heard each passing second go off in his head.

The police let her go after her questioning: Nothing to see here. *But Officer Thompson wasn't so convinced. She could see it in his eyes as he continued to look at her through his rearview mirror.*

It had been two days since she made the 9-1-1 call to report that her husband, Lucas, had struck her and then left. Soon after, someone called in a missing person report on him. Probably his whore, *Francesca thought.*

Officer Thompson was behind the wheel of the cruiser. A piece of bulletproof plexiglass separated the two.

Officer Thompson was one of the two responding officers who showed up to her house after she made the 9-1-1 call. He believed her every word that day when she told her sob story. "I have no idea where he may have gone, Officers, but I don't care. He hit me, that cheating bastard, and I hope I never hear from him again." They ate it up, Thompson and his counterpart.

But when he returned two days later looking for Lucas, he took a one-eighty. "Apparently no one has seen him since he 'left,'" he said, quoting the final word.

"Good," Francesca sobbed in her doorway while two officers stood on her doorstep. "I hope he's too embarrassed to ever show his face around here again. Look what he did to me!" She pointed to the swelling that had yet to go down – a few palms to her own face every now and then would ensure that puffiness stuck around longer than it had to.

But apparently this was something Officer Thompson had seen before. While his counterpart seemed empathetic, Officer Thompson put his foot on the gas, asking her a bunch of questions.

What brought about the fight?

Why did he hit you?

Did you attack him? Hit him with something first? We can't know these things until we find him and can speak with him.

Francesca remained quiet and with Thompson's counterpart telling him to take it easy, she was able to escape the on-the-spot interview.

Once that on-the-spot interrogation was over, the two officers asked her to come to the station for additional questioning. "We'll give you a ride," Thompson's counterpart told her. "Don't want you driving with that," he pointed to her eye.

Hours later, they were driving her back home.

"Don't you go far," the officer said to her from the front seat of the cruiser. "We might need to ask you some more questions." He looked at her through the rearview mirror as he pulled up to the house.

"Okay," she said as compassionately as possible. Once she agreed, the officer began to get out so he could open her door.

I could strangle him, she thought.

Brian slammed his laptop shut and threw his head against the back of his seat. He hated it. Strangle a cop? In the middle of the street? Right in front of her house? With his partner in the passenger seat? It made for a horrible story. Fake. No suspense leading up to it whatsoever. His time constraint was making him rush.

He sat with his hands on the steering wheel, fingers gripping the thing at ten and two, and thought of how much smaller the wheel of his forklift was. At that very moment, he thought, he was obviously no longer a forklift operator. He couldn't go back there.

Where *could* he go? If not to work, or home, or even live in peace in his car on the side of the road, where could he go? Was there some writer's safe house? Some place where he wouldn't be judged for what he'd done, but praised? After all, he was doing this for his career, going farther and studying harder than any other writer he'd heard of. Certainly not everyone who decided to write a murder mystery has killed someone in the name of authenticity.

He had no idea where he'd go from here, and he wouldn't have time to find out. He looked out the side view mirror of his car and saw what he was afraid to see: someone coming.

The person wasn't wearing a uniform and part of him let out a sigh of relief. The person was actually the same old man who'd lived at the house fifteen years earlier. He was older and walking with a bit of a hunch, but he was coming nonetheless. The sight of the old man walking down his driveway made Brian realize he needed to move somewhere. And fast. Before the old man even got a chance to read his license plate number.

He turned the key and fired up the engine, then pulled off, throwing some stones as the Civic moved down the narrow path and toward the asphalt road that led to the highway.

When he hit the end of the gravel driveway and his front

wheels touched the asphalt, he looked to his left and saw
the path he had lined up for himself: the highway.

42

The thought occurred to Detective Alicia Jones to drive back to the apartment complex's clubhouse on her way out. Poke her head in the property manager's office and let her know that "There's no need for me to get you that signed warrant you so desperately needed in order to give me the key. I got in myself." Maybe end with a wink.

The satisfaction of imagining the look on her face was enough. And instead, Detective Jones left the complex in her cruiser with a pocketful of notes and a strong feeling that she had just narrowed down the killer of two separate crimes. Her chin was high as she pulled out onto the main road.

"You have time?" she asked Detective Russell as he sat quietly in the passenger seat.

"Yeah, what's up?"

"Just one more stop," she said. Just one more stop before she could go back and start making the process official.

The parking lot of that one stop was empty and she was almost in shock when she saw the neon Open sign illuminated, along with some other drink options shining through the window and grabbing their weak prey: *Come on in. We're ready for ya.*

She pulled between two faded white lines, put the car in park, then walked across the empty and aging parking lot with Russell by her side. What was once a crisp blacktop was now a sea of cigarette butts and weed-filled cracks.

She opened the door that read *Duffy's Tavern* in white letters stuck to the door, and took in the aroma of stale beer and a blast of cold air.

"Whew." The smell shoved its way up Detective Russell's nostrils, too.

Jones turned and gave a wry smile. *Glad I asked you for the ride-along?*

The place was as empty as the parking lot, and there was no one on the inside of the enclosed bar, either. Alicia walked across the floor – surprised when her shoes didn't stick – and then took a seat at a wooden barstool and rested her arms on the green laminate bartop. Seconds later, a balding man in dirty sneakers and shorts came out from behind a swinging door carrying a plastic crate full of pint glasses.

"Mornin'," he said. "Can I getcha somethin'?" But as he got closer and saw the badge in her hand, he realized they weren't here to day drink. "Oh." He set down the crate on the bar and said, "Hey. I'm Melvin. How can I help ya?" He extended his hand for a shake.

"Detective Jones," Alicia said after the wet shake, and then she stood from the stool. The round man still had a good few inches on her, but she felt more professional when standing. "Were you working last night? Around five or six o'clock?"

"I was–," he stopped himself and gestured towards the glasses: "You mind?"

"No. Go ahead."

Melvin started to place the pint glasses in the freezer below him as he spoke. "I was here till six. Then Michelle came in. She works till two. Or whenever the place starts to empty, really."

"Is Michelle around?"

He shook his head. "She's probably still asleep. Works late and usually has herself a drink or two before heading out. Probably to erase some of the crap she hears from these old boys comin' in and out all night, tryin'-a pick her up."

"But you were here until six?"

"Just about."

If Brian Hart was here with Eric Millford, it was after work. They wouldn't get here until 5:30 at the earliest.

"Can you tell me if you saw this man?" She only had a picture of the deceased with her, so she held up the picture of Eric Millford to the bartender. It was his professional headshot, the one that lined the wall of executives at Eats-N-Treats.

He squinted, and for a second Alicia thought she might get something out of him. But then he shook his head and looked at her. "These boys here all look the same. I ain't lookin' into their eyes and they ain't lookin' into mine. Best bet would be Michelle. I can have her call you. Got a card?"

"I do." She reached into her breast pocket for a card and as she handed it to him, she looked up and around the drop ceiling to find what she hoped to see. "You have video cameras set up here?"

Melvin turned around and looked right into one of the black balls stuck against a ceiling tile. "We do," he said as if it was the first time he'd noticed them.

"You mind if I take a look?"

"Sure thing," he said. "Follow me." He grabbed the empty crate that once housed clean pint glasses ready to be dirtied up by the late morning and early afternoon stoppers-by and nodded for her to walk around the side of the bar. And then he himself popped out from behind a small gap in the green countertop.

With Russell beside her, Detective Jones followed behind the man who walked with a slight limp and wondered what life must be like as a lifelong bartender. The fights he must have seen. Must have had to break up. The drunks. The cheaters. The bimbos. The turn from a happy drunk to a sour one in so many people. The underagers and overdrinkers.

Interesting, she thought. But exhausting.

He pushed on the swinging door and held it open for the detectives to walk through.

"Right that way," he said, pointing with his eyes to an office door no more than five feet away, tucked into the corner. He dropped the empty crate onto a metal table and the sound amplified throughout the kitchen area. Had Detective Jones turned to the office door one second earlier, she wouldn't have seen the motion and the sound would have startled her to the point of reaching for her holster. But only a small flinch was the end result. And the bartender didn't even notice.

Of course not. He was used to chaos and noise.

She turned to Detective Russell who got a giggle out of her flinch.

She took a step into the office and then moved aside so Melvin the Bartender could show her what she wanted to see. But there wasn't much she couldn't see for herself.

The office was small, and the tiny, cluttered desk took up almost half of the space. It looked like an old coat closet, she thought to herself.

"Alright," Melvin mumbled and walked to one side of the desk. "You might hafta swing around here." He motioned for her to come around the other side and behind the desk. It was when she got there that she realized there was a door within this room. Somehow. A closet within a closet. The door and frame were painted the same dark green color as the walls so she told herself it was an easy camouflage. The only way to know it was there was from the golden doorknob hanging from the middle like some sort of misplaced towel rack.

Melvin reached for that towel rack and opened the door to a coat closet – a real one – that could hold no more than five coats. Sitting atop a shelf within this closet was a small tube TV. And on the black-and-white screen, the empty bar showed.

"You said you need yesterday about what time?"

"Any time between eight and ten should work," she said. She still hadn't gotten word back from forensics on a possible time of death, but from her own expertise and the body she saw lying cold and pale on his own driveway, she was thinking closer to midnight.

The bartender hit a button on the TV and two horizontal lines sent the time racing backward. Soon she could see herself on the screen, conversing with Melvin, and then walking backward towards the exit.

"Sorry 'bout this," Melvin said. "You gotta be the first

cop come walkin' through here askin' to see video. Usually it's just comin' in to check for no one underage," he said with a smirk.

You don't have anyone here right now of *any* age, she wanted to say. But instead smiled back and said, "Maybe I'll come back tomorrow for that." And then she asked, "Is this the only angle? I thought I saw two cameras out there."

"One's phantom," he said. "For a while there, this one was, too. Stopped recording because ain't nothin' happenin' and we were wasting money on a bunch of tapes." He kicked a box on the floor full of VHS tapes and said, "Just started recordin' over 'em."

Of course. She wouldn't say it out loud, but she was surprised a place like this even has *one* functional camera. Come on, they still had tube TVs in the bar area.

He nodded, and another fit of silence followed until the low buzzing sound made Melvin say he had to go to the front. "That sound means the front door's open. Someone needs their bubbles early today."

"Alright. I'll wait."

"Look," he said, and stepped aside as much as he could. "You can do it. Just hold down this button."

"Okay." She stepped toward the mini TV and when Melvin let go, she tapped the rewind button.

"You gotta hold it down. Thing's old," he said as he made his way out. "Just don't hit that record button. You'll erase everything," he said. "Be right back."

And then it was just Jones and Russell being detectives, watching the screen as the hours flew by in reverse. And soon it was at 2 AM, and then one, and the bar was surprisingly crowded for that hour on a weeknight.

When the ten o'clock hour wound down, she let go of the button, and the video ended up stopping at 9:56 PM. She squinted hard as the video played. The heads and faces were small and blurry, and it was almost impossible to see anything or anyone besides a few spots of teeth from people laughing and others walking to and from the bathrooms and exits.

"Can't see anything," Russell said from behind her.

"Tell me about it."

She rewound a little farther, seeing nothing intriguing. And then she stopped at the 9:12 mark. But the scene looked identical. She tried 8:30 next, and then 8:07... Nothing.

The kitchen door swung open and Melvin came strolling back in. "Any luck?" he asked, stopping and crossing his arms.

Detective Jones shook her head, and then hit rewind again. "Everything is just so small and blurry."

"Yeah, sorry. Like I said–"

"Wait." Detective Russell jumped in and moved closer to the monitor. "Go back."

She pushed her face closer to the screen as she obliged and hit the play button when Russell said to do so. She saw it at the 7:46 mark. Right there. A guy in a red collared shirt. He was just sitting there by himself, looking down at his phone. "Enhance that," Russell said.

"Enhance it?" the bartender asked, barely holding back a laugh. "Detective, we can't do that."

"Sorry," Russell said, stepping back into his backup role and shaking his head. "Force of habit."

"I do need this, though," Detective Jones said. She hit pause, pulled out her cell phone and took a picture of the screen. Horrible quality, but it'd do.

She needed to find out when Brian got there and when he left, so she hit rewind again, letting time roll back once more and waiting to see the moment he walked in. "You can go back out if you need to," she said to Melvin. "I'm okay."

"Nah," he said. "Just some couple. On a road trip and said something happened on the interstate. It's a parking lot."

"That's a shame," she said, but a majority of her attention was on this blurry man in the red collared shirt. The time was rolling back into the six o'clock hour and he was still sitting there. And then she found her time: 6:34 was when he arrived. She took out her notebook and wrote it down, then started to fast-forward to find the time he left.

"So the interstate's packed, huh?" she said to Melvin.

"Must be some sort of accident," he said.

"Must be."

Detective Jones found the time that her figure in the red shirt left the bar – 7:51 PM – and wrote it down in her pad. "Okay," she said. "I think I'm done. How do I get it back to where it was?"

"I got it," he waved her off. "You gotta fast forward all the way till the end then hit record so you don't..." He trailed off and shook his head. "I got it."

"Thank you, Melvin. We appreciate your help," she said, and shook the man's damp hand once more.

"No problem. Hope it helps," he said as he shook the hand of each detective.

"And you have my card to give to..."

"Michelle."

"Michelle. You have my card to give to her. If she has anything else, please have her call me."

"I will." He raised a finger. "Give me one sec; I'll show you out."

"Don't worry. We can show ourselves. I appreciate your help," she said once more.

Melvin nodded and looked back at the small screen. Detective Jones and her counterpart pushed through the kitchen doors and out to the bar. The couple that had just arrived gave them a glance, but within a second or two they were back to giggling about something they were discussing. Having fun. Enjoying each other's company. She almost had the urge to walk over to them and make sure neither one was pursuing a career as a police detective. *Because you'll never be able to have a relationship*, she'd tell them.

43

Damn you, Brian. You liar. Why didn't you keep your promise?

The promise of financial security. And getting the hell out of the apartment. Of giving the kids a house with a yard and a normal life. The life *Sarah* had. The life she told herself she'd give her kids.

Now she had to pick up her children – hers from now on, not his – and figure out a way to sugarcoat the situation. She needed to find a way to tell her children that their dad wasn't coming home anymore. And that they may never see him again. But she couldn't tell them where he was, or where he was going, because studies showed that children with an incarcerated father were much more likely to end up incarcerated themselves later in life. And she'd be damned if she watched her kids skate down the life of petty theft and crime as teenagers.

They'd drive somewhere. To her mother's maybe. Or to her sister's. Or maybe that lady detective that was at the apartment earlier would come back, or call, and tell Sarah that she and the kids must come down to the station while everything was being sorted out.

She knew one thing: she wasn't going to let her kids become scarred with memories of something happening to their father. She'd shield them from whatever she could.

Poor kids. Thrown into the middle of an adult world where happiness came in the form of money.

Sarah grabbed the lone suitcase that sat unused in the bottom of her closet, as well as the giant cloth bag she'd gotten as a *bring your shit to the hospital in this* gift when she was pregnant with Lacey – she reused it with Mason because no one else really gives a shit when you have subsequent kids.

She took the suitcase into her own room, thinking to herself that she may never be coming back here. *The zippers easily shut,* she told herself. She could pack more into the suitcase, but there was no urgency to do so. The urgency sat in getting the kids' stuff and then getting the hell out of the apartment before someone came: another police officer asking questions; the detectives, maybe; or worse.

She took the giant cloth bag into the kids' room and began to fill it with their clothes, filling *this one* to the point of its zipper busting. And even then, she wanted to grab more. All of Lacey and Mason's outfits from when they were kids were in this room. Shirts and pants too small to fit them now hung on tiny hangers in the back of the closet, or rolled up in balls in some bottom drawers. They may not have been put to use lately, but they all held meaning. Those clothes they no longer fit into were there as keepsakes for Sarah. She could look at them from time to time and reminisce about the days when they were younger.

Not anymore. These clothes would remain here now. Whether or not she'd ever see them again? Still unknown.

Sarah left the apartment with her head down. She fought her way down the staircase with the cloth bag over her shoulder and the suitcase on its wheels, smacking the top of each step as she descended. Back in the day, when she and Brian first met, she wouldn't have struggled, nor would she have even been short of breath. What a miserable change in life's momentum.

The trunk slammed shut and then she was in the driver's seat looking out the window and up to the porch she thought she may never step foot on again. She hated the damn apartment – the idea of a rental, living in someone else's property, where other people have laid, laughed, fucked – but found herself upset at the thought of never seeing the place again. Her kids had grown there. Played there. Matter of fact, their bikes still sat up there, rarely used, screaming for attention but they'd get none. Not until the apartment was wiped clean and they were given away to the Salvation Army and adored by some new grateful, underprivileged child.

As she slid the gear-shifter into reverse, her eyes welled with tears. The car rolled away from Building 500 and her vision blurred from her watered eyes. She kept looking at herself in the rearview mirror, telling herself not to rub the tears away: *You don't want the kids to see your red eyes.* She tried shifting her thoughts elsewhere during the ride to school, but nothing worked. The only thing that finally took her mind off of it was turning into the school parking lot and seeing that the bell had already rung.

Kids were everywhere, as they always were once the

doors flung open, and it scared Sarah to even put her foot on the gas pedal. Kids always ran out from between busses, not paying attention to their surroundings, as kids this age would do. Naivety. They'd learn about that in high school.

She parked and fought through the crowd of waist-high bodies to the front door of the building, then found Mason and Lacey in the after-school care classroom.

"Mommy?" Mason sounded like he could cry of joy. Her kids had to come here every day while the others got to get on the bus and go home.

Say goodbye, kids. You may miss it here one day. She didn't have the heart to say a word to either of them so she said nothing – a decision that has haunted her every day since.

It didn't take long for Lacey to realize they weren't headed home – a simple left-turn out of the parking lot instead of the usual right and *bam*, she was right on it: "Where are we going?"

"To Grandma and Grandpa's house."

"Grandma and Grandpa!" Mason yelled.

The kids weren't curious or skeptical. They didn't ask why or investigate further. They were simply two happy kids excited for a change of scenery. And Sarah was thankful they asked no other questions during the ride, because her mind was a whirlwind of thoughts and emotions and had they asked her any other questions, she's not sure what she would have said. It might not even have come out in English.

Sarah turned into the driveway of her parents' house to see her mom outside waiting. The kids were out of their seatbelts before Sarah even put the car in park.

"Hi, my sweethearts!" she yelled, leaning down to embrace one of them in each arm.

She was never anything but nice and supportive to Sarah growing up, Denise Wellington was. Even when Sarah and Brian first started dating and he'd come around the house, Denise was nice to him. She had her doubts – *that look in his eye*, she kept saying. Both of her parents did. But for the most part, they let Sarah make her own decisions...until the proposal came, at least.

Are you going to get a new job?

How will you support her?

Local union is hiring carpenters, you know.

Maybe it's time to put the writing aside; make it a hobby.

And it was that last one that Sarah thinks threw a dagger into the relationship between Brian and her parents. Because Brian despised people telling him that. Hated the idea. It would drive him crazy when people would suggest he give up working toward his dream.

"Why the hell would I settle for a regular job like them?" He'd point to the door, or the window, or somewhere behind him, but her parents were never around for these tirades. "To be mediocre? To be pissed off every day sitting in traffic with the rest of the settlers?"

It was an exaggeration, completely blown out of proportion, but it was done by a man who blew everything out of proportion.

"Some people enjoy their nine-to-fives," she'd say to him.

"Well I don't. And I'm sick and tired of people telling me what I *have* to do. Or what I *should* be doing. I'll do whatever the hell I want to do."

His passion annoyed others. But it drew her in. Every time. Whenever he'd get red in the face talking about his writing, defending it and protecting it like his weak offspring, it would make her fall even harder for him. His drive – his passion – was sexy. Intense. Masculine. He did what he did and wouldn't let anyone tell him otherwise. And she loved him for it.

"Oh, I've missed you," Denise said, eyes closed and grin wide as she embraced her grandchildren.

"It's been eight days, Mom," Sarah said. Always about *her*. Always little gut-jabs insinuating Sarah's a bad mother. What happened to the support? It went away. Gone the second Sarah said "I do" to a man who hadn't gained her mother's approval.

"Eight days too long," Denise said, eyes still closed and arms still locked around her grandchildren. "So," she said when she let them go and stood. "What do you want to do tonight?"

"Tonight?" Lacey turned and asked her mother. "Are we sleeping over?" Her eyes grew wider with each word.

"Yes," Sarah said with a smile, knowing the cheer from her kids that would follow. And it did. Screams and more hugs. Crazy how she pitied her children the whole ride here, thinking they'd be sad that they weren't going home. And now here they were, still oblivious to the truth, yet happier than they would have been had they spent a normal night at home.

"I've got popcorn," Denise started. "After dinner, we can watch a movie with popcorn and then maybe," she squinted, "maybe we can have some ice cream."

She hadn't seen them in eight days, yet she was spoiling them as though it had been eight months.

Sarah walked to the trunk to get the giant cloth bag. If the kids were a little older, and not preoccupied with the sugar offerings from their grandmother, they might realize this bag wasn't an overnight bag. They'd realize that this bag was full of most of their clothes and wonder exactly how long it would be that they were staying with Grandma and Grandpa.

"Come on, let's go say hi to Grandpa," Denise said, and the kids ran behind her, Sarah following behind and catching the screen door with her elbow before it closed.

Chaos. Pure chaos. Over M&Ms.

As he always did, Rick Wellington had a spread of the candies laid out for his grandkids so that when they walked in the door, they could scream at decibel levels bordering cracking every window in the house. It wasn't as if they were deprived of candy at home, it's just that they were surprised with it here. At home, it was a fight. Here, it was a treat. A surprise. And they apparently loved surprises.

Sarah watched the kids as they ate the sugar that'd have them running wild through the small three-bedroom house. She wondered why her parents did this to themselves, but it never failed. They always did.

Their grandpa wrote out their names in M&Ms on a cookie sheet, each one with the same number of pieces so not to cause a fight. And they stood on either side of him as he held the plastic cookie sheet in front of them. Christmas themed. Christmas was seven months away, but they didn't know that. And Dad didn't seem to care. He knew what they wanted, and what they'd be paying attention to.

"Hey, Dad," Sarah said.

He looked up from the top of his glasses. "Hi,

sweetheart." The rest of his body remained still, as if the predators in front of him tearing into their treats would confuse him with food if he moved a single muscle in his body. But when they were done and there was no candy left and they were onto something Grandma was now luring them into in the kitchen, he stood and gave his daughter a hug. "How are you, baby."

"I'm good."

He let go and grabbed her by the shoulders. "I don't know why I have to pry things out of you."

She smiled.

"You can talk to me."

"I can? You guys are always one-sided."

"You could kill him and I'd be on your side."

"Come on, Dad. Someone else could kill him and you'd be on their side, too."

He raised a brow and nodded. "Well..."

"Stop, Dad." She smiled at the one man who'd always been able to make her smile no matter what. "We'll talk about it later."

He pulled her in for a tight hug and told her he loved her.

"I love you, too, Dad."

Right on cue, the kids came back into the room, running around their ankles like swarming sharks.

"This is your fault," Sarah said to her father. Once she was able to get her kids to stop and pay attention to her, she said, "I have to go." She knelt down and gave them both a hug, a mirror image of their hug with their grandma a few minutes ago, only with much less enthusiasm on their end.

"When are you coming back, Mom?" Mason asked.

"Not sure, honey. Maybe tonight. Maybe tomorrow."

"What about Daddy?"

It must have come naturally. Maybe it was Sarah looking down. Or the pause itself before opening her mouth to answer. But Lacey felt something. "What happened to Dad?" she asked.

"Nothing! Nothing happened to him. Daddy's just fine," she said to both of her kids with wide eyes. "Daddy's fine."

Calmer, Lacey asked, "Where is he?"

"Well..." *Uh oh. Think before you speak, Sarah.* "Daddy lost his job." She looked at each of them. Neither gave a shit. Neither knew what a job was, or does, or its importance to their lives. *Where's Daddy?* That's all they cared about. *Can he play? Will he be here for dinner?*

Lacey was happy to learn, in her mind, that he wouldn't have to go to work anymore. She took the news as a positive, that he would be home all the time to play now. But Mason just stared into Sarah's eyes. He had no clue what was really going on, but he saw despair in Sarah's eyes and wouldn't relax until it was identified.

Sarah hated herself for not being able to wear a mask. She tried to comfort her son with words since she couldn't do so with expression. "He went for a long drive. He needed to get away. But he'll be back," she lied.

"When?" Mason asked.

"Soon."

"Who wants to go to Redbox?" Denise asked as if dangling the question in front of their faces would steer the conversation.

It worked. The kids both went crazy.

For someone who was all over the place emotionally with her daughter, Denise was amazing with the kids.

Energetic. Patient.

Thanks, Mom. She didn't say it, but she gave her mother the gracious look. She was hanging from a cliff and her mother pulled her up.

"Is your car unlocked?" Denise asked.

"Yeah," Sarah said.

It took Denise a few minutes to gather her things, but when she did, she was out the door with the kids, grabbing Mason's booster from Sarah's sedan and putting it into the back of hers.

Her dad took the Christmas cookie sheet from the couch where he'd left it and put it back in the cabinet, sitting right on top, waiting for another pile of M&Ms to be loaded onto it later that night, or, knowing him, in the morning for breakfast.

"I can't help if you don't talk to me," Rick said to his daughter once the house was empty and quiet.

"I know," she said. She sat on the couch and her dad came and sat next to her, wrapping his arm around her. She wished she could bury her face into his chest and tell him everything and hear him tell her that everything would be fine, but she couldn't.

He kissed her forehead and sat in silence, waiting for her to speak. He knew she wouldn't say anything, but he sat with her and held her tight anyway. She nestled in closer, thanking him with her actions for being there for her, though she never opened up about anything.

It was different, though. With anything else, she'd talk. But with this, she simply couldn't. What would he say to her if she did?

You really think some shrink's words made him this way? Honey, your mother and I have been telling you he's no good.

Seems it doesn't matter if she told him or not, because he had that fatherly instinct.

"Honey," he finally said. "If you're digging a hole, my suggestion is to get out now while you can."

44

This was no cute, conservative cry. It was everything coming out. All the guilt. All the buildup. She knew this would come.

She'd been driving around for nearly an hour at this point, but she felt like she was driving in circles. Brian had no friends. He had no local hangout. All he ever did was go to work and then come home to write. There were no avenues she could take that would lead her to him. This was a hunt without a clue, and it was going nowhere until her car's speakers shouted at her.

The radio station hadn't changed since the morning she'd heard that old man was stabbed in the neighborhood across the street. Each and every time she got into the car, this was on. Kids in the car or not, she listened. Waiting for it. Knowing it would come.

The show's host was going on a tirade, using phrases the FCC didn't take so kindly to, and bleeped them out. The guy called him a "sick fuck" and "they should fry this bastard." And all Sarah could think about was the man who stood in front of her on their wedding day. The innocent smile. The passion. The love. It was all there, in his squinted eyes looking at her above a wide smile.

At that very moment, on that very day, she would have never guessed this could have happened. Never would have known the proposition she was offered.

He promised her, Brian did. Promised her the world. Promised her that their kids would have the world. That he'd make it as a writer. That he'd do anything it took to make it. But she took that to mean he'd do anything to make money, and to provide for his family. She took those words to mean he'd do whatever it took to make sure his family lived the lifestyle Sarah had always wanted. A domestic life with Mom, Dad, kids, all inside a beautiful home with pictures and trophies and nice cars in the extended driveway and a happy puppy to jump on their legs when they came home.

The false promise began like any family's would, with an overpriced wedding attended by every family and friend they'd ever come across. It was beautiful. An outdoor ceremony in the sun followed by a cocktail hour in the garden and a reception inside the ballroom. It was any girl's dream to get married here and she did. Paid for by her skeptical mother and her adoring father, but that was how her entire relationship with Brian went up until her marriage: her mother approved of nothing and her father would give her anything.

Her wedding day was great, but the moment the reception ended and the lights began to turn on like a bar's last call, she felt something leave her. At the moment, she thought it was just the excitement leaving. Her wedding day over. The one day a girl thinks about from the time she's a teenager, gone. Even if she remarried one day, she'd never have this. Never have the glamor and the beauty. The next time – good god, she was already thinking about a possible next time – would be in a courthouse somewhere, no one wanting to witness.

Maybe it wasn't something *leaving* her at that moment the lights flicked on, but something *growing inside* her. Fear. And if that was the case, it would grow for the next eight years, because there was always a knot in her stomach. Always some sort of a financial burden in their lives and she would always want to confront Brian about his writing rather than just smile past a bitten tongue. Ask him how it's coming along. How the search for an agent was going. Or if there were any publishers that sent back an interest in his books. He was always so optimistic, but he never had the sense of urgency she had to get it done. *Let's go*, she'd think. *When can this damn thing be published?*

Brian claimed it wasn't that easy. That you don't just publish a book overnight. And her response would be that the bank *can* take your car overnight; the power company *can* shut off your electricity overnight. And what were they to do if that happened? Tell those companies to hold off until a book gets accepted and then goes through a production stage?

Sarah could debate all she wanted, but she knew what left her that night. It was hope. Hope had left her. Because although she hated when her mother had to give her opinion on her every move, she knew this time she was right. Sarah was rushing into a marriage for the sake of being married and nothing more. She just wanted to wear a white dress. She loved Brian, sure, but like her mother said, "When it comes to marriage, love is just the tip of the iceberg."

So this divorce Brian thought he was getting? The one that Dr. Epplestein had arranged? It was no surprise. It was no setup. A divorce between Sarah and Brian was imminent. He knew it and so did she. Which is why it was so easy for Dr. Epplestein to use it as a decoy. As some "phrase" to trigger Brian into becoming a robot.

She should have gone about it differently. Not only did she throw a dagger into Brian's heart when she mentioned a divorce and taking his kids away, but she let it sizzle in a hot flame before doing so, just to make the pain that much worse.

She wasn't divorcing him. She was deceiving him. And her deception led to Brian's latest act of violence. What the radio dee-jay was reporting as the worst thing to happen since the brutal Charles Manson murders.

45

Detective Jones was hunched over in her chair, eyes only inches away from her computer monitor. She studied the file on the screen in front of her. An image of Sarah Hart's dad was on the top corner. Beneath that, *Richard Wellington* was written in bold letters.

"Who's that? Richard Wellington?"

Detective Jones turned around to greet the voice she found familiar. "Hey, Captain." She turned back to the monitor. "Just trying to get a bit of background information about Hart's wife." She nodded toward the screen. "This is her dad, right here."

"Anything on him?"

"Nada. Squeaky clean."

"Good. Then you need to get your ass moving."

"Why?"

"I'm guessing you don't have your CB on?"

"It's in the cruiser." She stood. "Why?"

"Your guy Hart. He just took out an entire family."

"He what?"

"You heard me. Sick fuck drove through a rest stop on the highway. Took out a family of five walking back to their car."

"Holy shit." Her heart sank.

"Yeah. Went up the curb to do it, too. It's already been called in and all units are on the lookout."

"Any word?"

"None yet. Still on the loose. I'm heading over now if you want to come with–"

She grabbed the jacket off the back of her chair and ran out. Captain Furlong could have been yelling something to her on her way out, but she wouldn't have known.

Two at a time, she descended the municipal building staircase and hopped into her car. Alone. Detective Jones didn't even really know where the hell she was going, but she knew sitting in front of her monitor looking into the backgrounds of Brian Hart's in-laws wouldn't help find him. Of course, Brian had no immediate family left for her to look into. She learned that they were all killed in that horrible crash when Brian was eighteen.

How could someone like Brian do what he was doing? How could he kill? How could he strip families of loved ones? Hadn't he felt the pain that comes with losing people? Hadn't he been through the horror of having to bury family members before their time?

He had. And yet somehow, he showed no emotion. He was like some possessed killing machine that dangled himself right in front of the police only to safely flee.

Not this time, she thought. *Your ass is mine.*

The speedometer on the dashboard couldn't have been right. She had to be doing more than 120. She had to be.

Alicia Jones looked down at her speedometer as she traveled down the empty left lane of the expressway. The needle kept punching the 120 MPH dash and bouncing around. It reminded her of the cartoons she used to watch as a kid where a thermostat would rise and rise and rise and then the mercury would explode from the top like an erupting volcano. But those were back in the innocent days. Before she saw the world that adults live in. Before her innocent mind was stained and burnt with the images of death and despair and fraud and betrayal.

Brake lights began to flood the three-lane highway as she approached the rest stop. Blue and red lights spun in the sunlight up ahead and Detective Jones cut across the highway and onto the shoulder of the road, driving up to the scene on the shoulder's warning strips.

Two police cruisers blocked the entrance to the rest stop's on-ramp, but one pulled to the side when they saw her approaching. She drove by and into the long strip of asphalt and empty parking spaces until she hit the action point.

Forensics hadn't arrived yet so the scene was being blocked off by a few officers. Others in uniform were interviewing witnesses. Some were crying, some hugging, others wide-eyed and seemingly tranced. Sadly, scenes such as these were becoming all too normal for Detective Jones. She chose her line of business, but didn't realize that images that would haunt her would soon become the norm in her life.

"Anything confirmed?" she asked one of the officers guarding the scene.

"Nothing yet." His nametag read Cortez and the rank he wore on his sleeve indicated he was a Police Officer II –

the middle of the three Officer ranks. "Some officers over there," he nodded, "are conducting witness testimonials. No second round yet, though." When conducting witness statements, it was a requirement to interview at least twice to ensure the story doesn't change.

"How long have you been on scene?"

"No more than twenty minutes," Officer Cortez said.

"Have you heard anything on the suspect?"

"No." He looked over his shoulder toward the rest stop's exit. "I haven't talked to any witnesses myself, but from what I'm hearing, he took off right after. There's a 10-57 out to all units." A 10-57, she thought. Code for a Hit-and-Run.

As the officer was getting her up to speed, she looked past him and noticed the scene. There were black skid marks along the white sidewalk and those marks led to ruts in the grass past. Near the marks were three white sheets with what she knew would be underneath. One sheet took the form of an adult and the other two made her nauseous – obviously children.

"Where are the other two?" she asked Officer Cortez.

"Mother and son were still alive when we got here. They got taken to Kennedy down the street." He nodded his head in the opposite direction toward Kennedy Hospital, but he got his point across. "I saw them before they left," he said in a softer tone. Then he shook his head and didn't say another word.

Detective Jones thanked the officer and began her walk back to the cruiser. Forensics wasn't even on scene yet and it would take them some time to do their work. In the meantime, she had two options: Let her emotions carry her on an endless chase to find Brian Hart or pick up

where she left off with the investigation.
She knew where she was headed.

46

Get everything down on paper before you forget.

Brian was never this type of writer. He was never one of those authors who thought he had to write everything down the second he thought of it so he didn't forget. He always wondered why it seemed like so many others were. If you have a good idea, shouldn't it stick in your mind?

Since he'd started with this book, things had been different. Maybe it was the stress that was getting to him or the divorce – whatever it was, it was affecting his ability to not only write, but to remember.

Sitting where he was sitting was bold, and he knew it. But it was where he knew no one would look. He sat in his car in the Eats-N-Treats parking lot. The store had still yet to reopen since the death of their manager, but the store shared a lot with the neighboring Home Depot and those parking lots are always full.

Brian's sedan was parked near the contractor pickup

exit of the versatile store. He hid between a truck with a trailer attached and a large van owned by one of the million solar panel companies. He found it a safe place when he first pulled into the lot but realized after only a few short minutes that neither of these trucks would be there long. Cars and trucks pulled into parking spaces around him and left while he was still there. The whole image played out like the outside world was on a fast-forward track as Brian remained motionless in his car.

Only he wasn't motionless. His hands were moving quickly. There was still so much to write and he knew his time was winding down.

Taking down that family didn't help, he thought. *But I needed to. I needed the research.*

The main character in his novel, Francesca, was on the run from the police. After she murdered her husband and then strangled the next-door neighbor, she had to flee. The townspeople were starting to catch on, sort of like Brian's real-life story was at that point. At the moment, his life was a bit different.

Taking out that family at the rest stop was his final bit of research, though. It was all he'd need. From here, he just needed to let his prose do the rest of the work. He needed to show everyone that he did what he had to do to push himself over the hump.

He always did what he had to do. Always had the mindset that no one controlled his life but him. The idea of waiting around and being a subordinate aggravated him. So he took charge.

Take charge is exactly what he did. And now he was going to take charge of his writing career by writing a novel no one could put down. A novel that no one could critique as being unauthentic.

It was the car Lucas had bought her for their anniversary last year – a large SUV with third-row seating. Francesca took it as a hint that he was ready to start a family with her. Ready to have kids. But in reality, it was just his way of covering up the affair with his little slut.

With the nosey little weasel next door lying comfortably in the ground next to Lucas, she knew she had only one more person to rid before she could flee and find a new life. She'd already purchased the hair clippers, dye, undersized sports bras to constrict what was under her shirt, and some baggy t-shirts and jeans. Once she fled, she'd completely change her identity. She was going to pose as a man.

But not until she did what she knew she had to do.

Officer Thompson had been the one who was skeptical of her. It was like he could somehow see right through her, but he couldn't point a finger on exactly what happened so he held back. But he was onto her and she knew it. So she followed him.

It'd been close to 48 hours since Francesca was interviewed at the station and driven back home. "Don't you go far," were his patronizing words to her.

She didn't. She stayed close to home, close to where that nosey little shit of a neighbor watched her every move like a hawk. A smile came across her face as she thought about him. Damn, it felt good to wrap her hands around his neck and squeeze until the life came out of him. He tried to claw and scratch at her face as his brain strained for oxygen but received none. Any normal man would have been able to fight her off – hell, she was no more than 120 pounds. She almost felt bad, like she was picking on a child. But if the pathetic excuse for a man would have minded his own fucking business, she wouldn't have had to go to the extreme she did.

Too late now.

Strangling Officer Thompson would be impossible. It crossed her mind to do so back when he dropped her off after the interrogation. But he was a burly man. A veteran of the police force. Her manicured nails around his neck would be no greater disturbance than a pestering gnat. He'd whip her around and put cuffs on her before she could even manage to scream.

This big SUV, though... This big SUV, *she thought to herself.* This'll take him right down.

She'd been tracking him down since he dropped her off. She researched his career and family and address – amazing yet scary how quickly we can find out information on each other through the internet. She thought she might come across a way to hack into his phone camera so she could see exactly where he was, but going that in-depth was a bit out of her league.

His final killing scene. He had to take a breath to admit he was a bit nervous about writing this. For some reason, he felt fine writing the other scenes. Was it because this was the final scene? Or because he felt he had to top the other two? Or was it that this scene would need to be written under pressure? There was no one holding a loaded gun to his head and telling him to finish, but there were certainly at least fifty cops and hundreds if not thousands of citizens looking for him. If the citizens got to him first, they might take matters into their own hands. He smirked as he thought of it. He *did* do some pretty messed up stuff to some innocent people.

Wrong place, wrong time.

There was no time for regret. No time for what-ifs. Soon there would be a car that would pass him as he sat in this parking lot. They'd recognize him, looking in the windshield with wide eyes. And then they' call the police. He told himself this was true, though he had no idea that the person who would find him next would have strange intentions.

Time's running out, he thought to himself.

He kept writing.

She sat in the neighboring parking lot of the doughnut shop. It was a local place. Doughnut Drive-In, it was called. The entire shop was no bigger than a large shed, but that's because it was a drive-in only place.

She wished she had a CB radio so she could eavesdrop. Know if anyone was talking about her, her house, or if the wife of the weasel next door called in a missing person complaint yet. Without one, she simply sat in her car, observing the Doughnut Drive-In line across the street.

It seemed – from her observation, that is – Officer Thompson worked an eleven-to-seven shift. She saw him arrive at the Drive-In just after 11:00 on each of the last two days. And this day didn't disappoint.

His cruiser entered the Drive-In line a few minutes after the hour. Francesca noted the white-haired man through the windshield and the bumper number – #812 – in black letters by the exhaust pipe. Cruiser number 812 was the cruiser he drove to drop her off at her house after the interrogation.

He got his order and she could see him smiling as the young girl leaned out the window and handed him his coffee and a brown paper bag. His last meal, *she thought.*

After nearly an hour of following the cruiser, it dawned on her that it might be a while before he leaves the car. How would she kill him from inside his car? She had no gun, no knife, no way of running up and ambushing the man who was snooping around too closely into her secrets.

It wasn't until thirty minutes later that the door would open and the man built like a bear would step out from behind the wheel.

Brian hadn't realized until this moment that he should have been poking his head up every now and then. Having his face glued to the monitor on his lap for too long could lead to disaster. He could lift his head to find himself surrounded by cop cars and flashing lights.

He took a quick glance out of all windows, found himself to be safe, and dove into his story once more.

He pulled his cruiser up beside the curb in front of a single-story home in a residential neighborhood. All seemed calm, but he must have been here for a house call. Domestic disturbance maybe? Who knows? All Francesca knew is that this was her opportunity to close the loop on her potential arrest for the murder of her husband, the scumbag cheater. With the nosey neighbor out of the way, Officer Thompson was the only one remaining.

She was sure to follow at a distance throughout the day and this was the first time she was within two hundred feet of him.

Officer Thompson shut the door to his cruiser and began to walk up the driveway of the home. Still, no one had opened the door or come outside.

Good, she thought. No witnesses.

She pressed down on the gas and her SUV took off. This was it.

Brian wrote what he knew. He wrote exactly what he felt when he drove up the curb in the rest stop and his little sedan took on a family of five. He wrote about the last-minute scream, the thump, the additional thumps, and about Francesca's heartbeat thudding in her ears. He wrote the twisted scene with pleasure. And when he was done, he closed his computer and let out a cry of joy.

He punched at the roof of his car, smacked his palms on the steering wheel, and wanted so badly to lay on the horn. He wanted to scream, get out of the car and dance with the first person he saw.

Big old construction worker? Didn't even matter. He was ecstatic.

He did it. He'd just written the book he knew he needed to write; the book Sarah said he needed to write; the book the world needed to read in order to approve of him. This was going to be the story that sent him into *bestseller land.*

A part of him thought about his acceptance speech. The dream he had on so many occasions – the dream of him accepting an award from one of his literary idols– could now be a reality. He could envision it. And he was already beginning to write his speech.

He'd thank Sarah – *thanks for leaving me you dumb bitch.* He'd thank Dickhead Eric – *thanks for practically begging me to use you for practice*. And he'd thank poor old Thomas McMann and the family of five at the rest stop, though none of them had wronged him and he wouldn't have a bad thing to say, he could at least acknowledge them, right?

The adrenaline was pumping, but he knew this book wasn't complete. Sure, the most important parts were – the authentic murder scenes. But he still needed to write his closing. He needed to come up with a cliffhanger that would land him a multi-book deal with one of the Big Five publishing houses. Hell yeah, he did. Because this was going to be his big break. No more struggling. Step aside, Mr. Patterson. There's a new head-honcho in the game.

He took another look around to see if all was normal. Nothing seemed out of the ordinary so he opened the laptop again and started typing.

47

"I wouldn't give that son of a bitch the sock off my foot if he needed it. Damn kid hasn't done a thing for my daughter, not a thing. Never has. He's nothing but a damn talker, spewing bullshit from his mouth and into my Sarah's gullible ear."

It was clear from the second Detective Jones brought up his name that the man despised Brian Hart. Even though the last name was now his daughter's, it pained him to even let the name leave his lips.

Rick Wellington invited Detective Jones into the house and politely offered her a seat on the couch just a few short seconds after he answered the door. It was as if the sight of a police detective was expected. Like it was something he knew one day would come.

"We tried to stop her," he said. "Her mother, she pushed more than I did, but neither of us thought the boy was any good. Never even asked me for her hand in marriage." He looked down and shook his head when he said, "But she saw something in the boy. Something we didn't." And then he looked back up and said with the hint of a smirk, "Young love, I guess. Kids don't know what they're getting into."

Alicia couldn't relate. No relationship had gotten in her way. Her top priority had always been her career. That mindset was what got her promoted to Detective at age twenty-six, and what would continue to advance her career. No time for relationships. No time for kids or day cares or play dates. She continued to tell herself that she didn't want that yet. But part of that killed her inside. It killed her to see old friends and schoolmates getting married and having kids. Would she be lonely her entire life? And would Sarah Hart be joining her soon?

"So you don't know where your daughter is?" she asked.

"I sure as hell don't. But I'll tell you what, it makes me sick to think that son of a bitch is out there. After what he did?... Father of my grandbabies or not, he deserves what's coming to him."

"If you call your daughter, will she answer?"

"I'd sure hope so. But I doubt it. Detective," he leaned up in his seat and put his forearms on his knees. "My daughter is a sweetheart. Wouldn't hurt a soul or break a rule. I hope your being here isn't implying she's some sort of accomplice to something."

"Truthfully, Mr. Wellington, I'm not implying anything. I think it's pretty clear that your son-in-law" – he cringed at the term – "did all of this, but I don't think your daughter has anything to do with it. I think she's just a woman who's torn and thinks she's doing the right thing by helping out her husband."

"Maybe," he said, leaning back deeper into the couch.

On the opposite sofa, Detective Jones asked another question from the edge of her seat, notebook on her lap. "Mr. Wellington, do you know where your daughter is headed?"

If she'd been going with her gut instinct, she would have believed the face he made following that question meant his answer was bullshit, but she wanted to give him the benefit of the doubt. After all, they seemed like decent people, Sarah's parents. No record on either other than a careless driving ticket for the mister at the age of nineteen.

"I really have no idea," he said, looking right into her eyes. But his look was like one of a lying teenager. *Look, I'm looking right in your eyes and not even blinking so I must be telling the truth.*

He knew. And at that moment, Alicia knew it. But she didn't push. Turns out she didn't need to. Because he'd end up telling her exactly what she needed to hear.

"Hopefully she's going to talk to that shrink of hers. She usually talks to him after their fights."

Shrink?

"What shrink?" Alicia asked.

The big teddy bear who'd put a giant protective bubble around his daughter had just popped it.

48

Sarah hated the apartment, but at least it was a place to go. Now she had nothing and no one. The apartment was almost certainly a set trap by the cops at this point. She couldn't go to her parents' house because by now, they'd seen the news. Then what? What would they say? And how would they respond when Sarah told them she *had* to find Brian? *Had* to save him?

If only she and her sister were still close like they used to be. Back before they became teenagers. Back before the competitiveness in them took over. Who had more friends? Who had the cuter boyfriend? Normal sisters grow out of that phase, but Sarah and Bethany never did. She married someone who made more money than Brian and kept her snooty nose in the air ever since then.

What would she say if Sarah showed up? How would she react? Would she invite her in? Ask her what's wrong? Have her back when she said she needed to defy the cops and save her husband from prison?

It was doubtful. Sarah could already see the police coming to take her out of the house. *Sorry,* Bethany would say with a *fuck you* smirk. *Calling them was the right thing to do.*

Sarah knew her only options: Brian or Dr. Epplestein.

She knew what would happen if she went crawling back into Dr. Epplestein's office. She knew he'd lick his chops at her vulnerability. He'd push this little experiment of his even further, and she'd ultimately cave. She was able to stand up for herself the last time, but she knew she couldn't do it again. She couldn't go back.

Knowing Brian wouldn't answer, she picked up her cell to call him. Picturing the number of government ears listening to the call the second she found his name in her Recents and hit call, she held her breath but it wouldn't be for long. The call went straight to voicemail.

Sarah imagined he'd thrown it out the window while driving who knows where. On his way to his new life maybe. Gone forever, leaving Sarah and the kids in order to avoid prison. It didn't seem like a move the Brian *she* knew would make. The Brian *she* knew would do anything for his kids. He'd hold onto them as tight as he could while uniformed officers tried to pry him from their arms and into the back of a police cruiser.

But the Brian that Sarah knew was brainwashed. He was thrust into some psychological experiment by a man in corduroy pants and low-hanging glasses. And it was all because Sarah wanted more. Because she wanted the material things in life.

Jesus. She realized how horrible this was all sounding. She'd volunteered her husband – the man she laughed with, loved, cherished, promised to grow old with – for some sick mind game. It was like something out of a science fiction movie. And she allowed herself to be manipulated by the bait. The money.

She couldn't point the finger at Dr. Epplestein. Couldn't even point it at Brian. This was all her fault. She was the one that made it all possible. Her need for money. Her desire to have the life she expected to have. And for the first time ever, she realized that she may have been subconsciously wanting to compete and win against her sister.

Bethany had always been well-off. Whether it be with boys, grades in school, hell, she even won contests on the radio every other time she called. No matter what Sarah did, she could never keep up. And now here she was again, losing the battle of life to her younger sister.

Sarah had to get in touch with Brian. She tried to call again but only received the same response: straight to voicemail. She dropped the phone on her lap and threw her head back against the headrest. She was getting nowhere by sitting in her company's parking garage. It was a good hiding spot – no cop cars would come rolling through E-Co's parking structure – but with each passing minute, the authorities were that much closer to catching Brian.

One more time she tried calling and one more time she got the same result. Frustrated and not knowing what to do, she put the car in reverse, backed out of the spot, and drove toward the exit of the garage.

To hell with it, she thought.

The moment her hood hit the black tar of the street and the sun shone brightly in through the windshield, she felt vulnerable. She felt like the entire world could see her and they were looking in, judging. But she didn't care. She needed to find Brian.

And he would come right to her.

49

The fifth-floor suite 521 in the West Tower of *The Twins* belonged to Dr. James Epplestein. The first thought in Detective Jones's mind when walking into the doors wasn't the expensive décor. Mahogany everything, paintings lining the waiting room and dark, leather chairs lining the walls that led to the crescent reception desk. Instead, her first thought was *How the hell could Sarah Hart afford to come to a place like this?*

"May I help you, Miss?" an elegantly-dressed woman said from behind the desk. She was dressed so nicely that Detective Jones thought for a second she might be a therapist herself. Maybe just outside of earning her name on the entry door.

"I'm looking for James Epplestein."

"I'm sorry, Ma'am, but he's all booked up for the day. He leaves Wednesday afternoons open for new patients," she looked down and flipped through the pages of what Alicia assumed was a calendar. "But he doesn't seem to have anything open for a few–"

Detective Jones plucked her badge from her belt and held it up. "I'm not a patient."

"Oh." The badge sent the receptionist back a step, reacting to the thing like it had bullets and a trigger.

"I need to speak to him about something else."

"Okay." She tried as hard as she could to regain her composure but was still clearly flustered. "Let me...let me see if I can get a hold of him." She pressed a button that triggered a prolonged beep, and behind the double doors to the left of the desk, a faint ringing could be heard.

"What's wrong, Alex?" A man's deep and irritable voice came through the intercom. It made Alicia wonder whether this Alex woman was on thin ice and he was on his last straw with her.

"I'm sorry, Doctor, but there's a woman here you're going to... You might just want to come out here really quick."

There was no response through the speaker, but several minutes later one of the double doors swung slightly open and out walked the aesthetic definition of a therapist. Detective Jones thought to herself that these guys must have come off of an assembly line.

"May I help you?" he asked when he saw Alicia.

"You may," Alicia said, and she held up her badge for him to see.

"Alright," he said too calmly. "This way." The doctor guided her to the direction of his office with an extended arm.

They walked back toward the main entrance and into an office set along the wall with Dr. Epplestein's name displayed on a silver plate.

"You'll have to excuse the clutter," he said as they walked in. "I've been telling myself to come in on the weekend to organize, but it never happens." He smiled, but she didn't return the smile, nor the gesture of a friendly tone. She'd put herself in situations before where she needed to be firm, and wasn't, and it backfired. And this man had a Ph.D. in Psychology, displayed in several locations throughout his office. While she was trying to examine him, he was surely examining her.

"I appreciate you stepping away from your client to speak with me, so I'll make this as quick as possible. I'm here because of a patient of yours, Sarah Hart."

He gave nothing. No change in expression. Just walked around to his desk chair and gestured her to sit in one across from it. "Okay," he said. "She is...," he let his voice fade, as though he was going to say more but stopped himself.

"I'm aware of doctor-patient confidentiality, Dr. Epplestein, but this involves the murder of several individuals."

No expression. "Is Mrs. Hart a suspect in these murders?"

"Well no, but her husband is. And we have reason to believe she's trying to help him evade police."

"Is that so?"

"It is."

After a pause, he said, "And how can I be of assistance?"

"I need to know why Sarah was a patient of yours. What she was seeing you for."

"Detective...Jones was it?"

She nodded.

"Well, Detective Jones, I would love to help you fill in the missing pieces of your investigation, I truly would. But you see, unfortunately I'm not at will to discuss any patient information, especially reasons for her being here." He paused, leaning his elbows on the desk as he had been since he took his seat. Then he looked deep into her eyes as if she were a patient herself, looking to him for guidance. "So I won't be able to help you here. By law, I'm not allowed."

"Dr. Epplestein." She leaned closer, sliding to the edge of her seat. "This patient is involved in a homicide. Doctor-patient confidentiality goes out the window."

"You're correct, Detective. Patient confidentiality does go out the window when a patient is involved in a murder case. But you're not saying my patient is being accused of murder. You're saying that her husband was, and that...she's hiding him or something?" The ending question caused a slight turn of his head, which was the first sign of emotion since they sat down.

"Brian Hart killed five people including two children, and two more are in a hospital in critical condition. We have reason to believe your patient may be somehow involved. So I'll ask you one more time, doctor, to please cooperate with me so that this investigation can run smoothly."

"I'm very sorry," he said with a smile and the friendliest of tones. "But if I did, I'd be breaking the law. And then you'd be arresting *me*." He let out a whole-hearted giggle, as if the two were simply buddies shooting the shit.

"How many patients do you have, doctor?"

"Well I'm not sure of the total number, but I see about thirty patients a week."

"And you remember the background for every one?"

For the first time there was an affliction in his voice, and he said, "I remember all of my patients, Detective Jones. It's why I'm so good at what I do. I remember."

Playing Detective and playing Psychologist are essentially the same thing: you try to squeeze information out of people that they're hesitant to turn over, and then you listen, you analyze, and you report. These two could have held a respectable and educated conversation, but instead were in the duel of minds, one trying to outdo the other.

He was a little harder to read than she'd first anticipated. Either he was the most laid-back doctor who found pure joy in remembering each of his patients and everything about them, or he was hiding something behind those emotionless eyes. But that last comment struck a chord.

How could he so quickly and easily remember Sarah Hart and her file? Out of all his patients, Detective Jones walks in, mentions one name, and viola? He remembers everything? She wasn't buying it. Sarah hart was fresh on his mind for a reason.

"When was the last time Sarah Hart was in for a visit, doctor?"

"I can't recall," he said. "And I'm terribly sorry to cut this short, but I've got a patient waiting." He tapped at his watch. "On the clock."

"There's nothing at all you can give me from her file, huh?"

"Detective," he said as he rose from his chair. "I'm not even supposed to share the fact that she's a patient here. I did you a favor because I respect your badge. I see a lot of former military and police and I'm aware of the dangers of your profession. Unfortunately, I can't dive any farther into the history of my patient." He extended his hand to shake. "But if she somehow becomes the suspect herself...well now that might be a different story." He smiled but Detective Jones wouldn't acknowledge it with one in return.

She thanked him for his time, annoyed at yet another dead-end. But knowing that she'd be back. And this time, with a weapon. Something he couldn't say no to. Something that she'd hold in front of him and he'd gladly hand over the full file for Sarah Hart.

A warrant.

50

Detective Jones pulled her cruiser into an empty parking space in front of the municipal building. She threw her gear shifter up and into Park, thinking that with just an ounce more of might, she'd have ripped the thing clean off. She got out of the car and stormed the steps to the entrance, forcing herself to keep the shitstorm swirling in her head.

She was going through with this. No turning back.

She pushed through the double glass doors and walked through the lobby and into the back, where cubicles such as hers were set up, but mostly empty. At this time of day, all the detectives were out devouring cup after cup of coffee and filling their notebooks with useful information.

Lucky for them.

Captain Furlong's office was at the end of the hall and that's exactly where she was headed. Nothing was seen in her peripherals, because she didn't care what was there. To her, at that very moment, she and the Captain were the only two people in the building. And they were about to have a serious talk.

When she reached his office, she was glad to see him sitting behind his desk. *Good*, she thought. Because her emotions were running so high that she didn't want to have to wait. But shit, with every step she took, inching her way closer to the office door, anger began to mix with fear, and then fear took over completely. Her heart raced and her hands began to sweat.

Why? Why the hell was she nervous? She came here to prove to herself that she wasn't some weak woman in a place filled with men. She wasn't inferior. She wasn't going to be walked all over. She was just as tough as everyone else.

Once she'd hit the doorway, her mind was pulling itself so hard in two separate directions. She had no idea what would come out of her mouth if she'd open it. So she stood there, quiet, mouth pinched closed. But she couldn't stand there forever. And after only a few seconds, Captain Furlong made her speak.

"Can I help you?" he asked, looking down over the brim of his glasses at the scattered paperwork in front of him. And when she didn't answer, he looked over at her, still leaning his head downward.

"I need warrants," she said. On a scale of one to ten, the confidence in her voice barely tapped the chart.

He removed his glasses and rubbed his eyes. "For what?"

"For Brian Hart's apartment. And for his wife's shrink." She managed to get it all out, but felt stiff as a board.

"Her shrink?"

"Yeah."

"Why?"

It took her a while to get it out, but the lines going through her head were not coming out of her mouth. "I... I think I might have something. This guy...doctor...her doctor is, uh, it's like he's holding something back."

What the hell is wrong with you, Alicia. Get your shit together.

Why did everything flow so much smoother in her head? Why couldn't she relay it? Why in the hell was her brain shutting down at a time like this?

"That's patient-doctor confidentiality, Detective. He's not allowed."

"I know that, Captain. But it's different. He was holding something back. I know he was."

"A shrink holding something back isn't grounds for a search warrant," he said.

"But there's something–" she began her rebuttal, but was interrupted by two bodies squeezing past her and through the doorway: Perkins and Antini.

One little Irish, red-headed guy, followed by a taller, tanner Italian guy, but the smaller of the two had the shittier attitude towards his peers. Clearly, the guy thought highly of himself. Antini? Not so much. It's a wonder he even hung around the guy.

"Hey, Cap," Perkins says, stopping in front of the Captain's desk with his short arms and tiny hands placed on his hips. "Just got a new lead on the Jimenez case. Anonymous caller just dialed in and–"

"Excuse me," Alicia said. Did he really just cut in front of her like that? She felt like the shy, nine-year-old version of herself all over again, people cutting in front of her in the lunch line while she stood there doing nothing about it.

Perkins turned to her, but then carried right on talking to the captain, who seemed to give two shits about what just happened.

"Excuse me!"

She felt the heat rising into her face and she took a few steps forward. Perkins, the arrogant son of a bitch that he was, kept right on talking.

"Hey! I said excuse me. Did you not hear down there or are you just too ignorant to realize conversations happen in this world that don't involve you?"

Did you not hear down there? That's what did it. What got his attention. Whether or not it was because he took offense to it or because it was so far out of Alicia's realm that he wasn't prepared for it, that was the line that shut him the hell up.

"You were talking?" Perkins The Prick asked.

"I was."

"Well I didn't know. You see, normally when people talk to someone it's to their face, not fifty feet away almost in another room. What, you scared he'll yell at you or something?"

She took a few steps into the room, finally, and stopped just short of where Perkins was standing with her chest to his shoulder. "This better?" she asked, looking down at the short man.

Although at the moment she would have loved for him to turn and face her – size her up – Perkins didn't budge. He stood facing the captain's desk, his hands on his hips and his elbow within inches of Alicia's stomach. He looked at the captain and then back at Alicia.

"What's the matter? Afraid I'll yell at you or something?" Alicia asked.

He smirked, a sly little arrogant smirk, then looked to the captain and said, "I'll come back later." And then he walked out and Antini followed behind like some sort of pet.

Alicia followed them out of the room with her eyes, and then she looked over at Captain Furlong. She'd noticed he'd removed his glasses, serious now. Maybe wondering where this feistiness had been.

It was one of the things that helped her make detective, that feistiness. Word went around the precinct that she was fierce. That she was a go-getter. A sponge, taking in all the information she could get, trying her hardest to be as smart as the veterans of the force. He mentioned it to her during her interview, the captain did. How word was spreading that she was strong. *A tough cookie.* Those were his exact words.

She was. But for some reason she lost that spark when she switched from a uniform and into a suit.

That first morning after the switch was made official, she looked herself in the mirror. She can remember it like it was yesterday, and sometimes the fear creeps up on her just like it did that morning. There was something missing. Something that made her feel naked. Maybe it was the fact that her badge and gun were hidden. Or that she wouldn't be clearly labeled by passersby as a cop because of the suit. Maybe it freaked her out that she was once again vulnerable like she was before.

Whatever it was, she'd lost it that morning looking in the mirror. But today, standing up to Perkins and now looking over at Captain Furlong at his desk, looking up at her in astonishment, she knew she'd gotten it back.

"I need warrants," she said to him.

"This is all about the warrants?"

"Yes. I can't get shit done with this Hart case. I'm sick of it. I need some damn warrants."

She'd been a subordinate of Captain Furlong for years and she'd barely spoken more than one word to him in a tone other than inferior. But if she didn't start doing something herself, she might not be answering to him much longer.

"Alright." He pinched the bridge of his nose for a second and then stood from his chair and looked at his watch. "Court's still in session, but let me see what I can do." He walked past her, but stopped once he got to the door. He turned to her and said, "Grab a few officers and get ready to go. The guys are all out," he said pointing out to the empty room of cubicles.

He didn't want her to call another detective? Or wait until one gets back? She would have liked to somehow get her normal traveling partner, Russell. But there was no time to wait.

Captain Furlong must have known the urgency, too, though his expression wouldn't show it.

51

Judges are usually tense on days where court is in session. But this day must have been a good day. Either that or Captain Furlong has more authority than his team thinks, just doesn't boast about it.

But it only took him a little over an hour to get both warrants. And once they were in Alicia's hand, she was out the door and making her way down the stairs of the municipal building with Officers Gunther and Emans by her side. She hopped in her cruiser and had them follow her in their patrol car.

She was watching them through her rearview mirror the entire ride to the shrink's office. It wasn't that she didn't trust them, thinking they would veer off the road and take a shortcut to forewarn Dr. Epplestein. It was that she didn't know them. And they barely knew her, or the work and stress that had been put into this investigation.

Gunther and Emans were unfamiliar territory: Gunther a round guy with over fifteen years on the force, and

Emans a rookie, though, in his late twenties, was older than most rooks. Detective Russell was really the only person she felt comfortable with, so there was an awkwardness about the car with Gunther and Emans following behind her.

The officers followed, all the way to the pair of buildings, just as she knew deep down inside they would.

Detective Jones pulled her unmarked cruiser within an inch of the sidewalk's yellow curb just outside the entrance to the West Tower of The Twins. As she opened her door and stepped out, the patrol car behind her came to an abrupt halt, and out hopped Emans and Gunther – Gunther doing more of a roll out of the car.

Two blonde women stood in a makeshift gazebo about twenty feet from the door – the designated smoking area. They looked at the detective and her two officers, one with her mouth open and the other pulling on her cigarette, squinting to keep out the drift.

Then the detective was approaching the row of glass doors that made up the building's entrance. She heard the footsteps behind her but still turned to make sure her officers were keeping up. They were, and might have been a little too anxious.

"No need for that," she said to Emans with an extended arm. The rookie was reaching for his pistol. Over-enthusiastic maybe. Or maybe on the brink of shitting himself. He'd never met Dr. Epplestein before. Never realized the gray old man was no more a threat to his life than a leaf blowing in the wind.

The three of them walked into the empty lobby of the building where only a few single chairs sat unoccupied across from three elevators. When the first one opened, they all stepped inside and took a quiet ride up to the fifth floor.

When they stepped out, she led the way through the wooden door with the doctor's name on it. The door opened and Alex, the receptionist, shot an alarming look.

Alex opened her mouth as if she was about to greet the trio – her mouth was obviously a second or two behind her mind, or at least the expression on her face. Then she said, "Can I help you, Detective?"

This time there'd be no questions. There'd be no introductions and no gazing around the lobby in awe at the eliteness portrayed by the decor. This time, Alicia simply held out the warrant and said, "Where is he?"

It wasn't until Alicia reached the desk and the paper was in Alex's hand that she spoke again, though her mouth hung open for the entire length of the pause. "I...," she began. "I'll buzz him. He's with another client."

"Don't worry about it." Alicia snatched the paper back and walked toward the office. "Come on," she said to the officers.

"Detective, you can't go in there. He's with a client."

But there wasn't a damn thing stopping her. And as she approached the door, she heard the clicking of plastics as Alex plucked the phone from the receiver and called into it: "Dr. Epplestein, I'm sorry to interrupt, but–"

And then Alicia twisted the doorknobs and swung both doors open on their hinges. A grand entrance.

Dr. Epplestein stood from his chair with a stern look on his face. In front of him was a patient. A woman. With eyes now as wide as the lenses on her face. And she sat up from her leather recliner as her doctor stood.

"The hell?" the doctor said.

"I have a warrant," Alicia said. "A search warrant. I want to see her file."

The patient's eyes opened even wider, and she placed her hand on her chest and turned around to look at the doctor: *She wants to see my files?*

A quick glance down at her was all Dr. Epplestein needed, and she dropped her hand. "Marybeth," he said, looking at Alicia now and locking eyes. "I'm sorry to do this but I'm going to have to cut this short. We'll reschedule a time to make up next week."

"Oh. Alright." She wanted to dispute, but one more quick glance down at her from her shrink was all it took for her to submit, grab her coat and head for the door. Alicia watched her as she passed, head down, sliding against the frame of the door as if she and the cops had some contagious and incurable disease.

Once he knew his patient was a safe distance away, Dr. Epplestein squinted through his bifocals at the sheet of paper dangling from Alicia's hand. "Search warrant? You're going to rip my whole place apart now?"

"Not quite. Just your office. And we're not going through anything. You're going to do it for us."

He seemed frustrated. An old, aging, gray, overworked man. The stress of his patients seemed to have rubbed off on him. And this was just another event in his life that drove him up a wall. With a loud sigh, he shook his head and said, "Let's go."

Last in line behind Dr. Epplestein and both Officers, Alicia walked out of the office and into the lobby where Alex stood looking as if she was about to be smacked across the head. But no one was even close enough to do it. They scaled the line of chairs against the wall and followed the path to the shrink's office. Alicia kicked the door shut with her heel once the four of them were inside. The chances of Alex barging in were about as slim as a single strand of hair on her head, but Alicia didn't want to risk it. With the door closed, it was just the doctor, Alicia, and the two officers in the room.

Dr. Epplestein walked beside his desk and stood there, acting as if he had no idea what he needed to do next. "Where is it," Alicia asked. "Sarah hart's file." She followed up with the instruction, knowing the doctor would play coy.

"I don't have it," he said.

"Where are your files?"

No answer. And then a loud bang echoed through the room. The sound came from Officer Emans' foot, and then he said, "You keep files in here?"

Dr. Epplestein looked over at him and said, "I don't know. Find out."

Find out she did. Alicia walked over to the side-by-side cabinets and pulled open each drawer, searching for a tab with Sarah Hart's name on it. All she really found was that the man was highly organized. His patients were listed in alphabetical order and each had a color-coated tab – for diagnosis maybe? But his organization worried her all the more when she was unable to find a file for Sarah Hart. Because there's no way a man this organized would have a file out of place.

"Where is it?" she asked. "Where's her file?"

"It's not the file that you should be looking for," he said. His tone was patronizing and Alicia felt her face grow hot.

"I'm not one of your fucking patients, Doctor," she said, and the entire room seemed to stand still. "Where is Sarah

Hart's file?"

He didn't answer, and Alicia didn't want to show how angry she truly was. Displaying anger to a psychologist with a Ph.D. would only encourage him to take over. He'd start spitting out his jargon and feeling like he was in control of the situation. As the lead detective on this case, *she* was in control. And she wasn't about to turn it over.

This case had been a drain on her. It was a roller coaster. Every time she thought she'd made progress and turned a corner, she found that the new road she was staring down was even longer than the first. But now, with a warrant being executed, and the warrant for the Harts' apartment in her coat pocket, she finally saw the end of the road. A closed case. The images of the men in her precinct laughing at her and shaking their heads at her inept performance...they all disappear when she hits the end of this road. So she must hit it.

"Detective Jones." The call came from the other side of the desk: Officer Gunther. "The computer," he said with a head nod toward the large monitor sitting on the polyurethaned desk. "You want to check his files in there?"

Smart thinking is what she wanted to say. But she needed to keep control. Needed to show she was still in the lead here. Calling the shots. So she nodded and walked to the brown leather chair. She sat in it and her first thought was that she should have aspired for a different career. The chair she had back in her cubicle sported yellow padding hanging out of frayed cloth. This one was heaven. Like sitting on a cloud.

The doctor had no response to her actions without permission. It could have been his awareness of the warrant's abilities or that he had nothing to hide.

His computer fired up with the movement of his mouse under Alicia's palm. The three men stood around her – Gunther by her side, Emans and Dr. Epplestein still standing several feet away beside the file cabinets. She could feel them breathing down her neck. Watching her every move.

Gunther must have been in IT in a prior life. Alicia knew how to navigate his documents folder, but Gunther started looking into online sites where he could have them stored: Dropbox, Google Drive... Still, after what felt like hours of searching, there was nothing. Not one file in his computer that would indicate Sarah Hart's information was included. There were PDF ebooks, his mortgage documents, business plans and financials, but nothing to do with patients. Not one. It blew her away how organized this guy was. At the same time, it gave her relief to know that she couldn't have simply missed something. It wasn't there and she knew it.

"Where the hell is her file?" Alicia asked the doctor, swinging around in the man's chair. "Why the hell don't you have a file for her?" She said it as calmly as someone holding a conversation in a library.

"I have nothing for you, Detective."

"You know I could have this place ripped apart, right? With one phone call, I could have all the drywall ripped out of this building. Floorboards removed. I could have access to every single file in your computer and in your receptionist's. You know that, right?"

"I do," he said as if exhausted. "But I ask you not to do that. I assure you, Detective, that I have nothing for you here. But may I suggest trying the Hart's residence? Do you have a warrant?"

It's none of your fucking business, she thought. But said, "I do. Is her file there?" Pure sarcasm and he knew it.

"It isn't. But it seems her husband spends most of his life in their bedroom at his desk. Many people have skeletons in the closet and maybe–"

He kept going, but she didn't need to hear anymore. What he just said was all Alicia needed to have an image placed in her head: *Many people have skeletons in the closet.*

And that's when she remembered the odd box collection Brian had in *his* closet.

52

It was a risk and Francesca knew it, but she had no other choice. She couldn't take off in her car or the now-dead neighbor's car. She needed something new and her choice was the only way to go about it.

Nerves struck her as she pulled open the door to Frank's Used Cars. A salesman that looked like a former cop walked up to her, but maybe his looks were swayed by the nerves and the fear that this one final move could get her caught. If she could find a way to pull this off, she'd be free.

"My name's Carter," the man said with an extended hand. "How can I help you?"

"I saw that Fusion out there and was wondering if you could tell me a little more about it."

"Sure. You want to take it for a ride?"

"Um..." No. No, she didn't. She wanted the keys and to be off and on her way. "I actually had another one before," she giggled – flirtation always throws a man's mind askew.

"You did?" He asked with a smirk rather than with an

intent to investigate.

"Yeah," she said. "My husband got me this thing," she turned to point at her SUV, then turned back to him. "Ex-husband, actually."

"Oh, I'm sorry to hear."

She waved him off. "No, don't be. It's for the best. But I want this thing out of my sight. I want the Fusion so I can feel like I'm going back in time, you know? Forget all about him, like he was never in my life."

"I see. So..." he trailed off and then said, "You want to take a look inside the car, at least?"

"No, I'm really okay. Anything is better than sitting in that gift from him."

"Alright." He trailed off again and the look of skepticism came back.

"I'm sorry. I know it's a lot to take in," she said. "And I'm sure you wouldn't know – you and your wife probably never fight, huh?" She knew there was no ring on his finger. She was bringing the flirting back into this little back-and-forth.

"Oh, I'm not married," he said with a smile.

"No? Well I bet you have a fiancée. Or someone special."

"Nope. Just me."

"Wow," she said, turning up that flirting knob from Low to High. "That's shocking, but I guess it's good; you won't have to go through what I'm going through right now."

He apologized to her once more out of courtesy and then asked, "Do you want to look into financing options?"

"Well I was kind of hoping," she looked to the SUV in the parking lot again and then back at him, "that I could just make an even swap.

Carter looked over her shoulder and out the window,

then back at her. *"That a Denali?"*

"It is."

"What year?"

"It's only three years old."

"You realize that Fusion is a previous model, right? It's eight years old."

"I know." His eyes squinted as he tried to read the situation. "Like I said, I just want it gone. I know that trading it in won't get the value it's worth, so I figured trading it for that Fusion would maybe be about the same money...?" She threw her palms in the air to play dumb. Come on, man. Just give me the damn car and let me leave.

"Do you have the title?" he asked.

"I do. It's in the car. Spare key and manual, too."

"Oh...okay...You just want an even exchange?"

"Is that possible?"

"Sure. We're just going to have to fill out some paperwork and then call your insurance company to switch vehicles."

"Oh, we have to do all that?"

"In order to legally drive that car off the lot, yes we do."

"Can we do it illegally?" She almost whispered it.

"I'm afraid we can't." He took a step back and Francesca feared she was losing him. She could envision him picking up the phone to call the police as soon as he told her to leave. Read her license plate as she pulled away in the Denali and give it to them. The authorities would be on her before she could make it a mile down the road.

"I'm sorry," she said, and she turned flirting into sulking. "I'm not trying to do anything crazy or get you into any trouble. It's just...this car. This fucking car. Every time I get in it, it reminds me of that cheating bastard. It smells like

his little whore. I want it gone. I don't ever want to look at it again. I'd take the oldest car you have on your lot if I could just get this thing out of my life." She wiped the tears that welled in her eyes – natural and unforced, which even came as a surprise to her – and apologized again.

"You said you have the title?" Carter asked.

"Yes," she said, wiping away the last of her tears. "in the car with the spare key. I have it in an envelope in the glove compartment."

"You go get me those and I'll get you situated with the Fusion."

She lit up, and once again the naturality of her excitement was a surprise to her. Moments before, she envisioned this man calling the police on her. And now he had a change of heart.

Francesca went to her car, grabbed the envelope and brought it in to Carter. Within ten minutes, he did what he had to do and handed her a manila folder. "Keys and title," he said.

She hugged him. The flirting game was over, but she knew that her plan had worked and she could now leave freely. For a split-second, she thought that maybe Carter would call the police anyway – as soon as she left in the Fusion, he'd call with its VIN and whatever plate number she was driving off with. But then she thought better, or maybe thought that it was something she couldn't control anyway. This was a risk and she was well aware of it.

Carter walked outside and went right to the Denali as she went to the Fusion. It was as if he wanted nothing to do with the illegality of what he'd just done – just get the hell off my lot.

Off the lot she went, turning right and taking a short

drive down the road before she hit the entrance ramp to the highway. Her next stop: Who the hell knew. She just hoped it wouldn't be prison.

He'd done it. Brian had finally done it. He wrote the closing words of his novel. An authentic novel with authentic murder scenes.

He shouted again, looking down at the final words of his manuscript. He'd written books before and had this elated feeling when done, but none to this extent. Maybe it was because he hadn't done thorough research like he did with this one, or maybe he thought the story was the best he'd written. At this point, he didn't care *why* he felt this way. He was simply happy *to* feel this way. He wanted to share this with the world. Wanted to share it with somebody. Anybody. But there was only one person he ever had to share his work with.

He reached into his pocket and pulled out his cell phone. The screen was black – turned off after his rest stop incident. Phone off meant GPS off, and if the GPS had been enabled, there was no way he could have had this time to finish his story.

Now he was torn. What to do? Turn on the phone to call Sarah or keep it off and risk the possibility that no one ever reads this story? What would happen if – and when – the police found him? Would they confiscate the laptop? Destroy it? Keep it as evidence and maybe, just maybe, if he ever got out of prison he could have it back and try to sell it then?

Sarah deserved to read this. Up until recently, she'd stuck with him throughout his life. She watched him as he worked a low-paying job so he could write as much as possible. She watched as he wrote every morning and suffered through rejection letter after rejection letter when trying to sell his other books. This was not only the book that Brian had been waiting to write, but it was the book Sarah had been waiting to read. It was the book she'd been waiting to be excited about. The one where she knew, as well as Brian, that it was their ticket out of poverty. Their bestseller.

He made his decision. She deserved it. He powered on his phone.

Once light illuminated the screen, he had this sudden fear that he just shone a spotlight down on him. *Here I am, Coppers. Come and get me.* But it was too late for regrets. Too late to turn it off. All they needed was one second to see the little GPS bubble of his flick onto their screen and they'd have him.

Knowing time was dwindling down, he called Sarah.

After less than half of a ring, she answered: "Brian?" She almost screamed it into the phone.

"Hi."

"What are you doing? Where are you?–"

"Hey."

"–Listen. Everything–"

"Sarah."

"–that's been going on, it's–"

"Sarah!"

"–not what you think. There's a lot more to it–"

"Sarah! Listen to me!" He shouted it into the phone. The yelling actually made him angrier. She was stealing his moment of glory. This was supposed to be a happy phone call and she was shouting all over it.

She finally paused.

"Sarah," he said. "I'm done! I wrote it! And it's amazing!"

"What?"

"The book. I just finished it."

"You did?"

"Yes! And this is it. I know I've said it before, but this is it. This is the one. This is going to sell. We can have a happy life. You don't have to leave me!"

"Brian."

"Yeah?"

"Where are you?"

"Do you want to come read it?"

"Sure," she said.

Something about her voice didn't click, but he didn't mind. Her eyes would be the first of many to read this fantastic story.

"I'm at work," he said.

Brian tried his best to keep his head down, but he had to keep an eye out for Sarah. He pictured her driving through the lot in a different car. One of her parents' maybe. Or maybe she was driving around expecting to see *him* in another car. Maybe she thought he was smart enough to swap cars somehow, seeing that cops from every county in the state were looking for him.

He continued to look around but saw nothing but burly men in work boots walking in and out of the Home Depot's contractor entrance. Lucky for him, most of these men neither paid attention to the news nor cared for it. They were out to get supplies for their work and that was all.

Finally, Brian spotted Sarah's car coming out from behind the rear of the Eats-N-Treats building. He *had* told her he was at work so he can't fault her for checking the employee parking lot. But now he was nervous one of the cameras might have spotted her car. Maybe someone from corporate would take a look and report it.

As her car came closer, he spotted her and began to wave from within the windshield. Her eyes grew wide and she looked stunned. Yes, he was still in the car he used to run over an entire family.

She pulled up in the spot next to his and rolled down her window. He mimicked the action in his car and his window wasn't even halfway down when he yelled to her, "You have to read this! Come here." He motioned with his head for her to come join him in the passenger seat of his car.

Sarah climbed out of her car and walked around the front of Brian's. While walking, she did everything in her power not to look at the hood of his car and he knew why. She was afraid of what she'd see on that bumper: blood, hair, or something much worse. Brian didn't even have the courage to look.

"Here," he said before she was even fully in the seat. "Read this." He placed the open laptop on her thighs.

"The whole thing?" she asked as she pulled the door closed. "How the hell am I going to read the whole thing?"

He shrugged like he hadn't even thought about it. "I don't know. Just read what you can."

She shook her head. "Brian, I–"

"Please, just read it." He looked at her with wide, excited eyes and nodded.

"Okay."

She began to read. He was watching her every reaction. Analyzing. But he could tell she was hardly paying attention.

After what felt like an hour, she wasn't even through the first chapter yet, and then she stopped altogether.

"Brian," she said without looking away from the laptop.

"Uh oh. What'd you find? Something wrong already?"

"No. It's not about this."

"Then please wait," he said. "This is important. I'm running out of time."

"I know your time is running out and that's why I need to tell you this."

"It can't wait?" He tried remaining calm. How could she not see the need for urgency?

"It can't." She shut the laptop and handed it to him. He took it with a sigh, aggravated that she didn't share his enthusiasm for the story.

"What is it?" he asked.

Her hands began to shake in her lap and the volcano that was forming on the tip of her tongue was about to erupt. He could sense it. Lava would soon come spewing out toward him in the form of words – words he would have never imagined he would hear come from her mouth.

"I didn't realize it would work," she started. "I thought it was bullshit. All bullshit. Some dumb tactic from a man who thought he was more powerful than he really was." She paused again. She started bouncing her leg, adding to the nervousness her shaking hands were displaying. The truth was brewing. He thought it might have been about the divorce. Or about her parents or the kids. But he wasn't even close.

"He just wanted me to start saying these words to you. Dumb words. Here and there. *Say this* or *Say that,* he would tell me. He said it could make you do things. Crazy things." Her shaking got worse. "Said that it would make everything better. Make you a better writer. Make you a professional writer like you always wanted. And then you could make money with your writing. We could finally get out of the apartment. We'd have a life. A house. The kids would have their own rooms. A yard. They'd have a yard." She looked over at him. "The kids were going to have a yard!" She yelled it. Her eyes were wide and that crazy shaking had made it all the way up to her head.

"Sarah." He said her name calmly and quietly, but she didn't stop.

"You killed those people because of me," she said softly. "It was my fault. It was some psychological trick. A game. An experiment. And I played into it. I played along. I didn't want to, but I played along."

"Sarah, what the hell are you talking about?" It wasn't shock in his tone when he asked. It was more of a reprimanding one. Talking to her like some kid telling a tall tale and swearing up and down it was true.

"Dr. Epplestein. My psychologist. He has this theory that he's trying to prove. To use words. Trigger words. He told me to use them. He said it would make you a better writer, and then you'd finally start making money off of your books."

"Oh, that easily?" he asked.

"Have you heard of the Misinformation Effect?"

"I'm not a goddamn shrink, Sarah."

"It's this idea that you can sway someone's story. Make them tell you a story that they don't really mean to say. It's like...it creates false memories or something. Apparently cops use it when questioning witnesses and stuff. If the witness tells the cop that 'The car was driving up to the red light,' the cop will sort of re-ask the question in a different way: 'So the car was speeding up to the red light?' The witness will think about it and then agree, thinking that maybe they *did* see the car speeding but forgot to say it.

"I don't really know. It's crazy psychological stuff. But he has this theory, Dr. Epplestein does, that it can be taken further and that the human mind can be manipulated in sort of the same way. That you can...make people *do* stuff and not just *say* stuff."

"What the hell are you talking about?"

"I told him no," she said like she didn't even hear him. "I thought it sounded stupid, too. How could saying some words to you make your books sell? It sounded like some sort of a hypnotizing thing.

"But...he...he convinced me. Brian," she looked at him. "He paid me."

"Paid you? Your therapist?"

"Yes. I was so confused. Just sitting in his office and he's talking to me about saying these trigger words, and how it'll help, and as soon as I gave some push back and said no, he told me something. He said he and some other colleague of his were working on research. Some nonfiction book they had a guy ghostwriting. That they could pay me if I helped. It could all be part of what they were working on.

"I told him 'Absolutely not,' but then he came back and started saying things like they would never use your name in the book or in any kind of documentation. That they only wanted to document the results."

"Sarah, am I some sort of a fucking test dummy?"

She didn't say no. Just looked down into her lap. He waited for an answer and saw a tear fall from her face and into her waistline. With a sniffle she said, "I don't know."

He put the laptop in the backseat, then laid his head against the headrest and looked out the windshield. Cars came and went in the parking lot. Life outside this car went on as normal. Surely, not one person in a passing car thought to themselves, *I bet a wife is explaining to her husband why he's a murderer in that little car parked there.*

All around, more cars passed. More people moved on about their merry lives. Some might have been bored. Some might have been mad. Frustrated. At their spouse. Their kids. Their job. But certainly no one around them could be in the same situation Brian and Sarah were in. Hell, no one in the *world* could be in the same situation right now.

Sniffles and choppy breathing were the only sounds inside the car until Brian finally spoke. "Trigger words, huh?" But that only seemed to set Sarah off again.

"I had no idea it would work like they wanted it to." She shook her head, still looking down at her lap. "I thought it was stupid. So fucking stupid. But the money." She finally lifted her head. "The money that they paid me...I was able to pay things off, Brian." A smile faintly made its way across her face. "The calls stopped coming in. No more Citibank. No more Chase. My call log was no longer bleeding red with unknown numbers. And the bank statements stopped showing bounced checks and non-sufficient funds fees. Do you know how relieving that was?"

The weight of the world seemed to be coming off her chest as she said this. But Brian felt as though she was taking the weight and throwing it on him. With every relieving word that left her lips, added balls of weight were being thrown at him. And he was forced to catch them. Even if he didn't want the weight, it was sticking to him like some sort of glue.

"Did you notice the letters stopped coming from the apartment office?" Sarah asked him. "Did you notice they stopped calling, too?" Her smile grew larger now and he ground his teeth. "You were able to write, Brian." Maybe she knew she was pushing a button. Or maybe she didn't. But that sentence extinguished any flame burning inside him. "You were able to write without me bitching at you. I no longer had this hatred towards your writing."

"I figured you didn't care anymore because of the divorce," he said, and a smile crawled up his cheeks, too. Now a married couple, soon to be divorced, one telling the other that she was responsible for him murdering several people, were smiling at each other as they spilled their feelings. Sick world.

"The divorce was one of the triggers," she said simply. "I've always cared about you. I just didn't have to think about money anymore. Didn't have to worry that every hour one of us wasn't working was one hour farther from being able to pay the bills."

The thought did make him happy. Without bills and debt and the fear of being evicted looming in the back of his mind, writing would be easy. It would be fun again. He'd still wake up at three or four in the morning to get it done, but it would be done with a smile. Life would be easy again, just like it was when he had his mom's life insurance money. And like it was when he sold the family home.

But that wouldn't happen. It was too late because he murdered five people. He left a family to die on the sidewalk of a rest stop. And there was nothing discreet about it. Not this time around. There was nowhere for him to go but Death Row.

"How much was he paying you?" Brian asked.

"A lot. He started paying me a grand a week. That only lasted two weeks because when I came back in on the third week, I told him I wanted to stop. It felt wrong. I felt like I was in high school again, manipulating some stupid boy into thinking one thing when reality was another. And you aren't some boy, you're my husband."

"*Was* your husband."

"*Are* my husband. For now, at least."

Until I rot away in some prison cell because of what you've done. Some part of his subconscious screams this at her. But the smiles are still on display. Everything is fine and dandy on the outside, but some darkness is clawing its way up on the inside.

"When I did that, he told me he'd pay me more. Two grand a week." She must have seen his eyes shoot open because she shook her head emphatically and said, "I know, right. I couldn't say no. So, like every week, he gave me some new set of words to tell you. Then at my next appointment, he'd ask me things about you. And I did. Two grand a week, Brian. I was getting ahead on all of our payments. Do you believe that right now we're caught up on everything? We even have some spare money in our bank account?"

"Not in *our* bank account," Brian said. What he was really asking was where the hell the money was.

"It's in a separate account. I had to, Brian. Come on. If I had to hide this from you, I had to do that. But it isn't just my money. It's *ours.*"

Easy thing to say to a person about to go to prison for life. *No* money is Brian's money.

"What happens now? Since I'm some fucking experiment, what happens now?"

"I don't know," she lowered her head again. "But Dr. Epplestein promised. He promised me. Promised me that he'd help in any way if anything happened."

Yeah? Well tell him to help me stay the fuck out of prison.

There it was again. The little voice. The little subconscious making its way up. Clawing at Brian's chest and neck and pushing aside anything holding it back. It was coming out of him like some demon. Coming to the surface.

"Why are you smiling?" Brian asked, yet he still wore a smile on *his* face. They'd both been smiling for some reason, like this was a long overdue conversation that they both needed in order to save their marriage.

"What?"

"Why are you smiling?"

She paused, shrugged. "I don't know. This is relieving, I guess. Telling you all this. Being honest."

"That true?" he asked.

Her smile turned to a frown. "Brian, I'm sorry. I never meant for any of this to happen. Look," she looked over to the road. "I'll take you anywhere you want to go. Buy you whatever you need and drop you off at some bus station. You can still see the kids once this blows over."

There it was. His perfect escape. He was so close. In the getaway car with someone willing to be an accomplice. But it was too late for apologies. Too late for plots and escapes. The demon made its way out. Brian was no longer calling the shots.

"I'm sorry, too," he said. He started to move across the

center console, and as he stared into her, he saw the fear jump into her eyes.

Sarah leaned back against the door and put up her hands, but it did nothing. Brian moved toward her, slowly – almost too slowly, unless it just felt that way to him. He moved his hands past hers and wrapped them around her neck, squeezing. Her face went red almost instantaneously and she grasped at his wrists, pulling and scratching.

"Brian," she managed to get out in a croak. "Brian, the kids."

54

There were a lot of naysayers back at the precinct, and a beautiful scene kept playing itself over in Alicia's head. In the scene, she walked in the entrance with Brian Hart in cuffs. Perkins and Antini stood there in their plain suits, jaws dropped, wondering why they ever doubted her in the first place. And then Captain Furlong gave the slightest *atta-girl* nod as she walked on by with her perp.

With the paper sitting in her passenger seat, she drove to the apartment complex. That bitch of a property manager wouldn't have a damn thing to say when she saw this warrant. She wouldn't be able to. She'd end up caving. Hand over the keys like a good little girl. Something she could have done in the first place and saved them both the aggravation.

Mercer Street was as empty as it ever was at this time on a weekday. Normal people were out and about, working their day jobs and waiting impatiently to drive down whichever roads led to the comfort of their own home. So Alicia had the road to herself, and as she approached the entrance to the complex, she glanced at Building 500 on her right, separated from her by a strip of grass and an asphalt parking lot. She leaned over the center console to get a good look inside one specific second-story window. She knew she wouldn't see anything, but she still tried. She knew she wouldn't see Brian and Sarah Hart moving around inside like two anxious dogs in a cage, but she looked anyway. And just as she'd expected, she saw nothing.

The cruiser turned the corner and rounded the curve that would bring her to the community's clubhouse. Felicia, the property manager, was surely still sitting inside. Still sitting in front of a locked key box feeling like she had authority over the detective.

Well, Detective Jones thought, *she sure as hell didn't.* And she would prove that to be true. She walked into the building once more and found her way back to Felicia's office. This time, the lady who dressed like she was still twenty years old placed the key in Alicia's palm.

"I'm sure you can appreciate the fact that I was doing my job," Felicia said as she handed it over.

She sure as shit wasn't. She was pissed. Had to go all the way back to the captain to get warrants, taking time out of both of their days. This all could have been avoided. But in reality, she really wasn't mad at the woman. After all, she *was* just doing her job. Not only that, she was abiding by the law.

"No hard feelings, ma'am."

"You need me to show you how to get there? I can give you a ride if you want."

"No, thank you." Detective Jones held up the key and

said, "This is all I need." And then she was out, and driving too fast inside of an apartment complex, and then pulling into one of the many vacant spots outside of Building 500.

As she ascended the steps to the second floor in the open, outdoor stairwell, two thoughts popped into her head. The first was wondering where the Harts could be right now. Together? Apart? Running? Hiding? What about the kids? And the second thought: Dr. Epplestein's words, *Many people have skeletons in the closet.*

She knocked at the door, knowing there would be no answer. Even with the thought that there would be no answer, she told herself to take caution. Brian Hart was obviously not stable, and nothing more could be said about his harboring wife. Who knew what they could have planned behind this door? Anything from a simple booby trap or a camera to a hired, trigger-happy gunman.

As suspected, no answer.

She slid the key into the doorknob, slowly, feeling the catch of every groove, and waiting to hear some sort of a click. *Boom! There goes Alicia.* She was able to breathe again once the key was in and the knob turned.

The door moved open without a sound. With her fingertips, she pushed open the door and took a step to the side, pressing her shoulder into the siding. Once a few seconds passed and bullets hadn't come flying through the doorway, she found it safe to enter.

With her gun drawn, held tightly with both hands by her waist, she tiptoed into the apartment. "Police," she announced. "Anyone here?" More silence. She took another couple of steps in, checked behind the open door and then walked into the kitchen and checked more blind spots. There was no sign of anyone. But airing on the side of caution, she kept her weapon drawn.

She moved slowly through the living room, where the remote control sat on the couch. On a normal day, the kids might run in from school and fight for it. But this wasn't a normal day. She thought the same thing as she made her way down the hallway and looked into the kids' bedroom. Two twin beds, one on each side of the room. One comforter red with race cars, the other purple with princesses. Hopefully no important dolls or blankets were left behind.

She poked her head through the doorway of the master bedroom, hands gripping her gun a little tighter this time, finger on the trigger. Brian could be behind the bed. Or Sarah could jump out of the closet. The kids could even come running out from underneath Brian's desk, armed with sharp objects, brainwashed. The house had been empty until now, but Alicia wasn't taking any chances. This family might seem normal to an outsider, but she knew what had happened over the past few days, and nothing was impossible.

She checked those spots – under the desk, behind the bed – and then came up to the door leading to the walk-in closet. Once she found it safe to enter fully, she did so.

Only the rich have organized closets. You know, the gigantic ones you see on TV, when they bring the camera crew through and shoes are aligned on shelves, clothes neatly hung and sorted by color or style. The rich person before the camera shows viewers a glimpse of what it's like to have the money to hire someone to keep up with your closet. For the rest of us, a walk-in closet becomes another place for storage. We throw shit in there and shut the door, telling ourselves that one day we'll set aside time to organize it, but we never do. Brian and Sarah Hart were apparently the same.

The closet was bare and messy. Clothes hangers crisscrossed on the wire shelves, and other loose articles sat scattered across the tops of the shelving and along the floor. She knew what she was here for, but she had to check her surroundings first. Diving right into what she wanted would be like running right into a trap.

She began to move around some of the scattered clothes on the floor with her foot, gently but swiftly, never letting her guard down and keeping the mindset that there could be anything lying underneath. But with every shirt or pair of pants she moved, she only found worn carpet. Her hands scaled the drywall and patted the floor. Nothing.

And then she came to the stack of boxes stacked neatly in the corner. She remembered being in here with Detective Russell and Sarah Hart, and Sarah explaining to her that her husband had a thing for keeping boxes. He felt like he might need them again. *Bullshit,* she thought. *This is his skeleton in the closet.*

Alicia got on one knee and took a handkerchief from her coat pocket – the thought was that this might end up being a crime scene and she didn't want to contaminate anything. She brushed aside some clothes and started lifting lids from boxes. Some had shoes in them, some were empty minus tissue paper or Styrofoam. Alicia continued to go through, and on her sixth or seventh box, she found herself becoming complacent. She was opening and closing too quickly. So on this particular box, she stopped and examined closer. And on this particular box, she found what it was Dr. Epplestein said she should look for.

A clear, plastic pocket was taped to the inside top of the box – a shoe box – like something you'd find on the inside of an old library book. Inside this clear pocket was a folded white paper, yellowed on the edges. With her handkerchief on her fingertips, she pulled out the paper and opened it up on the carpet beneath her. It was a note.

To whomever it is that may find this:

Suicide was my only option. I kept trying to tell myself that last night was a dream. But it wasn't. I know what I saw.

Every Friday night, Linda and I asked our two children if they wanted to go out to eat with us. They always said no; both too busy. But last night, Christina said yes. And we were so excited.

Bones Out is where we almost always went. Linda loved their riblets and I could always find something I liked on the menu. It was a safe bet and right around the corner, so we decided to go there. Christina didn't really seem to mind where we went. I remember going into her room to ask if she was okay with Bones Out, and she just sort of nodded, head buried in her phone like every other nineteen-year-old.

It takes one exit to get there. I get on the highway, get off at exit 8, and we're there. And it's the way I took last night. We were all talking, asking Christina how her semester was going and if she still wanted Marine Biology as her major.

And then these lights came up behind me. Some guy in a truck, brights on and all. I moved over into the right lane and it pulled up next to me. It was dark so I couldn't see inside. I tried looking over, and by this point we were all yelling at whoever the driver was.

Wasn't sure why they were being such an asshole. Then the next thing I know, this truck slams into the side of the car and I almost veer off the road. Then it moves behind us, slams into the back bumper, pulls up and sideswipes us again. The girls were screaming and cursing but all I could think about was keeping the car on the road and keeping us alive.

The truck was next to us again. Linda was leaning across my lap, yelling, and I could hear Christina in the back, too. They were leaning over, yelling at whoever it was behind the wheel. And for a split second, the driver was visible. Maybe it was the lights of a passing car on the other side, or maybe a street light. I don't know. But when he looked over, I saw. I saw my son. Brian was behind the wheel of that truck. I'd never seen the truck before in my life, but I know my son's face.

Maybe Linda and Christina saw him, too. Maybe they were yelling at him and yelling his name, but it was all a blur to me. Pure chaos.

He hit us again and I lost control. It felt like whichever way I turned the wheel, it forced us the other. We swerved and the girls screamed, and then all went black.

I woke up to some firemen pulling me out of the car. It was flipped over and they pulled me out through the shattered rear window. All I remember was blurriness and then seeing two bodies still in the car. I didn't yell or scream or fight with them to get them out like I should have. Maybe I somehow already knew they were dead.

I went to the hospital and had some tests done. They wanted to hold me there this morning, but let me go because of everything I was going to have to do with the funeral arrangements. But I can't do it. I can't go on acting like I didn't see my son behind that wheel. I don't know where he got the truck or how the hell he got away with it, or why, for Christ's sake. But he killed them. He killed my wife and my daughter. His mother and his sister. And I don't know what to do. He's still my son. My blood. I used to play ball with him in the yard or put together puzzles on the kitchen table. I'd look into his little eyes and my heart would melt. So I can't turn him in. I can't send him to prison. But I can't die with this inside me. For Christina and for Linda, I have to tell someone. So whoever you are reading this note right now, know that Brian killed his mother and his sister. I don't know why and I don't want to know why. But I can't go on. I can't live in this world when the one person still alive in my family is the one who killed the others. There's no need for me here anymore.

And whatever happens to my son, I hope he finds peace. I hope he one day admits what he did.

- Kurt Hart

Once Alicia can get beyond the shock, there are so many questions. How could this have happened? Was this case closed? Who closed it? Was anyone charged? Was it documented as an accident? Kurt Hart's fault?

But she couldn't concentrate. Because there was only one thing running through her mind. "He kept this," Detective Jones said to herself. "All these years...this sick fuck kept this."

55

There are times in every person's life where emotion takes over. Maybe it's a sadness and all you can do is curl up and cry. Or maybe it's excitement and your body seems to leap itself off the ground – you have no control. In Brian's case, it was anger. And it controlled him. Possessed him. It was an out of body experience, as if he was looking down on himself from above.

Brian had never felt this before. Not when he stabbed the old man who was prepping for a peaceful fishing trip. Or when he strangled the life out of his boss, Eric. Or even when he ran over a family full of innocent travelers on their way to see Grandma and Grandpa, or wherever the hell it was they were headed. Shit, he didn't even feel this way when he slammed into the side of his dad's car seventeen years ago. No. None of those experiences felt like this. This was true anger. True grit. He wanted to squeeze his hands so close together that Sarah's head would pop clean off of her shoulders. And if it wasn't for the force pulling him back, he might have.

As he was being pulled back, he took her with him. Sarah's limp body came awkwardly across the center console as he fell from the car, never taking his eyes off of her. The face that was once a pale and soft white was now a purplish-blue, and her eyes were no longer visible, rolled up into the back of her head. Brian only let go when a feeling of cold steel came across his forearms. He hadn't noticed until several long minutes later that one broken arm and one severely bruised one would be the result.

He felt the jolt of his body hitting the ground, and saw the limp body is his soon-to-be ex-wife crumble overtop the center console – her head on the driver's seat and her legs on the passenger seat. Was she dead? He sure as hell hoped so.

Then all of a sudden the commotion came back. His hearing came back. His vision no longer tunneled. The world was sprouting again before his eyes. And the first thing he saw was a balled white fist coming from the sky, connecting with his face and giving the back-to-life shock of cold water on your face first thing in the morning. Except this splash of water made a crunching noise, and sent his head back into the tar parking lot.

Brian heard another voice, a man's asking him if he was alright, but he couldn't see anything. His world was a blur again. He tried to open his eyes wide, but everything was spinning. He tried to get to his feet but couldn't. The guy's voice was frantic: "Hey! Are you alright? Wake up! Hey!" He sounded so scared. Angry. Persistent.

"I'm okay," Brian said, trying again to stand to his feet.

And then miraculously he was helped up. The blurriness began to subside after about fifteen blinks and in front of him stood a large man, white, burly, with overalls and a baseball cap. He had to bend down to look into Brian's eyes and when he did, he said, "You think he was fuckin' talking to you, you piece-a shit?" And he was pointing at something. Something next to Brian. So he looked. And he saw another man. Identical in dress, but this man was much thinner. He was leaning inside the driver door of the car. *It was his voice*, Brian thought. *He's the one asking if I'm okay.*

"Hey, I'm okay," Brian repeated, still woozy like a college drunk.

The man turned around and it was clear through his burrowing gray eyebrows that he wasn't happy to hear Brian's voice. He said nothing and began to talk into the cell phone pressed against his ear. And that's when Brian finally sobered up and realized the man was talking to Sarah. Unconscious Sarah, lying lifeless in the car. Asking her if she was okay. Trying to help the woman who might have been killed right before his eyes.

Brian lost his breath. Couldn't breathe. Couldn't inhale, couldn't exhale. The burly man's bear paw was wrapped around his neck. One single hand wrapped almost entirely around Brian's neck. He looked at the long, thick, hairy arm attached to the hand, and that arm led back to a face full of hate. Of rage. Of wanting to squeeze the life out of him right then and there. Like the face Sarah must have looked into just minutes ago.

How the hell did they see this? No one else batted an eye in his direction the entire time he was there. And right as he had his hands on Sarah, someone noticed?

"I can't tell! She looks dead! She ain't breathin'!" The skinny guy's voice was frantic. But it didn't faze the burly one.

The pudgy face looking back into Brian's eyes was full of anger. Brian could feel him squeeze harder and harder and Brian wondered if *his* head would pop off of his shoulders. He wished at the time that it would have. Simply to alleviate the pressure building up. To end it. End the pain. But it didn't happen that way. The pressure was relieved when the man opened his palm and Brian fell to the ground without the slightest effort to catch himself.

There was only commotion. Grunting. Feet moving. And then a thump. Brian finally managed to look down past his feet where the two men had dragged Sarah from the car and onto her back. They were both hovered over her. The thin man was getting more frantic with each passing second. Sirens faded in. More bodies began to surround the area – other bystanders offering to help.

Brian sat up and took in his surroundings. The fuzziness was gone, but now everything felt like a dream. Men and women surrounding a car; helping a lifeless victim on the ground in a parking lot; red and blue lights swirling as they came storming into the scene.

He was back, Brian was. Back to that night. Back to the night where his family died. To the night he ran them off the road. And here he was, the bad guy again. Only this time, there'd be no walking away. No playing the victim. The burly man hovering over his wife wouldn't allow for it.

Chaos intensified yet the noise never seemed to grow louder. Brian sat there, watching the replay before him, feeling the shooting pain in his broken forearm and holding it in his other hand. Medics with their duffle bags came running up and moved the two men in overalls out of the way. Bystanders who'd left their cars had begun to surround Sarah as the medics were working on her. And then cops showed up and began to push them back, yelling something that sounded only like echoes to Brian.

Brian looked around to take in the scene again. Flashing lights. People running around, scrambling, hurrying. A woman in a suit came running up to the scene. Her open suit jacket revealed a badge on her beltline. *Detective Jones*. He recognized her. But she wasn't looking at him. Wasn't even running towards him. She was running near him. To some place between where he sat and where Sarah lay with an army of people around her. And when he looked over, he could see who she was running after. It was the burly man, angry again, balling that hairy bear paw and coming straight for Brian.

Was Sarah dead? She had to be, right? Why else would the burly trucker have lost his shit again? Brian wondered if he'd killed again, and why killing again didn't seem to matter.

"Don't!" The first word Brian could clearly hear in quite some time, and it came from Detective Jones's mouth.

But it was too late. The burly man's fist came crashing down into Brian's face again, but this time it didn't send him into a daze, it sent him into a sea of black.

56

For a moment, he thought it was the gurney. Directly above him was a bright white light and he looked around the perimeter expecting to see clear glass windows, spectators looking down, watching his very last minutes and wondering what his final words would be.

But no, he was not in an execution chamber. Not yet, anyway. He was lying in a hospital bed when he finally awoke from the burly man's blow to the face. Machines beeped beside him and a small flat screen hung so high on the wall it looked like the top may have disappeared into the drop ceiling. On it, some soap opera played. A love story had just taken a turn for the worse, apparently, and a woman was overacting in the arms of her male counterpart.

Out of the corner of his eye, he saw a cop sitting on a chair by his door. He was a tall guy with a skinny neck, but somehow had arms the size of logs coming out from beneath his short-sleeve button-up. He was looking down at his cell phone, laughing at whatever it was he was seeing. Brian could feel his heart begin to race – he needed to get out of there. He looked down at his arms and his chest at all the wires binding him to the machines around him, and then he saw that his wrists – one covered in a white cast – were shackled to the sides of the bed and his ankles bound together. Then he heard a deep voice say, "Don't even think about it." He looked to his side and saw another cop sitting in another chair, but this one was not on his phone. He was older. Wiser. Not as much muscle but made up for it with his sternness. He was sitting with his back straight – at the position of attention – with his eyes glued on Brian.

"What's going on?" Brian asked. How the hell had he gotten from the parking lot to here? What happened? The last thing he remembered was that lady cop running his way. Was it Detective Jones? The one who he talked to during the whole Eats-N-Treats interrogation after Eric's death? He couldn't remember for some reason. But she wasn't running at him. She was running to someone else.

And then he remembered. The balled-up, hairy bear paw that came flying into his face like a bowling ball shot from a cannon. Then darkness.

"You're going to prison, that's what's going on," the cop by the door said without lifting his head from his phone. Brian looked back to the other cop, as if for approval, and was given a reassuring head nod.

"Think you can just kill people and sit comfy in a hospital bed while you get all fixed up?" the younger one said. "Nah. It doesn't work that way." He finally lifted his head and looked at Brian. "Matter of fact, I think I'll call Detective Jones right now and let her know you got your boo boos taken care of and you're ready to go to your new home."

"Already did," the older cop said. And all Brian could do was plop his head back down on the pillow and wait.

It took less than ten minutes for Detective Jones to come walking through the doors of the room. And she stormed in like a lawyer walking into a courtroom for the thousandth time. She didn't stop to take in her surroundings, or even break stride. She came in with her suit jacket open and almost blowing behind her. "Brian Hart," she said when she finally stopped, leaning over and placing her hands on the plastic foot of the bed. "You sick fuck," she said. She took a deep breath and then told the two officers to leave the room. When they did, she continued.

"I've never met someone like you in my life," she began. She held up a manila folder and then threw it down onto his shins. Brian could do nothing. The wires connected to his body were like knotted rope binding him to the bed, and the blanket felt like it was made of lead. All he could do was listen and remain motionless as the woman who'd been chasing him for nearly a week unleashed her rage.

"Let's see what you did," she said. She reached down and opened the folder, and when her hand came up, there was a picture – a full sheet image – of Thomas McMann, the old man he'd stabbed. It was a picture his family must have taken, him out on a boat with his fishing hat on and an ear-to-ear smile. "Thomas McMann," she said. "He was sixty-four years old. He had a–"

Brian looked away and shut his eyes. He didn't want to look. Didn't want to stare straight into the energetic and gleeful eyes of a man who just wanted to go fishing one morning. All he wanted to do was sit on a small boat somewhere near the coast and listen to the waves as they crashed into a marsh not too far from where he'd be anchored. Maybe he'd have an early morning beer or a cigar to celebrate the retired life he no-doubtedly worked so hard for.

The next picture she held up was of Eric Milford, his old boss at Eats-N-Treats. He couldn't look at that either, but she forced him to. The detective walked to the side of the bed and held the picture in front of him. He could have squirmed. Could have turned side to side, making her run back and forth to chase his eyes, but there was no point. "This was your boss. A twenty-six-year-old college graduate who you strangled after purposefully getting him drunk. You knew you couldn't overpower him without it, huh?" She smirked, getting the last laugh. "Coward."

"And then, Mr. Hart," she said as she walked back to the foot of the bed. "And then you had the courage to go run over an entire family. Hunt them down like you were in some sort of video game." She held up the picture, but this time didn't show Brian anything besides its solid white back. "I won't give you the pleasure of showing you their smiling faces," she said as she herself was looking into the snapshot. "Because you're sick, and you might get some sort of enjoyment out of it. And I won't let that happen."

She placed the pictures back into the folder with the calm demeanor of a teacher straightening a stack of papers on her desk.

"Two of those family members survived, you know. And now they'll have to live knowing that the rest of their family will never be with them again. You feel good about that?" she asked with a nod. "Feel big and bad? Feel like a

God, killing people at will?"

No answer.

"Your wife survived, too. And I pray for her sake that she removes any trace of even being involved with you."

And when she was done, she tucked the folder beneath her arm and crossed her hands in front of her waist.

"I know what you'll do," she said with a smirk. "You'll find a lawyer who'll tell you to plead insanity and you'll oblige. You'll sit in the courtroom and hear the comments and snarls coming from the families of the people you've killed and you'll hang your head low. You'll pout and expect pity from some people. And you know what? Some dumbasses will give it to you. They'll say you've got some screws loose or some psychological terminology and that all this wasn't really your fault." She bent down to try to meet his sagging eyes, but he wouldn't look at her. Somehow he knew what was coming. He knew she had him. *Checkmate. You win. I'm doomed to rot in prison.*

"You can't even look at me?" she asked. "Can't look at the images of the people you killed and can't even look at me? Maybe you *are* the coward some people will call you. Maybe you're not even worthy of being called a murderer. Just some worthless, pathetic excuse for a man."

He heard a piece of paper crumbling in her hand and shut his eyes. He knew what she'd found.

"You can't even look at it?"

He could see it as she pulled it from her breast pocket. The paper had yellowed pretty significantly over the years. But apparently the ink had stayed firm and intact, because she knew everything it said.

"You're fucking sick for keeping this," she said, leaning into her words and thrusting the paper at him with the word *sick.* "But you know what?" she asked, standing straight again and with the smirk back on her face. "Your ego just landed you in prison for the rest of your life, at the very least. My guess? You'll get death." He looked her in the eye as she continued. "They'll strap you to that gurney." She squeezed her wrist to emphasize. "Put those needles into you as the families of the dead watch. Hell, they might even cheer. I know I would. I'd bang on the glass like I was at a fucking hockey game."

Heat began to fill his face. The pity ran out of him with a single exhale and he was now ready to wrap his hands around this woman's neck. Cop or no cop, she'd crossed the line.

"Mr. Hart," she walked to his bedside and leaned toward him. The brown skin around her eyes wrinkled as she squinted. "That anger and rage you feel now? Well that's what I've felt for you the past few days, you sick fuck. Chasing you around like some wild damn goose chase while you killed innocent people. I hope the rage kills you. I hope you meet your match in prison and you don't even last long enough to see the needle." His muscles spasmed as he tried to break free from the cuffs attached to the sides of the bed, but he got nowhere. His skin grew hotter and hotter, but the detective never flinched. "I hope you rot in hell, you sick son of a bitch. I wish everything bad on you that one person could wish on another."

The detective stood again and the squinting went away. Brian tried hard to follow – to sit up and grab her by her hair and smash her fucking head into the frame of the bed. But he could go nowhere. The only part of him that could move was his waist, and he raised it high but found no relief. He thrashed, squirmed, wore himself out. And when he lay there, exhausted and defeated, the detective said one last thing to him that he'd hear in his mind over and over again:

"I'll see your ass in court, Mr. Hart."

EPILOGUE

It wasn't a typical visit. He'd only gotten two visits in the three years since the judge slammed the gavel and sealed the fate the entire courtroom knew he'd have: *Death by Lethal Injection.*

It was close to the two-year mark when Sarah finally showed up. It was his first visitor and shocked Brian almost as much as it shocked the guards who were set to escort him. She didn't have much to say when she showed up. Couldn't look him in the eye and mentioned a few times how she felt bad for what she let the shrink talk her into. But it had nothing to do with that. A normal person wouldn't have taken the trigger word of *authentic* and turned into a serial killer.

I like this chapter, but make it more authentic isn't enough to trigger a sane writer to go on a killing spree. It was in Brian's blood beforehand.

Sarah was kind enough to show Brian pictures of the kids when she came. They both looked so much older. It made him sad to think that he'd never see them again. Sad to think of them eventually calling another man Dad and soon forgetting all about their real dad, the one who worked hard but always found the time to come home and play with them at night. But in the end, he knew they'd be okay.

Sarah's visit was his first, and now this would be his second.

For this visit, there were lights and a backdrop and an entire crew setting up the visitation room. Two large cameras were brought in and set up on tripods. One of these cameras pointed to the metal chair Brian would be shackled to and the other to a black stool set up a few feet from it. The two chairs were aligned just as any would be for a one-on-one TV interview, and this was no different.

Brian was allowed to switch out of his orange jumpsuit for this occasion and was permitted to wear his denims: jeans, jean jacket, white t-shirt – something he'd never wear in the free world, but felt relieved to wear in prison when he could.

The guards guided him to his chair and shackled his ankles to its legs, and those legs were bolted to the floor. His hands were shackled as well. The guards joked with him and told him not to make an ass of himself. By this point, the guards and prisoners were almost...not exactly friends, but they were acquaintances – there was no rivalry like you see in movies. Not on Death Row, at least.

It only took a few minutes until Sharon Jacobsen walked into the room, and she was followed by her crew of cameramen, producers, staff, and two armed bodyguards. Between the prison guards and her personal security, there were four pistols ready to fire at him at any moment.

His execution date was still three weeks away, but he could have made it this very day if he wanted to.

Her crew took their positions, but Sharon walked right up to Brian and extended her hand. "Hello, Mr. Hart. My name is Sharon Jacobsen of Spotlight News. I want to thank you for taking the time to interview with us," she said.

"You mean instead of any other channel?" he joked, but her only response was a smile. "You're welcome," he said. "It's an honor to meet you."

Ms. Jacobsen took her seat and several minutes of small chit-chat between some people behind the cameras was the only noise in the room. A makeup person came out and gave one last touch up to Sharon before the director of the whole ordeal indicated that he was ready to go.

"This whole thing is prerecorded, Mr. Hart," Sharon said. "So no need to feel tense and worry about messing up. Our director over there, Larry, will yell cut if there's something he doesn't like. Other than that," she shook her head. "You can just talk to me as if we're two people having an everyday conversation."

"Except we're in a prison and we're here to talk about why my life comes to an end in twenty-one days."

She nodded. "Well we're also here to talk about your book."

"For so many years, that's all I ever wanted to hear," Brian said, shaking his head at the irony.

"Well, better late than never," she said, and the uncomfortable aura hung in the air until the interview began.

"Welcome to Spotlight News," Sharon looked into the camera on the director's cue, "and our exclusive interview with Brian Hart from within the walls of Haverton State Prison. With just three weeks left until his execution date, Brian has agreed to speak with Spotlight exclusively to tell us about his book that has just recently sold its one-millionth copy." She turned to face Brian, and although she told him to be calm because this wasn't live, he felt himself tense up. "Mr. Hart, first of all, we'd like to thank you for taking the time to speak with us."

"You're welcome," he said. Somehow the two simple words gave him relief.

A sixty-minute interview felt a lot shorter when you were the one being asked the questions – and when there are no commercial breaks. But once the overbearing questions of *What made you kill your family?* and *Why did you kill those people?* and *Do you regret it?* and *Why not plea insanity if your wife's psychiatrist knowingly put these thoughts into your head?* were done being asked, Sharon went into the book.

"So...one million copies." She shook her head in awe. "A man in prison writes a book and sells a million copies. How does that happen?"

"Well I wasn't in prison when I wrote it," Brian responded with a slight laugh. "I was a free man who woke up early every morning to work on what I always thought would be my family's escape from a little apartment. I was going to be a full-time novelist."

"You wanted to be the next big thing?"

"No. I didn't need fame. Didn't need to be filthy rich. I just wanted to make a comfortable living writing. I wanted to make enough money to where I didn't have to say no to my kids every time they asked for a candy bar at the checkout line of the grocery store. I wanted to have enough money to where we could eat healthy dinners and not macaroni and cheese and hot dogs. I just wanted a better life for my family, that's all."

"Well, you've sold a million copies of your novel, Heat." She points to a copy of the book on a small table beside her. The hardcover stands up on its spine. Brian envisioned this so many times during his writing career: being interviewed with his hardcover between him and the interviewer. This scenario was just a bit off. "I think if your family can put your past aside for just a moment, somewhere deep inside they can be happy for you."

"I doubt that very much, Ms. Jacobsen, but thank you. To be honest, though, I don't want anyone to be happy for me. I'm just glad my family will be financially stable."

There was a slight pause and then she asked, "On the subject of money, let's talk about your family – and I mean your immediate family of your mother, father, and sister. There was a letter found that was written by your father, and there's been much debate as to your objectives for that night. What do you say to the people who think your mental status is clearly unstable?"

"You mean am I a psycho?" A grin appeared on his face and would be the eerie snapshot posted on the home pages of several news sites in the following days. "Maybe I am. But what I say is I was a guy chasing a dream and there wasn't a damn thing that was going to get in my way."

"So, it was your family that was getting in the way of your writing?"

"No. Not them, although my dad would constantly hound me to 'give the shit up.' But it wasn't them in particular – more about society as a whole and how they could help me avoid it."

"Are you saying you're a socially anxious person, Mr. Hart?"

"No. If society's label on every little human trait as a *disease* were true, I just may be sitting in the comfort of a cell with padded walls and not three weeks away from my death, Ms. Jacobsen. What I mean is that society was driving me into this idea of growing up. Of getting a nine-to-five and sharing the highway with angry commuters every day. And I wasn't ready for it – not at the time. I wanted to sit and write. I wanted to share my thoughts with the world and I needed more time. The only way I could get more time was if I could get more money. And my parents had life insurance policies."

You could hear a small gasp from someone behind the camera, but the director let the video continue to roll. This was the first time Brian had made any of this public. He said nothing in court when asked about why he killed his family, saying only that he had to. But with his fate so close by and given the platform to come clean with everything, there was no better time than now. Let all the friends and distant relatives know exactly what happened and why so they wouldn't walk this earth for the rest of their lives wondering. This would allow them to have some closure.

"Money is the root of all evil, right?" Brian continued. "It really is. People kill for it. They steal for it. Women sell their bodies for it and men actually kidnap women and children and sell them for it. Money really is evil. Sick. Had we as a society not tried so damn hard to constantly be on the rise with every aspect in our life, so many issues would disappear. If we bartered everything, there would be no central currency to pursue. If we bartered everything, there would be no comparison to others and no feeling of self-doubt when you couldn't accomplish the great wealth of another."

"Are you saying a Socialist society could have prevented you from killing your family and five other innocent people?"

"No. Not at all. I'm not trying to get political. What I'm saying is that I knew what I wanted to do with my short time on this planet and society's view of how someone should live their life wasn't going to stop me. I wasn't going to get some job I dreaded, waking up miserable every morning for the rest of my life."

"But you had a job, did you not?"

"I worked at the pet store, yes. But it was a *job*, not a *career*. There's a difference. With a job, there's a light at the end of the tunnel. For me, it was publication. But with a career...just the word career makes me cringe. The thought of it, of this word defining *what you do* for the duration of the one life you get on this planet. I can't imagine how people live their lives knowing this. It's like we're slaves to our society's norms. We must get jobs we don't like because we must make the world go 'round. Well." He shook his head. "Not me."

The interview went back and forth more on this topic, and then Sharon Jacobsen used her expertise and talents to begin winding down the interview. Brian could feel it coming to an end and it felt like a door closing. He was able to get so much out, but still felt so much bottled up inside. Maybe it wasn't fair of him to feel he should be able to get everything out, but he still wanted to. He'd only have one more opportunity to do so, by answering the question Ms. Jacobsen stated as her final. "Mr. Hart," she asked. "Do you have any regrets?"

He did. Of course he did. He'd taken the lives of so many people and ruined the lives of many more, especially the lives of Sarah, Lacey, and Mason. But to go back to his teenage years and begin to list all of his regrets would take another one-hour special. So he thought of right now, of the people alive while he sat in this chair, bound and shackled. At this very moment, he was a published author whose book hit the New York Times Bestseller list and sold over a million copies. He thought of the money going to his estate, which would go right to his kids. It would go to Sarah, also, and to the inevitable new man she'd bring into her life, but he was okay with that. Sarah was a great mom and would spend the money spoiling her kids after what they'd been through.

So to answer the question of regrets, Brian responded, "No. At this very moment, I have no regrets. My family will never have to worry like I did. They won't have to struggle and wake up at 4 AM to do what they love or stock shelves at a pet store like I did. They've got a head start in this money-rules-all society and I did what I had to do to ensure that. It's a kill or be killed world and in that sense, I think I came away a winner."

It would be ratings gold, surely. Everyone would list him as an obvious psychopath, but Brian knew deep down inside that he wasn't. Deep down he knew that this weakening society just couldn't grasp the idea of extreme Darwinism: survival of the fittest.

Sharon Jacobsen shook his hand once more and then left as the crew began to break down their equipment. The prison guards came back over and unbound him from the chair before walking him back to his cell. They joked with him and told him that his answers were going to drive so much debate.

"You're crazy," one of them said.

You see, but I'm not, Brian thought. It wouldn't matter what he thought, though. In twenty-one days, he'd be dead.

Special Thanks

First and foremost, I'd like to let you know that I've never considered taking my research to the extreme Brian had in order to write better. I don't need to...I have Google!. And if that doesn't suffice, I have a good ole library just over a mile from my home.

Jokes aside, I would like to sincerely thank everyone who has taken the time to read this book. I hope you've enjoyed being on this journey with me because I'm happy – and blessed – that you have decided to do so. My hope is that you find my stories enjoyable enough to follow me on the many journeys I have planned in the coming years.

Also, I thank my family members at the conclusion of every book and this will be no different. Their sacrifices are the only reason I'm able to do what I do. My wife and kids, my parents, my grandparents, aunts and uncles, sisters and their families, friends and distant relatives – I can honestly say my support system is amazing. Thank you to each and every one of you who have supported me along the way.

A note from the author

As you may know, reviews can make or break an author and their work. So if you enjoyed this book, I'd be eternally grateful for a review on Amazon, Goodreads, or anywhere else you feel comfortable leaving one. Every review helps! (Well, the good ones do.)

Please feel free to find more information about books or following my blog at www.johnfeldman.com. You can also email me directly at: askjohn@johnfeldman.com.

www.Facebook.com/JohnFeldmanAuthor
Instagram: @JohnFeldmanAuthor
Twitter: @AuthorFeldman

www.ingramcontent.com/pod-product-compliance
Lightning Source LLC
Chambersburg PA
CBHW020554120726
47903CB00001B/258